BARD ON THE RUN

A Dark Elf laughed. A hand clamped roughly on his left arm, but Kevin gave in the direction of the pull, spinning left and driving his elbow into his invisible assailant. He was rewarded with an "oomph!" and a loosened grip that allowed him to tear free as he continued his leftward spin until he was facing in his original direction. He plunged on, struggling through forest so dense it was as if he were caught in a nightmare, gasping, aching, legs trembling, unable to hurry even though something monstrous was right behind.

But the Dark Elves, quicksilver though they were, were still in tangible bodies; they couldn't get through that tangled underbrush any faster than Kevin—or not much faster. His lead had narrowed dangerously, but it remained a lead, and maybe he could—

"Aie!"

He'd slipped through another shard of Gate—and suddenly his feet trod emptiness. He was sliding over a cliff's edge! A river roared far below. Kevin twisted desperately about, grabbing blindly at whatever came to his hand, releasing as it gave and grabbing at something else, clawing his frantic way back up—

He made it. For a

nothing but lie flat, cl

When at last he felt stro

wall of coldly smiling Da

THE BARD'S TALE SERIES

Castle of Deception by Mercedes Lackey & Josepha Sherman
Fortress of Frost and Fire by Mercedes Lackey & Ru Emerson
Prison of Souls by Mercedes Lackey & Mark Shepherd
The Chaos Gate by Josepha Sherman

JOSEPHA SHERMAN

THE CHAOS GATE

This is a work of fiction. All the characters and events portrayed in this book are fictional, and any resemblance to real people or incidents is purely coincidental.

A Baen Books Original

Baen Publishing Enterprises
P.O. Box 1403
Riverdale, NY 10471

ISBN: 0-671-87597-3

Cover art by Larry Elmore

First printing, April 1994

Distributed by Paramount Publishing
1230 Avenue of the Americas
New York, NY 10020

Printed in the United States of America

Acknowledgment

With thanks to Jim Baen for the tone-deaf elf!

Chapter I

Old Friends

Swords clashed together, the hard, clear sound cutting through the cool morning air, echoing off the castle walls. Kevin, once merely a lowly bardling, now Count Kevin, Bard Kevin, struggled to keep the upper hand, but the dark-clad, hooded figure he fought continued to drive him inexorably back across the smooth cobbles of the courtyard. All around him, Kevin knew, various guards and servants were keeping a bemused eye on their lord as they went about their work.

Wonderful. And all I seem to be doing is parrying and parrying again. He's just too inhumanly fast, *curse it!*

All at once, though, his opponent stepped back and lowered his sword. "Not bad, Kevin. Not bad at all."

"Not bad!" Kevin echoed wearily, brushing back damp reddish strands of hair from his face with his free hand. "Naitachal, this is ridiculous. All we did just now was wear ourselves out. It wasn't working at all!"

"Hush, now," the other murmured. "It was."

"Oh, nonsense."

"It was, I say." Naitachal pushed back his hood, shaking

free a silky, silvery fall of hair, revealing a dark-skinned, ageless, sharply planed face: the classic, coldly elegant face of a Dark Elf. Only the clear blue eyes, bright with joyous life, proved that he, alone of all his kin, belonged to the Light. Slipping a companionable arm around Kevin's shoulders, the elf added softly, "We agreed that till we had hard proof no one else should think this was anything other than a duel between friends."

"Well, yes, but—"

"And it was only a theory, after all."

"Yes, but . . ." Frustrated, Kevin let his voice trail off as a servant approached, and he wiped his blade clean with a soft scrap of cloth the man offered him. This wasn't a war sword, of course, though for a practice blade it was sharp enough; the White Elves never did anything by half measures. Still, Kevin admitted, glancing down at the intricately woven guard, he never would have dared study advanced swordplay at all if it hadn't been for this beautifully wrought gift of theirs. It very cleverly shielded his precious hands, which, along with talent, were a musician's most important asset.

The practice blade, and its matching war blade, had come from the Moonspirit Clan in gratitude for the kindness he had shown their deceased kinsman. *Eliathanis*, Kevin thought with a sudden sharp little pang of sadness, remembering the proud, heroic, doomed elven warrior, then determinedly blocked the past from his mind. It had, after all, been over four years since he and a mismatched little group of adventurers, including Eliathanis, had set out to rescue a count's stolen niece and ended up defeating the half-fairy, thoroughly evil, Princess Carlotta.

"Naitachal," he said suddenly, "this isn't all some sort of elven jest, is it? Do you really believe we can turn my swordplay into a form of Bardic Magic?"

Naitachal shrugged. "Why not? It's not any stranger than a Dark Elf turning Bard!"

Kevin had to grin at that. Naitachal was most certainly the only one of his kind ever to harbor a love of music, let alone show a blazing talent for it. "Yes, but—"

"You're beginning to sound like a poorly trained parrot," the Dark Elf teased. "'Yes, but, yes, but.' Why do you think Master Aidan let me come here?"

Kevin laughed outright. "Because you've been driving him mad."

"Oh, I have not!"

"Don't give me that look! I received a message from him a few months back all about you." The message, conveying the Master Bard's wry tone beautifully, had told Kevin, *"A fanatically determined elf with equally phenomenal raw talent can learn a skill far more quickly and thoroughly than any mere, lowly human. He's a full Bard now, just like you—and he's just as much of a 'let's go have an adventure' nuisance!"*

"Never mind. Kevin, we went over this before: Since swordplay has its own definite rhythm, and since you are a Bard who has mastered the basic moves quite gracefully—for a human—you may very well be creating a new form of Bardic Magic just by duelling. And it *was* working," Naitachal continued seriously before Kevin could interrupt. "*Something* happened when you used the Maladan Maneuver."

Kevin raised a skeptical eyebrow. "Such as what?"

"Such as the fact that just for a moment I found you drawing me into a dancelike pattern I couldn't help but finish. For that matter," the elf added thoughtfully, "at that same moment it was actually difficult to look at you."

"That's because he's a human!" came a shrill taunt. "The ugly things are always tough to look at!"

Kevin glanced up at a small, sharp-faced figure, her glittery wings an iridescent blur as she hovered just out of reach. By now, he knew better than to retort. These days Tich'ki might be the aide of D'Krikas, the castle seneschal, but that rank had hardly dampened her quirky, nasty sense of humor. She remained as fiery-tongued a little menace as ever; as far as Kevin knew, only the woman warrior, Lydia, Tich'ki's sometime travelling companion and now the castle's commander-in-chief, had ever managed to get the last word.

"Not all of us have the elegance of a fairy," the Bard told the fairy with wry courtesy, and heard her snicker.

"Or the nuisance factor," Naitachal added drily, brushing Tich'ki away as if she was a bothersome insect. "Kevin, if you can do that sword-dance to an enemy, entrancing him into predictable moves . . ."

"I'd have him," Kevin finished, then shrugged. "It's a nice thought, but who knows? We're making up the rules here, and—ah, *now* what?"

It was usually pleasant being a count; Kevin couldn't deny he enjoyed holding a noble title and overseeing the running of a castle, particularly since in these four years he hadn't made any really bad errors. People here seemed to truly like him. But there were times when he could almost wish he was a nobody again, responsible for no one but himself. Folks were always *after* a count! If D'Krikas wasn't cornering him to discuss in tedious detail this edict or that, it was Commander-in-Chief Lydia wanting him to oversee the new guard's testing. Or maybe it was the castle baker, bypassing the seneschal to complain directly to the count about the quality of wheat (arguing that since D'Krikas didn't *eat* bread, D'Krikas could hardly understand the fine points of its baking), or the farrier worrying that the current shipment of iron was underweight (even though D'Krikas could judge each ingot's weight to a hairbreadth's accuracy), or—or—

Kevin bit back a frustrated sigh. First and foremost, he was a Bard, with the music burning in him, aching to be used. But now that he'd finally earned that status, now that he'd mastered Bardic Magic, there was barely enough free time in a day for him to keep his fingers nimble enough to play anything!

And now here came this messenger from the royal court—no. This road-weary man wasn't wearing King Amber's livery. Puzzling over just who outfitted their servants in quartered blue and yellow, Kevin watched Lydia, her decidedly female form nicely outlined by her just-this-side-of-tight leather armor, her curly black hair barely restrained by a leather circlet, lead the man this way. The woman was a coolly competent warrior, but she had her rough, bawdy side. And Kevin didn't like the mischievous glint he saw in her dark eyes.

"That would be Count Trahern's livery," a dry, precise voice said suddenly. Kevin glanced back over his shoulder to see a tall, never-human form towering over him, its shiny, chitinous green skin glinting in the sunlight. D'Krikas, seneschal to Kevin and the two counts who'd preceded him, was Arachnia, not human, totally honorable and as coolly logical and fastidious as all that race. "And that is most certainly Count Trahern's coat-of-arms on the man's breast," the being continued. "You do remember who Count Trahern is?"

It was impossible to read expression in those glittering, segmented eyes, but Kevin frowned at the touch of condescension in D'Krikas' voice: the Arachnia had a seemingly inexhaustible knowledge of courtly detail—and expected the same of Kevin. "Of course," the Bard said shortly. "His lands lie due north of here."

"Indeed. Now, let us see. . . . His messenger carries no parchments with him, nor do any of his servants. Count Trahern has one child, a daughter. I believe her name is Gwenlyn, and she is of what humans consider marriageable age. Therefore," D'Krikas decided, "the man has most likely come to this castle with a miniature of that daughter, and most probably an offer of marriage."

Kevin groaned. "Not another one!"

Lydia had come close enough to hear that, and grinned widely at him. "That's it. Another lovely, lonely lady languishing for your love."

Naitachal, eyes full of amusement, gave her a sweeping bow of appreciation. "Couldn't have said that better myself."

Kevin glared at him. "I thought you were on my side."

The Dark Elf blinked innocently. "But I *am*! I think a bit of romance would be just the thing for you."

"A bit of romance!" Kevin squawked. "Naitachal, they're all trying to get me *married*!"

"Indeed." D'Krikas, segmented arms folded neatly, was the very image of propriety. "Have we not been discussing this matter for some time?"

"Ohh yes." The seneschal had been insisting for days that it was high time Kevin found himself a bride.

"Surely you see the need for such a thing?" D'Krikas asked in a voice that said he'd be a fool if he didn't. "After all, you are a count. A count must have an heir, and as quickly as possible, to ensure the succession and protect his people."

"I know, I know." For some time Kevin had been flooded by other miniature portraits of other unmarried daughters. He might, the Bard thought cynically, be of humble origin, but there wasn't a nobleman out there who didn't think this upstart young count, King's friend that he was, would make a valuable political ally. "I understand the whole thing, believe me. It's just . . ."

"He's scared!" Tich'ki jibed from overhead. "Poor little boy doesn't know *what* to do. Wouldn't even know what to do if a woman was plopped down in his bed!"

To his disgust, Kevin felt his face reddening. At nineteen he was hardly the innocent he'd once been, but he had yet to learn how to keep his cursedly fair skin from betraying him. "I am not scared. I'm merely—"

"Terrified!"

"No! I only meant that—"

"I'm right, he *wouldn't* know what to do! Woman had better bring a deck of cards to keep her amused—"

"Enough, Tich'ki!" Kevin snapped, and heard Lydia chuckle. Furious at himself for getting so flustered, Kevin snatched up the miniature the bewildered messenger was offering. Like all the others, the small portrait was far too stylized to show the young count much: the usual perfectly oval face, the usual perfectly groomed hair, dark and wavy in this case. Kevin was about to hand the miniature back with the blandly polite refusal he'd perfected during the last deluge of miniatures, but to his surprise found himself glancing down at it again. Funny, it really didn't tell him much, but there was something hinted at in the set of those deep blue eyes that—

"You don't have to memorize it," Lydia teased. "No matter how hard you stare, it isn't going to move."

"Naw, it's not that!" Tich'ki sneered. "He's too scared to think, that's all. Doesn't know which end is which!"

"I said *enough*, Tich'ki!" Kevin snapped, glaring up, staring back down at the miniature, praying to stop blushing. There really was something intriguing about the set of those blue eyes, but he could hardly change his life because of a stylized portrait. He'd give it back and—

But just then Tich'ki drew in her breath for yet another taunt, and Kevin, to his shock, heard himself blurt out, "All right, the Lady Gwenlyn it shall be!"

Oh curse it all to Darkness, what made me say that? What have I gotten myself into now?

Too late to back down. Everyone around him was cheering, and Lydia was slapping him joyfully on his back. The messenger, face wreathed in smiles, bowed and bowed again.

"My master, Count Trahern, will be truly delighted, my Lord Count. As soon as I may, I shall return to him with the joyous news. Oh, and a portrait of you, of course, Count Kevin."

"Of . . . course."

But Kevin couldn't help repeating in silent panic, *What have I gotten myself into now?*

As the days passed, Kevin found himself growing increasingly nervous. What had he done, what? A betrothal was as good as a marriage, everyone knew that, and by making that stupid declaration he'd as good as betrothed himself to—to whom? The Lady Gwenlyn? All he knew about her was that she was Count Trahern's daughter, and he didn't even know anything much about Count Trahern!

Meanwhile, of course, castle life had to go on. He had to continue being Count Kevin. Even if it meant being faced with the most awkward, embarrassing tasks. Like this one:

"Uh . . . Naitachal."

"I'm glad to see you remember my name," the Dark Elf said drily. He sat sprawled at his ease, looking impossibly graceful even so, making Kevin feel very clumsy by comparison.

"Do you . . . have you any idea why I . . . uh . . . asked you to meet me here?"

Naitachal glanced about the private little audience room, with its one window overlooking empty space and the bare stone walls that offered no hiding space for spies. "Offhand, I'd say you wanted to discuss something in private." Irony dripped from the elegant voice.

"Uh . . . yes. You—you've been living among humans for four years now."

"So I have. Bracklin has proved most . . . interesting."

"Interesting" was hardly the word Kevin would have applied to the quiet little backwater village that was the home of Master Bard Aidan. But that very peacefulness must have been wonderfully soothing to a Dark Elf trying desperately to turn from the necromancy that had been all he'd known for untold years to the magic of music instead. "I—I'm sure it has," Kevin said belatedly. "But I didn't mean to ask you about that. Your people don't believe in—in love, do they?"

The bright blue eyes turned suddenly hard and cold. "You know that," Naitachal said flatly. "No *Nithathil*, no Dark Elf, trusts another. No one of us dares. We come together only for mutual profit or procreation."

Kevin winced. "Then human ways must still seem very strange to you."

The coldness faded. "After only these four years or so of living freely among your kind? Oh, yes. Kevin, what is all this about? You didn't ask me here for lessons on *Nithathili* life." Naitachal paused, studying the young count thoughtfully, and a slow smile formed on his lips. "So-o. Judging from the embarrassed looks you're giving me, this has to do with those happy, silly games human men and women love to play together: the not-quite-true flattery, the not-quite-true lust."

"You've been playing those games, too."

"Flirting, you mean? That *is* the term? Why, yes." Naitachal's teeth flashed in a quick grin. "The good folk of Bracklin don't go in for such silliness. But the women here seem to enjoy it. And frankly, so do I. It's such a novelty to try such a frivolous thing."

"Ah well, yes, but . . . it's not a matter of the—the games themselves, but—"

"But of whom I play them with? Yes? I thought that didn't matter with such frivolities."

"Well, no—yes—" Kevin floundered to a stop, all at once aware of the amusement flickering in the elven eyes. "Naitachal . . ."

"I know, I know. Stay away from the married ladies. I'd already come to that conclusion after some idiot man tried to challenge me for smiling at his fat little hen of a wife. And it's not fair of me to tease you, not when you're being so earnest. Not," the elven Bard added delicately, "when you have your own potential romance to concern you."

"Oh. That."

"The thought does frighten you, doesn't it?"

"Gods, yes!" The words burst out before Kevin could stop them. "I—I know I'll have to wed sometime; that's part of the duties of a count, after all. B-but I never thought, not really, that I'd wind up tying my life to a total stranger!"

"You're about to suggest something. What is it?"

Kevin licked suddenly dry lips. Leaning forward in his chair, he said, "I was playing with the idea of—of going off, secretly, that is, to Count Trahern's castle, so I can meet the Lady Gwenlyn for myself." He sat nervously back, watching Naitachal intently, half hoping the Dark Elf would talk him out of it. "So. What do you think of that?"

To his shock, he saw Naitachal grin. "I like it. A most excellent suggestion."

"What—"

"What better way for you to get to know your lady than to appear on her very doorstep after a weary journey to meet her? What young woman could refuse you after that? Why, it's the very essence of romance!"

Romance, Kevin thought drily. He should have known better. Naitachal, of course, could never have known romance, not with his harsh background, but now that he'd discovered the joys of flirtation, his quicksilver elf mind must be full of fancies worthy of any lovesick minstrel.

"Don't you think," Kevin began warily, "that maybe we should think this over? It might be dangerous to—"

Naitachal waved that off impatiently. "What danger could we possibly run into on a short trip through civilized lands?"

"Ah—'we'?"

"You didn't think I'd miss a chance to see human courting behavior, did you?"

"There may not be any courting," Kevin reminded him between clenched teeth. "And isn't it going to be risky for you?"

"As a Dark Elf, you mean?" Naitachal shrugged. "I've hidden my true identity from humans easily enough before this with long sleeves and a hooded cloak. No insult meant, Kevin, but your folk really do see only what they expect to see. So. When we leave, we can't let Lydia know what we're doing."

"Why not?"

"Do you really *want* to meet your lady fair surrounded by a battalion of armed guards?"

Kevin held up a hand in wry surrender. Lydia was an efficient commander-in-chief, all right, far more efficient than Kevin could ever have predicted four years back when he'd appointed her. She had most definitely taken her job to heart!

Ah well, Naitachal was probably right. What danger could there possibly be for two full Bards trained in Bardic Magic? Besides . . . he really did want to see this Gwenlyn . . . find out what he was facing. . . .

"All right," Kevin said sharply before he could change his mind. "We need some good excuse. Ha, I have it." Snatching a pen from an inkstand, he hunted for a scrap of parchment and began to write. "I'm leaving a note claiming you and I are . . . mmm . . . going off into the surrounding forest to . . . to . . ."

"To practice music and Bardic Magic," Naitachal continued, and Kevin nodded eagerly.

"Exactly. To practice our Art without any distractions." He stopped short. "Oh, what a wonderful thought that is."

Naitachal smiled softly. "No reason we can't include some music in our journey."

"No reason at all." Kevin bent over the parchment, scribbling hurriedly. "There. I'll just sign it, thus, mark it with my seal, thus. A servant can deliver it to D'Krikas." Kevin grinned. "Shall we be off?"

Naitachal bowed extravagantly. "We shall, indeed. Come, my friend, romance awaits you."

"Uh . . . sure," Kevin said in sudden wild doubt, and followed.

Chapter II

The Battle Is Joined

The young page stood frozen in horror, listening to the sounds of violence in disbelief, then turned to run for help. But before he'd gotten more than a few steps, hands clamped down on his arms, dragging him to a halt.

"Whoa, now," amused voices asked, "where do you think you're going in such a rush?"

"There—the sounds—battle—my Lord Trahern is being attacked, and Lady Gwenlyn is—" The page broke off to stare at the squires who'd caught him, trying desperately to place them; pages didn't associate much with squires, who were, after all, several years senior. A stocky towhead, a skinny, brown-haired boy, a dark-haired, slender fellow: Ah, he had it! "Matt, Garin, Wellan—what are you laughing at?"

"That's no enemy, you idiot!" said towheaded Matt. "That's His Lordship, yes, and Her Ladyship, too, having at each other."

The page blinked. "A—a family quarrel? Is *that* all it is?"

"You new in this castle? You *must* be new if you

haven't heard them fighting before this. Those are two of the most hot-blooded stubborn folk you could care to meet, and when they disagree—whee!"

"B-but they're *noble!*"

The squires laughed. "Does that mean they aren't allowed to get mad at each other?" brown-haired Garin asked.

"Well, no, but . . ."

A crash made them all start. "Now what?" Wellan wondered, quickly brushing wild black hair out of his eyes. "Have they started throwing things at each other?"

Matt shook his head. "Not a chance. Throwing things isn't their style. They *are* noble, as the kid here says." The squire hesitated, listening. "Can't quite make out what they're saying. What do you think they're fighting over this time?"

"Her betrothal," Wellan said with certainty. "What else could it be?"

"Her betrothal," Matt echoed with wonder. "Who would dare marry a fierce one like that?"

Garin shrugged. "Someone 'smitten by her charm,' as the minstrels put it. Hey, don't give me those looks. Our Lady Gwenlyn may not be one of those pretty little perfect creatures the minstrels rave about—"

"You mean, those perfectly brainless creatures," Wellan corrected drily. "One thing our Lady Gwenlyn isn't is brainless."

"She sure isn't. And maybe she isn't a raging beauty, or whatever they call it, but Lady Gwenlyn isn't exactly hard to look at, either."

"Besides," Matt added, "she's got a good heart underneath all that fire. A pretty clever wit, too."

"Right," Garin agreed. "Our Gwenlyn can manage to charm anyone she sets her mind to, and you all know it."

"Huh. Anyone save her father," Matt muttered.

Angry voices still roared and rumbled in the background. Garin shrugged. "Five to one her ladyship wins this one," he said.

"This is ridiculous! Ridiculous, I say!" Count Trahern, tall and elegant and blazing with rage, was as impressive as a great, handsome bird of prey.

Gwen—Lady Gwenlyn Mared Rhona Gwinerya—wasn't impressed. "Ridiculous, is it? This is my *future* we're discussing, my *life!*"

"Don't be so melodramatic!"

"What do you expect of me? You've bargained away my entire future!"

Her father gave a great sigh, visibly struggling to calm himself. "You knew the day of your betrothal would come eventually."

"Of course I did, curse it!"

"Gwenlyn!"

"After all," she forged on, "I'm nothing much, am I? Nothing but a *girl*. Why should I expect to have any say in what happens to me? It's not as though I was actually worth something. Except as a pawn in political games, of course. I'm just a—a—cursed bargaining chip!"

"Don't be a—"

"Don't try to deny it! We both know—"

"Stop this stupid self-pity right now!"

"It's not—"

"I said, *stop it!* Gwenlyn, I could have married again, I could have fathered another child—"

"I wish you had!" But then Gwen added, almost softly, "I know you've been lonely since—since Mother died. And I—I hate seeing you alone. It's been nearly twelve years, Father. I wish you would let yourself find someone else to love."

She saw pain flicker in his dark eyes, but the count answered with cold dignity, "What I do or do not do with my life is not your affair. I have no other child, and that is as it is. I raised you as my heir, I gave you the best education. I even, curse me for a fool, encouraged you to use your brain."

"Yes. That's why—"

"Then use it!" he shouted. "I *could* have married you off to some doddering old idiot or a monster who'd beat you every day. Instead, I go out of my way to arrange a fine match for you—"

Here we go again. "A fine match!" Gwen yelled back. "He's nothing but a *boy!*"

"Ha! That *boy*, as you call him, is a full year your senior."

"But he's a nobody," Gwen protested, "a commoner without one drop of noble blood."

"Let me remind you," her father countered, "that he is both a full Bard and a hero."

"Some hero," Gwen sniffed. "He was made count just because he happened to be in the right place at the right time!"

"And knew what to do about it when that time came. *And* won royal favor, I might add. Gwenlyn, like it or not, he is an important political figure. And I will not have you make us both look like idiots!"

"Idiots, is it? *He's* the fool if he thinks he'll marry me!"

With that, Gwen stormed off before her father could shape a suitable retort, hardly noticing the squires she hurried past. But their whispers reached her: "A draw, by the gods, a true draw!"

Why, those little idiots were wagering *on us!*

For an instant she wavered, torn between raging at them and laughing at their nerve. But if she stopped now, her father would almost certainly overtake her, and Gwen just did not have the heart to continue the battle.

We're always fighting these days, she thought wearily. *Over politics, over castle affairs—even over the state of the weather!*

It hadn't always been like this. Gwen could barely remember her mother: twelve years was, after all, a long time. But surely there had been peaceful days back then. She seemed to recall days when father and mother and daughter were one harmonious, cheerful family. And even after, there had been times when she and her father had laughed together more than they fought. Days when they weren't always challenging each other. Days when they were happy. Her vision suddenly blurred, and Gwen fiercely blinked and blinked again, refusing to weep.

I don't want it to be like this! I don't want either of us to be unhappy, truly I don't. I try to be properly meek and submissive, but I—I just can't be that way. Father, Father, I love you dearly, but if this goes on much longer I swear one of us is going to kill the other!

How could she possibly escape this tangle? By forcing herself into a submissive mold, no matter how much it hurt? Gwen snorted, refusing to lie to herself. As soon ask a hawk to turn into a dove! She was never going to fit into the dull little niche society seemed to demand of a noblewoman. But what else was there for her to do? Marry? Marry that *nobody?*

Ha. He'd probably try to rule over me like a tyrant, the arrogant son of a—

"Bah!" Gwen said aloud and, heedless of her fine linen gown, threw herself down on her knees. Every castle had its herb garden, ruled over by the castle lady, and she, perforce, ruled this one—and spent a good deal of time taking out her frustration on it. Tossing her wild black mane impatiently back over her shoulders, Gwen began savagely to pull weeds.

But slowly her fierceness faded. What *was* to become of her? A commoner could do pretty much anything she dared. Gwen had even seen a few women warriors.

Oh, right. Some warrior I'd make. What would I do, terrorize enemies with my little belt knife?

No. A forced marriage or a cloistered life—there really weren't any other choices for a noblewoman. There certainly wasn't any choice she could imagine that included . . . happiness.

Surrounded by greenery, Gwenlyn saw none of it. She sat staring instead at a future that looked all too bleak.

✧ ✧ ✧

"Oh no, my lord, oh no, my lord,
I shall not marry thee.
For I shall bed my bandit bold
And live both wild and free!"

Kevin and Naitachal, riding side by side through the forest, roared out that last stanza together, then burst into laughter.

"Fortunate none of the courtiers heard that," Kevin gasped out, and Naitachal corrected:

"Fortunate Master *Aidan* didn't hear that!"

"Oh, yes!" Kevin agreed. "I can just see his scowls. 'Trying to prove Bardic Magic doesn't work on the tone-deaf, are we?' But hey now, a Bard can't be elegant all the time!"

Naitachal grinned. "We just proved a Bard can't be in tune all the time, either! Lucky our horses didn't throw us in indignation."

"Speaking of horses," Kevin added, patting the neck

of his mount, "it's time to give them another rest."

Naitachal slipped gracefully to the forest floor. "They earned one, listening to us."

Kevin followed, stretching stiff muscles. "There's nothing wrong with the occasional bawdy ballad, and—what is it?"

The elf had been glancing warily about, alert as a predator. "Nothing," he said after a moment. "I was just being cautious. Remember how Lydia would scout out escape routes every time we stopped?"

Kevin nodded. "I thought it was silly back then. Not any longer." He snapped lead ropes to the halters the horses were wearing under their bridles, then looped the ropes securely about a tree near a good stand of grass. "There. Graze a bit."

The journey so far had been more like one extended camping trip than anything else. Kevin paused, realizing with a jolt of surprise that he never *had* had a chance to travel just for the joy of it. Now, alone with a good friend and the chance for good music, the Bard could almost trick his mind into thinking this was a light, rambling-for-the-sake-of-rambling trip.

Almost. If it wasn't for the nagging guilt he felt at up and abandoning the castle that had been given into his charge—even if said castle could function quite well without him.

And if it wasn't for the quiet little fact that there was, indeed, a goal to this trip: a dark-haired, keen-eyed potential bride to whom he just might have to tie his life forever—

Oh gods.

Naitachal had settled himself comfortably on a grassy knoll, fingers idly running over the strings of his travelling harp, waking soft, sweet falls of notes. Kevin forced thoughts of What Might Be out of his mind as best he could, and sat beside the elven Bard, taking his lute out of its protective case, tuning it with what was by now unconscious ease. There weren't too many compositions for harp and lute, particularly since the little travelling harp had no sharps or flats, but that hadn't stopped them so far. After a few false starts, the two Bards improvised a cheerful, deceptively simple melody that sent a small shiver of delight up Kevin's spine.

What of Gwenlyn, though? Did she like music? What if she was tone deaf? Worse, what if she actually hated music and—and—

Kevin's fingers stumbled on the strings. "Thinking about your intended?" Naitachal asked slyly.

"Trying not to. Naitachal, what do I do if I can't stand her? Or if she can't stand me?"

"Don't look at me for an answer! I'm hardly an expert on your human romances. Or on *any* of your human ways, for that matter."

"I thought at Bracklin—"

"The folk of Bracklin accepted me because I was clearly a friend and student of Master Aidan, but that didn't mean they took me into their confidences. Besides," the Dark Elf added with a grin, "I doubt that the matters of commoners and nobles have all that much in common."

"But I'm not—I mean, I wasn't born noble, I don't understand how nobles think, either, and—and—"

"Hush. From everything I've seen, Kevin, you're doing a fine job as count. And if this Gwenlyn doesn't appreciate what she's getting," Naitachal continued, humor glinting in his blue eyes, "well then, she doesn't deserve so fine a lad!"

"Huh." Studying his lute, Kevin said with forced lightness, "What do Dark Elves know about human women, anyway? They're so wrapped up in their sinister plots they wouldn't know a pretty woman from—"

"Stop."

Kevin glanced up in surprise at the chill tone. Naitachal's face had suddenly gone cold and still. "Do not jest about them," the Dark Elf warned quietly. "The *Nithathili* are still my kin. And they hate me for escaping what they saw as my destiny as a Necromancer—and for denying them my share of Dark Power."

"They . . . aren't hunting you, are they?"

Naitachal shrugged slightly. "Not yet. Not as far as I know. But who knows what may happen? In their eyes, particularly those of my own clan, I am the worst kind of traitor, one who has willingly turned from the Darkness they worship to the Light. If they ever should choose to hunt me, if they should catch me . . ."

He shrugged again, eyes so bleak and empty that Kevin shuddered, remembering with a shock, *this is the sorcerer who could age a man to instant death with a touch,* just for a moment not at all sure that Naitachal had quite banished all traces of Necromantic magic. "Well, then," the young count said with all the defiance he could muster, "we won't *let* them catch you!"

To his relief, he heard Naitachal chuckle and saw life come back into the blue eyes. "Thank you, oh great and mighty hero." The elf got to his feet, slipping his harp back into its protective covering. "So now, our horses look rested enough. Come, let's continue our ride."

Kevin scrambled up. "Ah, wait, I have a thought. We're pretty well travel-stained by now."

"True," Naitachal agreed with a fastidious sniff. "And we reek of horse. I trust your lady will have enough patience to let us clean ourselves up a bit before you start your wooing."

"She's not my lady. And you're missing my point."

"Which is?"

"We were planning to arrive at Count Trahern's castle as Count Kevin and Bard Naitachal."

Naitachal raised a wry brow. "Which, I take it, we're not going to be any longer?"

"No. I've changed my mind about that. If I meet Lady Gwenlyn as a count, as her—uh—her betrothed-to-be, we're not going to be able to be honest with each other. We'll be forced to play the roles noble society insists upon: polite, formal and totally artificial. But I—I want a chance to judge her honestly, and to let her judge me, without rank getting in the way."

"I don't think I like the sound of this."

"Wait, hear me out. We won't enter Count Trahern's castle as nobles, but as common musicians, wandering minstrels, the sort of folk who are usually welcome anywhere but who aren't really noticed unless they're actually performing."

"And you think your lady won't notice you until you want her to notice you." The Dark Elf's voice was carefully empty of emotion. "So you'll have a chance to watch her without any artifices getting in the way."

"She's not my lady. And yes, that's exactly it."

"I'm not too sure about this. If—"

"It'll be easy!" Kevin interrupted hastily. "We've done enough successful role-playing when we were out trying to rescue poor Charina."

Humor flashed in Naitachal's eyes. "Indeed. I seem to remember that you made quite a fetching dancing girl."

Kevin shuddered. "Uh, well, we did what we had to do. We won't have to do anything as drastic as that this time around."

"Count Trahern has never actually met you, has he?"

"He's never even seen me. Except, of course, for that stupid, stylized miniature his servant insisted on taking. And as for you . . . well . . . you aren't the easiest person to ignore," Kevin said tactfully, "but . . . ah . . ."

"But four years isn't enough time for everyone to have heard of the oddity, the Dark Elf who's turned Bard," Naitachal finished blandly. "The one who was the companion of Kevin, the hero Bard. True enough. Our clothes look tired enough to be credible as minstrels' wear, and it's simple enough for me to hide what I am with a hooded cloak and a long-sleeved tunic. But how are you going to explain away our swords and these fine-blooded horses?"

Kevin grinned. "That's easy. They're the gifts of grateful patrons. You see? It'll all be just as easy."

Naitachal shook his head. "You make it all sound so simple. But I think you're missing an important point: starting off a relationship by pretense just doesn't seem wise to me."

"It's not pretense, not really. And there may not be any relationship unless I get that chance to know Lady Gwenlyn fairly."

"Fairly," the Dark Elf echoed.

"Oh, come now, Naitachal! It's only a small deceit, a very small deceit. And . . . well . . . things will turn out fine, you'll see."

"You hope," Naitachal said drily, and swung into the saddle.

Chapter III

In The Realm Of Darkness

The cavern was dark and chill, far below the world's surface as it was, lit here and there with the dim, smokeless, sorcerous blue flames that were all the light the Dark Elves, the *Nithathili,* needed. No ornaments marred the smoothness of the stone walls, no noise marred the heavy quiet. Servants moved with silent, careful grace through the dimness like so many black-robed shadows. These were men and women of the lowest castes, coldly beautiful as their betters but expendable, subject to regal whim or sacrifice. They glanced warily at the regal figure slumped on the obsidian throne as they passed him, sensing the dark waves of his thoughts, not daring to disturb him, not daring to do anything at all that might rouse his interest in them.

Another had no such fears. Tanarchal strode boldly forward, black cloak swirling dramatically about him. He stopped at the proper Distance of Respect, which was technically just out of reach of thrown weapon or spell, and granted the enthroned figure the Ninefold Dignities bow, not quite showing respect, not quite showing contempt. "Greetings, my Lord Haralachan."

Haralachan, lord of the Nightblood Clan, was tall, ageless and elegant in a hard-edged, chill, predatory way, as all his kin. His skin was dark as his silky robes, his hair a startling mass of silver; his sharply slanted blue eyes, fully adapted to the darkness, glinted with reddish light. He did not stir at Tanarchal's greeting; to have straightened would have shown too much respect to this arrogant creature.

This ambitious creature, Haralachan thought. *Walk warily, Tanarchal.*

Tanarchal showed no such inclination. "My lord, I was wondering when you were planning to hold a new hunt."

"When it pleases me," Haralachan murmured.

"Ah, of course. But I—and I speak for many of the clan in this—I was wondering when one specific hunt would be held. A hunt for the traitor, for Naitachal."

Haralachan betrayed nothing of his inner start. "That will come."

"But when, my lord? You are far too wise and cunning to let the traitor escape vengeance. Your kinsman," Tanarchal added delicately, "though he is."

Now Haralachan did straighten on his obsidian throne, casting chill waves of menace at the nobleman, seeing him flinch ever so slightly. "Vengeance will be taken," the Dark Elf lord said flatly. "Do you doubt me?"

"I? Not I, my lord." But the glint in the slanted eyes said otherwise, and Haralachan added coolly, "Do you not? Do you not, indeed?"

"My lord?"

Haralachan rose, drawing Power about him in a swirl of Darkness. "Do you challenge me, Tanarchal? Do you dare?"

He felt the other give way before the display of greater Power. "No, my lord," Tanarchal murmured, and it wasn't quite a snarl. "Of course not."

"Wise." Haralachan settled back in his throne. "Be assured that treason shall be punished. All treason, Tanarchal."

Tanarchal's bow of submission was perfect and precise. "Of course, my lord. I never did doubt it." But as he left, the nobleman added one final sally: "And may the day of vengeance come soon."

Haralachan slumped, losing himself in brooding once more, only vaguely aware of the wary servants. No, they were nothing, hardly worth a thought. Even Tanarchal was barely of importance; he could always meet with a quiet accident should the need arise, or be tricked into outright treason. It was the true traitor who held Haralachan's attention once more, the traitor Naitachal, he who had been of such a high caste that treason—particularly of such a disgusting, formerly unthinkable form—had seemed impossible. After all, had any *Nithathil* ever considered, even for the slightest moment of softness, turning from the Darkness that was his proper heritage?

There was worse than the existence of a traitor, Haralachan thought bitterly. As Tanarchal had so graciously reminded him, as many a *Nithathili* nobleman had been reminding him all along—as if he'd ever thought to forget—Naitachal was his clansman, his kinsman. To be kin to such a one was to come perilously close to weakness. While Tanarchal had, of course, not dared risk a challenge, knowing Haralachan to be so much the more Powerful, he'd issued a very clear warning: even the mightiest of lords could be overthrown were that treacherous kinsman not punished.

Always assuming, of course, that the traitor could

actually be located and captured. In all the days since the betrayal of his people, not one trace of Naitachal had been found.

Haralachan straightened with a hiss. Enough of this useless brooding! "You."

His hand stabbed out at one servant. The chosen one froze in such wide-eyed, total terror that for a cruelly delicious moment the Dark Elf lord toyed with the thought of saving this one for the hunt.

No. Not yet. First let the creature serve a more current use as messenger. "Bring Rualath to me."

No *Nithathil* trusted another; such a weakness as trust was the essence of stupidity. But of course as clan lord he had his consort: Rualath, chosen as much for her sorceries as for her caste—almost as high as his own—and her potential fertility, so important in a predominantly infertile race. Rualath specialized in strange, experimental magics. Sometimes they failed in most bizarre ways, but just as often those magics resulted in new, deliciously twisted forms of Power: Power which of course she shared with her lord in exchange for the political pride of place he deigned give her.

The servant cringed even further. "B-but, lord, your lady consort is in the midst of her sorceries. . . ."

Aaah, yes, this one would make fine hunting prey. "I have given a command," Haralachan said with deceptive mildness. "Obey it."

Slumped on his obsidian throne, he watched with half-lidded, predatory eyes as the terrified servant scurried to obey.

The room was small and dank, further below the surface even than the audience cavern; the thin drafts of air that stole their way within smelled strongly of ancient rock and older sorceries. There were no furnishings save for heavy, unornamented chests full of sorcerous scrolls and artifacts, sealed tightly against damp and possible spies. The only light was cast by three dull red flames from candles of black wax set in a carefully spaced triangle on the bare stone floor.

Tall and coldly lovely, Rualath stood precisely in the center of the triangle, her dark skin and robes a darker mass in the dimness, her long, straight fall of silver hair tinged as red as her eyes by the candle flames; she smiled thinly in satisfaction. Before her, a book lay open to a page marked in convoluted sorcerous equations in her own handwriting, and a little ground squirrel squealed in terror in her hand as she stroked it absently.

Yes, and yes . . . the spell had all the ingredients it needed, or so her experiments had revealed so far, all the ingredients save one, and the small creature she held would provide that.

Rualath took a deep, steadying breath, cold blue eyes shutting for a moment as she focused her Power, then began her chant. The twisting, ugly syllables whispered and echoed through the chamber as the magic grew . . . grew. Without slowing her chant, she drew a knife of black obsidian, caught the squirrel in a firmer grip and—

"My lady! My lady Rualath!"

Her concentration shattered. The channelled magic spilled away and was lost. The squirrel twisted in her hand, sinking sharp little fangs into her thumb, and Rualath snarled in frustration, hurling the animal aside so hard it broke against a wall. She whirled on the servant, who sank to his knees in abject surrender.

"What? Speak, fool, or you take that beast's place now! What do you want?"

Head bent to the stone floor, not daring to so much as look up at her fury, the servant stammered out, "Th-the Lord Haralachan bids you c-come to him."

Rualath glanced about her sorcery room impatiently. That he should call her *now*, when he knew she was in the midst of her experiments, and call her as if she was some erring subject! And yet, and yet . . . was this, she wondered warily, a trap? Rualath never considered that he might have tired of her; there had never been anything like the soft stupidity of love (she thought the word with distaste) between them. No, no, just as Haralachan needed her sorceries, so much greater in their way than his own, so he had his uses. *Power*, Rualath thought, and for once didn't mean sorcerous strength.

Ah well. Haralachan's summons was inconvenient at best and a marginal insult at worst, but she would answer his summons for the sake of that power. With a glance at the shuddering servant to fix his face in her mind for future use (how much stronger the life force of even such an inferior *Nithathil* than a mere animal), Rualath swept from the chamber, which neatly locked and sealed itself away as she left. The corridors of the Nightblood Clan realm were as blank of any wasteful ornamentation as the audience cavern, barely lighted since any who belonged here knew every trap and every safe way. Any who did not—such fools never regretted their mistakes for long.

Rualath entered the audience cavern with every sorcerous sense alert.

There sat Haralachan on his black throne. Her own throne, ever so slightly smaller, stood empty beside it. As Rualath entered, *feeling* his wary sorcery sweeping over her, hunting for spells, weapons—even as she, equally wary, was doing the same to him—he gestured to her to sit. So. He had no intention of replacing her. If he had, another would have already held that seat. Rualath sank with conscious grace to the smooth, cold hardness of the obsidian, smoothing her skirts about her slender form. "What troubles you, my lord?"

"Thoughts of a traitor."

"Ah?"

"One particular traitor." Haralachan paused deliberately, then continued, "One who is—was—of our clan, our caste."

"So . . . Naitachal."

"Naitachal."

Rualath smiled without humor. *The nobles have been after you again, my lord, have they?* "A waste, that. He had shown signs of being one of the mightiest Necromancers our clan had ever known."

Haralachan glared at her, eyes like blue ice. "More than a waste! Do you not realize what his loss means to us? With all that Power at his call, he willfully betrayed us, his blood-kin, his people! He deprived us of that Power and the chance to use it against the humans and those soft, Light-loving White Elves."

"Yes. There is that, of course." Rualath winced delicately in distaste. "Why did he do it?" she wondered softly. "What appeal could the weak, garish Light possibly hold for him? And this . . . *music*." She used the human word, since the Dark Elves had no word for something that was unknown to them; they alone of all the elven folk had no music. "How could he take pleasure, and to such an unseemly extent, in—in mere sound?"

"You wander from the track." Haralachan's voice was chill. "He betrayed us. He stole Power from us. He turned from his clan and honor to the soft, foolish forces of Light—and by all the Ways of Darkness, we must see that he pays for his treason."

"Oh, indeed. But how?" Rualath paused, considering. "Naitachal is skilled enough in magic to have kept us from tracking his aura all this while, and by now it has become hopelessly entangled with that of the humans with whom he consorts."

"That," Haralachan said coldly, "is your concern. Your sorceries are stronger than his." He glanced her way, elegant silver brow raised. "They *are*, are they not?"

Rualath met that suddenly speculative glance with a firm, chilly stare. "Of course they are. What would you have me do?"

"Snare him, bring him to us, I care not how. Only do it."

Oh, so easily said, my dear lord, Rualath told him silently. *As if you didn't know I have already tried, and failed, to catch the traitor. Yes, my lord, snap your fingers and watch the trained animal run through its paces. If I did not need you, my lord . . .*

But she did, for now. The nobles would follow Haralachan till they found some weakness in him. And neither they nor she had found that weakness yet, so: "I accept the challenge, my lord," Rualath said, carefully putting into her voice not the servant's humility but the hunter's eagerness. "I shall bring Naitachal before you."

Oh, yes. I shall. Somehow.

Chapter IV

Minstrels

"Pacing back and forth within a confined space seems an odd means of relieving tension to me."

Lydia stopped short at D'Krikas' quiet words, turning to glare at the seneschal where the Arachnia sat neatly folded behind his desk. It was often difficult to tell from that dry, clipped voice whether or not D'Krikas was being sarcastic, but those insectlike eyes were blinking in what was very obviously false innocence. "Where are they?" she snarled.

"To whom do you refer?" D'Krikas asked with infuriatingly precise Arachnia logic. "Do you mean Count Kevin and the elven Bard?"

Lydia just barely kept from spitting out a sarcastic, No, I mean the Two Lost Kings of the Western Empire. "Of course I mean Kevin and Naitachal, blast it! Where *are* they?"

The Arachnia paused to choose a sugar cube from the small bowl on his desk and pop it into his beaked mouth. Lydia knew his kind needed to eat frequently, but that didn't make waiting for him to finish his deliberate munching any easier. At last D'Krikas swallowed, wiped his beak delicately with a scrap of cloth, and said, "We have their note."

"Yeah, sure. 'We've gone off into the forest to practice our Bardic Art.' That tells us a lot, doesn't it?"

"It tells us everything." D'Krikas paused again, folding his segmented arms precisely across his chitinous chest. "The creative mind is an odd thing; particularly, it would seem, in a human. Such a mind cannot thrive under close confinement. And it is quite true that Count Kevin has had scant time to be what he primarily is: a Bard."

"And you aren't even a little bit worried?"

"Why, no. He is not in enemy territory, after all, nor is he alone."

"Sure," Lydia said flatly. "He has Naitachal with him. Now that really fills me with confidence!"

D'Krikas cocked his head to one side in the sharp Arachnia fashion that meant surprise but always reminded Lydia of a predatory insect about to pounce. As she schooled herself not to flinch, the seneschal asked in what sounded like genuine confusion, "Why should it not? The elf is no longer a Necromancer."

"That's exactly my point! At least while he was practicing that cursed death magic, he kept himself rigidly under control. Maybe you couldn't *quite* trust him not to work Necromantic spells, but at least he acted like a responsible adult! Now that he's turned into a Bard, he's gotten just as unpredictable as Kevin."

"Ah. No. You misunderstand. The elf is acting like one newly released from prison, drunk with freedom. It is a temporary condition and does not make him untrustworthy. And at any rate," D'Krikas added severely, "Count Kevin is no longer a child in need of care."

"Why, that's ridiculous. He's still just a kid."

"He is nineteen. In human society, that makes him quite legally responsible for his actions, does it not?"

Lydia hesitated, then sighed. "You know it does," she admitted reluctantly, brushing a straying black curl back from her face with an impatient hand. "And yeah, I guess you're right. He doesn't really need watching over, not anymore. He and Naitachal are probably off in some nice, pretty grove playing nice, pretty music together."

"Exactly. They will surely be back in a short while. And then," D'Krikas added with the slightest edge to his voice, "it will be time for worry, for then we shall have to listen to whatever new songs they have composed."

Lydia, who had heard in her travels some of the atonal dronings the Arachnia considered the only proper music, barely managed to bite back a laugh. "You got it," she said.

But for all her amusement, for all D'Krikas' inhuman calm, a shadow of worry remained to haunt her.

Kevin craned his head back and back again, looking up at the grim grey walls towering over him on the equally grey rocks. "Now that," he said, "is most definitely a war castle."

"Oh, indeed," Naitachal agreed. "Count Trahern's ancestors must have led some interesting lives. But times are far more peaceable these days, the lost, unlamented Princess Carlotta notwithstanding. Are we still going to keep up this ridiculous pretense?"

Kevin shot a glance Naitachal's way. The Dark Elf was completely shrouded in his cloak, only the harp slung across his back breaking the somber, anonymous mass. "We are, indeed. Unless, of course, you'd rather not continue with me?"

"What, and give up the entertainment business?"

Ignoring Naitachal's sarcasm, Kevin kicked his horse forward and started up the twisting road to Count Trahern's castle.

And, he thought uneasily, *to Gwenlyn.*

Now, where were minstrels supposed to enter? At his own court, he gave wandering musicians a friendly greeting, being a Bard himself. But who knew how Count Trahern felt about such folk? For want of an answer, Kevin rode right up to the main gate, a massive thing of heavy oak beams and heavier iron grating. Beside him sat Naitachal. The Dark Elf had slipped into the role of a hunched-over, submissive nobody with the ease, Kevin thought bemusedly, of someone who'd once managed to fool an entire squadron of guards into thinking him no more than a harmless dancing girl.

Two great watchtowers loomed over the gate, and the young count glanced up, suddenly very much aware of watching eyes. *So. Here we go.* "Ho, the castle!" he yelled.

"Who calls?"

"Two minstrels," Kevin began, "who—"

But before he could get any further, the unseen guard's voice cut in flatly. "Servants' entrance is around back that way. Use it."

Kevin sat gape-mouthed, taken aback by the unexpected rudeness. Beside him, Naitachal murmured, "This was your idea." Such amusement hinted in the elven Bard's voice that Kevin said shortly, "It's all right. A little humility isn't going to hurt us."

"Oh, indeed."

But as they rode along the curve of the castle towers, Kevin couldn't quite quench a hot little flame of anger, remembering all too clearly another time when he'd ridden just as boldly up to a castle, only to be humbled just as thoroughly. Ah yes, but back then he'd been truly naive, those four incredible years ago, back when becoming a Bard was only a dream and he'd never imagined such folk as warrior women or Dark Elf allies could exist. He'd been plain Kevin in those days, a lowly bardling sent on what he'd thought was a boring errand to copy out a musty old music text.

Ha! Boring was the last thing that *errand turned out to be. What with sorcery and undead and—*

"Kevin."

"Ah." Lost in memory, he had almost ridden right past the servants' gate. Standing in the stirrups, the count rapped sharply on the thick oaken door. "Anyone within?"

"Who's there?" The voice sounded thoroughly bored, as though, Kevin thought uneasily, its owner might bar strangers from entry just for the sake of something to do.

I don't need this. I just want to meet Gwenlyn and get it over with. I don't need anyone playing games with me. "Two minstrels," Kevin answered as pleasantly as he could, "come to entertain Count Trahern and his folk."

"Why?"

That was the last thing he'd expected. "I . . . uh . . . I . . ."

Was that a chuckle from Naitachal? The Dark Elf wasn't making the slightest move to help him at all, so Kevin said defensively, "Why, because we're good at what we do! We are—we are fine musicians and talented entertainers. And I assure you, Count Trahern will enjoy meeting us."

"True enough, that last," Naitachal murmured wryly, so softly Kevin almost couldn't hear him. "Even if it's for different reasons than you claim."

"We've had musicians here in plenty," the voice continued from the other side of the door, "some good, some not. Lady Gwenlyn loves music, and so does her noble father."

Well now, that sounded hopeful enough. But before Kevin could reply to that, the voice added scornfully, "So why do we need *you*?"

Oh, this is ridiculous! "Because, curse it all, we're *not* like other minstrels—"

"Clowns, are you?"

"No!" Naitachal was definitely chuckling now, and Kevin only just kept from childishly kicking the door—or the Dark Elf. "We," he said with great restraint, "are true musicians, not mountebanks, not street corner entertainers, and as such are covered by the Laws of Hospitality." Kevin was aware he was bluffing wildly now, but hopefully the guard on the other side of the door knew even less than he about archaic points of law. "If you wish to examine us, fine. If you wish to hold our weapons for security, fine. Just *let us enter!*"

There was a long pause. Then the door slowly groaned open. "Enter," the bored voice said as though doing them a favor. Kevin bit back a sharp retort, knowing all too well why the unseen guard had let them in. It hadn't been because Kevin had convinced him of anything, but simply because the guard had gotten tired of his game.

Never mind, never mind. We're inside, and that's all that matters.

Kevin glanced quickly about the castle courtyard, trying to orient himself. The yard, like that of his own castle, was full of people, stablehands, farriers, merchants, servants rushing here and there on mysterious errands. Not all were human; Kevin spotted two Arachnia traders chirring and clicking to each other in their native tongue as they strolled along.

Huh. Bet they *didn't have any trouble getting in.*

At the far end of the courtyard rose the massive keep, square-sided and several stories high, topped by lead sheathing. This building would surely hold the audience chamber and Count Trahern's private living quarters. And those of Gwenlyn . . .

"That's what we want," Kevin told Naitachal and dismounted, tossing the reins to a stable lad. Suddenly overwhelmed by the need for this whole business to be over, he strode fiercely forward—

"Hey! Watch it!" a woman's voice snapped. Kevin, caught off balance, staggered on one foot for a moment, struggling not to fall. "Look out, you clumsy oaf!" the woman shrilled. "You're stepping all over them!"

With a wild, graceless lunge, he finally recovered his footing and glanced down to find himself standing in the middle of an herb garden, some of the tender green sprouts crushed under his boots. A young woman in the worn, plain, comfortable clothes of a gardener was kneeling to one side, trowel in hand. She was no great beauty: her face was red from work and sun and streaked with dirt, unkempt strands of hair were straggling out from beneath the faded blue scarf covering her head—

And she was glaring up at him with undisguised rage. Embarrassed, Kevin began, "I'm sorry—"

"You should be sorry, you lout!"

It was bad enough to lose dignity in a fight with a gatekeeper. He was not going to let a—a common gardener yell at him like this. "It was an accident," Kevin said carefully. "Besides, these are just plants, and—"

"Hmph." Studiously ignoring him, she tried to straighten the seedlings he'd crushed. To his surprise,

Kevin found himself staring at her hands. These weren't the elegant white fingers of a lady who'd never done a stitch of work in her life, but underneath all the dirt they were charmingly graceful and amazingly gentle—

Far gentler than her tongue. "'Just plants,'" she muttered. "Say they're 'just plants' when you've got a wound that won't heal and there isn't any comfrey to soothe it because some stupid idiot of a—" She glanced sharply up at him again, blatantly disapproving of his travel-stained, rumpled self— "Of a whatever you are—"

"A minstrel."

"Good for you. It took me weeks to get some of these seedlings started, and here you come along and—"

"For the last time," Kevin snapped, "it was an *accident.* If you'd put a fence around the whole thing, this wouldn't have happened!"

"Hah! You'd probably have fallen over it!" Her eyes were the most astonishing shade, the exact indigo he'd seen in summer thunderclouds. Gwenlyn's eyes were blue, too, at least according to the stylized miniature that had started this mess, but they couldn't possibly be this wild, this fierce. . . .

"What are you staring at?" the young woman snarled, and her eyes lost all their appeal for him. "Go on, get out of here!"

"Gladly!" Gods, what sort of place was this? Were *all* the servants in the castle this obnoxious? And if so, what oh what could the count and his daughter be like?

"If you've finished arguing with the help," Naitachal murmured smoothly, suddenly at his side, "follow me. I've arranged lodging for us. Tonight we are to sing before the count and his court."

"Wonderful," Kevin muttered.

"There's still time to give up this masquerade."

"No!"

The dining hall was as crowded as his own, lined with rows of trestle tables covered with white linen and set with bowls and ewers of dully gleaming pewter and brighter silver. *Not ostentatiously wealthy,* Kevin thought, *but wealthy.* Fresh rushes rustled underfoot, giving off a clean, herbal scent as he and Naitachal, the elven Bard still so shrouded in his cloak and long-sleeved tunic none of his telltale dark skin could be seen, wormed their way through to a place at one of the lower tables. Sharing the table with them was a mixed lot of servants, merchants and entertainers, one of whom kept nervously juggling whatever bits of bread came his way and dropping most of them.

"I hope no one lets him too near any knives," Naitachal murmured wryly.

Kevin hardly noticed. He was too intent on staring at the two blue-canopied chairs there at the far end of the hall. "Where are they?" he asked uneasily.

"Where's who?" a red-bearded servant sitting to his left asked without much interest. "Ah, you mean Count Trahern and his daughter! They'll be here shortly, never fear." He looked Kevin up and down. "You a minstrel, huh? Don't worry. You'll get fed proper before you have to perform." A blare of trumpets broke into the last of his words, and the servant glanced casually up, adding, "See? Here they come now."

Kevin looked, looked again, and nearly shot to his feet in shock. Only Naitachal's hand clamping firmly about his wrist kept him in his seat, staring wildly at the two elegant figures who'd entered. Count Trahern was a tall, lean, handsome man in his richly blue, gold-embroidered robes, his glossy black hair and beard dramatically touched by grey. He looked every bit the sort of man about whom ballads should be sung.

But Kevin gave him only one cursory glance. For at the count's side sat a slender, dark-haired young woman, her sleek, silky gown as deeply blue as the count's robes, a woman with the most incredible indigo eyes, visible even at this distance, a woman who—

"Dear gods," Kevin breathed.

Naitachal glanced his way. "What's wrong?"

But Kevin could do nothing but shake his head in silent, dazed disbelief. Though her clean-scrubbed face no longer showed the slightest streak of dirt, though her black hair now flowed smoothly down her back, that finely dressed young woman was none other than the sharp-tongued, shrewish gardener with whom he'd fought.

"No, oh no . . ."

With a groan, Kevin hid his head in his hands.

Chapter V

Young Love

Head buried in his hands, Kevin moaned, "What am I going to do?"

"Eat," Naitachal said without a trace of sympathy. "Then perform. That is what common minstrels do, isn't it? And we are common minstrels, are we not?"

"Yes, but I—she—I—"

"That is the young woman gardener, is it not? The gardener who is also, it appears, Count Trahern's daughter. The one with whom you argued so strongly." Naitachal paused, then added with just the faintest touch of delicate elven malice, "My, what strange judgment you humans show."

Kevin looked sharply up at that, glaring at the elf. "How was I to know who she was? You saw what happened. She looked and acted like—like a filthy gardener!"

"Hey," a servant two seats to the right complained, "watch it. *I'm* a gardener."

"Sorry," Kevin said tightly. "I didn't mean any insult."

He heard the faintest of chuckles from Naitachal. "Awkward situation, isn't it?" There still wasn't much sympathy in the elven Bard's voice. "The sort of awkwardness that seldom happens to nobility. Only to . . . common minstrels."

Kevin winced. "You're not going to let me forget my mistake, are you?"

"Minstrelsy wasn't my idea, now, was it?"

"At least she hasn't recognized me yet. I . . . uh . . . don't suppose you'd care to lend me your hood?"

"And reveal to everyone that a Dark Elf sits among them?" Naitachal murmured drily. "Not a chance."

"Ah. No. Of course not." Kevin shook his head ruefully. "Sorry. I wasn't thinking."

"That much seems clear."

"All right, all right, you were right about the whole thing and I was wrong. Naitachal . . . what *am* I going to do?"

The bright blue gaze softened slightly. "Why not just go up there and confess the truth to the young lady and her father?"

"How? Without looking like an idiot? More of an idiot than she already thinks me, I mean," Kevin added bitterly. "Besides, you saw what happened earlier between Gwenlyn and me."

"To paraphrase what I said a moment ago, you two didn't exactly seem to be getting along."

"Ha! She has the sharpest tongue I've ever heard: I swear, she could give Tich'ki lessons!"

"And you, of course, were the model of gentility."

Kevin ignored that jibe as best he could. If only he could just quietly sneak out of here . . . no, that was ridiculous. Even if he got out of the hall, he could hardly sneak out of the betrothal. Might as well make the best of this uncomfortable situation. Maybe Gwenlyn had just been short-tempered because of the heat and—and—

"And maybe swine can soar," Kevin muttered.

"They're roosting in the trees right now," Naitachal said. "Waiting to hear us perform. Courage, my friend. Into battle we go."

Ah well, maybe she wouldn't recognize him.

Not a chance. Kevin saw her indigo eyes widen as he approached and waited for her to tell the world he was the lout who'd stomped all over her herbs. But she said nothing. *Probably waiting for me to make a fool of myself all over again.*

Well, he wasn't about to oblige her. Kevin swept down in as elegant a bow as he'd seen a minstrel perform. "My lord, my lady, thank you for the most gracious kindness of your hospitality." Was that suitably minstrel-like? "But now my partner and I would try to repay you, at least to the best of our humble abilities."

He saw twin spasms of distaste cross the faces of both the count and his daughter: too late, Kevin realized they must be thoroughly bored with such flowery nonsense, the sort of thing they'd hear from every courtier seeking favors. *Wonderful. Another blunder.*

Nothing else to do now but play. Kevin ran a hand over the strings of his lute, then made hasty, delicate refinements to the tuning; lutes went out of pitch fairly easily. Beside him, he could hear Naitachal doing the same with his small harp.

"'The Lover True,'" Kevin murmured to him as the elf finished, and they broke together into the opening chords. As they finished the introductory measures, Naitachal gave a little dip of the head, saying as plain as words, You take it.

Good enough. As he'd reached his majority, Kevin's voice had darkened ever so slightly into a deep tenor that still secretly delighted him. As he sang the gently tender verses, he subtly studied

Gwenlyn for a reaction. She wasn't pretty, not by the bland, conventional standards. No, there wasn't anything bland about her at all, least of all those incredible eyes.

The eyes that right now were sparking with something approaching contempt. Kevin finished his song to enthusiastic applause—save from her. Hers was slow and deliberate enough to be blatantly sarcastic. "You didn't like the song, my lady?" Kevin asked wryly.

"Very pretty, minstrel," she said without expression. "Not as—"

"Oh, please. You're not going to say, 'Not as pretty as you,' are you?"

"I *was* about to say," Kevin lied hastily, "not as pretty as the song itself."

"Ah, clever. The minstrel is more graceful with his words than he is with his feet."

"I could say, my lady," Kevin began with a desperate stab at gallantry, "that I was clumsy only because your beauty dazzled me."

"That's rot."

"Gwenlyn!" Count Trahern whispered in disapproval, and she glanced his way. "But it *is* rot, Father. I was covered with dirt and wearing my oldest clothes." Gwenlyn turned back to Kevin. "I hear false praise enough from your betters, minstrel. I don't choose to suffer it from you, too."

Fighting back sharper words, Kevin said carefully, "If you consider my words, my lady, you'll see I didn't actually cast false praise on you."

Dark brows raised in surprise. "No," she admitted drily after a moment, "you didn't. I could say 'how flattering.' "

Her sarcasm stung. "If you want flattery," Kevin exclaimed in a sudden burst of impatience, "you aren't going to get it from me. A rose with too many thorns isn't going to have too many admirers."

"A rose with too many thorns," she snapped back, "retains its freedom."

"Freedom to wither on—"

"That's enough!" Count Trahern cut in angrily. "I've tried to make excuses for creative foolishness, but minstrel, this nonsense has gone too far!"

"I didn't mean—" Kevin began, only to be interrupted by Gwenlyn's indignant, "Father, I can take care of myself!"

But the man silenced them both with an angry wave of his hand. "I cannot allow a commoner such license. Minstrel, you surely know you cannot be allowed to insult a woman of noble blood like this. My regrets, but I must ask you to leave before I am forced to—"

Oh, curse it all! "But I'm not a minstrel," Kevin admitted reluctantly.

"What are you, then?" Gwenlyn's voice dripped scorn. "A Bard?"

"Exactly!" Too late to stop now. "I am also not a commoner, but Count Kevin, your—the one who—the one who accepted your portrait."

"So much for dashing disguises," Naitachal murmured, with just a touch too much amusement in his voice for Kevin's liking.

Count Trahern and Gwenlyn both were sitting bolt upright with shock. "The portrait," the man whispered fiercely to his daughter, "his portrait. Let me see it."

"Do you think I carry it with me?" she hissed back.

Kevin sighed. "I know I don't look particularly noble right now. I don't *feel* particularly noble. But I can at least prove my friend and I really are Bards."

Count Trahern raised a skeptical eyebrow. "Do so."

With a wary glance at Naitachal, who looked the

very image of innocence—if innocence were shrouded in solid black—Kevin lifted his lute once more and began the gentle song known as "Quiet Friendship's Melody," which held within it the possibility of soothing roused emotions and allaying suspicions. Naitachal added his harp's counterpoint to the soft, intricate melody but nodded at Kevin, signalling him once again to carry the words. As he sang their gentle simplicity, the young count felt Bardic Magic rousing within him, warm and heady as wine, and had to fight with himself to keep the power of the spell-song at only half-strength. He wanted to soothe the count and his daughter, not ensorcel them! Kevin saw Count Trahern settle back in his chair, saw even Gwenlyn's fierce blue stare soften, and dared a small smile.

But just as the magic was taking full control, Gwenlyn shot to her feet with a frantic "No!" Her shout was fierce enough to break through Kevin's Bardic trance. Startled, he lost his hold on the song and the fragile spell, and the music faltered into silence. Before he could recover, Gwenlyn raced from the room.

"What did I say?" Kevin asked in confusion, dazed from the suddenness of the spell's breaking, struggling to reorganize his thoughts. "What did I sing wrong? I didn't mean her any harm."

Count Trahern shook his head. "Nothing was wrong, save, perhaps, my daughter's fancies. You sang most wondrously fair, Count Kevin. And yes," he added wryly, "I do believe you are who and what you claim; I felt the power of your song." Almost apologetically, the count added, "My daughter is a fiery spirit; I can't always understand what moves her. Go after her. Speak with her. See if, perhaps, *you* can soften her heart."

Oh. Of course. Just what I want to do. Kevin glanced

at Naitachal, uneasy about leaving a Dark Elf—Bard or no Bard—alone among possibly hostile strangers. But Naitachal, still virtually radiating elven amusement at human foolishness, waved him on.

Human stupidity, rather, Kevin thought drily. *I don't even* want *the woman.*

But he couldn't very well say that to her father. "I can only try," the young count said evasively, and set out after Gwenlyn. After some quick questions to various guards and servants, he finally caught up with her on the castle ramparts. She was staring fiercely out into the surrounding forest.

Now, what? Kevin wondered doubtfully. "My . . . uh . . . lady."

She turned sharply to him, her eyes so wild with rage that for a moment he was sure she was going to try tossing him over the rim. "How *dare* you!"

"I beg your pardon?"

"How *dare* you not tell me who you were right from the start!"

"I—"

"What were you trying to do? Let the silly girl make a fool of herself?"

"No, I—"

"That's exactly it, isn't it?"

"Why would I want to do a thing like that?"

"Why? Because you wouldn't be the first! Men don't like women who aren't properly meek, do they?"

"That's the most ridiculous thing I've ever—"

"No, no," Gwenlyn rushed on, "all they want of a noblewoman is that she not be noticed except as—as a prize to be shown off like a pretty, brainless brood mare!"

"I would never treat a woman like that!"

"Ha! You certainly aren't going to treat *me* like that!"

Gwenlyn broke off to catch her breath, then continued in a slightly calmer voice, "Look you, I know I have a sharp tongue. But what other weapon is there for someone like me? You don't really think you're the first of my would-be suitors, do you? The others have come wooing my father's wealth and status practically since the day I was born. But all of them raced away the minute they found out they couldn't cow me—after each one of them did his best to humble me. And that's exactly the path you were following!"

"No!"

"Yes! You wanted me to make a fool of myself so you could laugh at me and be oh so superior!"

A stab of sympathy shot through Kevin. "I'm sorry you think that way. But I swear I didn't mean to hurt you."

"Oh no, of course not," she drawled. "You were playing that ridiculous false role because you were trying to make me feel at ease."

"I was trying," Kevin said with as much self-control as he could muster, "to give us both a chance to know each other without rank getting in the way. But I can see that isn't going to work out."

"On the contrary," Gwenlyn snarled. "It's worked out all too well. I've already learned I'd as soon link my name to—to a dog baying at the moon as marry you."

"How poetic. And *I* would much prefer to hear that dog howl at me than listen to one more word from Your Thorniness."

"Oh, be wary of my thorns, indeed!"

They broke off, glaring at each other. "Better to know how we feel about each other now," Kevin said at last, "before it's too late."

"Much better. And since we do know it, you have no excuse to linger here. So go!"

"Gladly!"

Kevin bowed his curtest bow and stormed off, swearing under his breath. Curse the woman, curse his own stupidity, curse this whole idiotic business! Part of him still couldn't help but feel sorry for Gwenlyn, trapped in the snare of her social status as she was. But he didn't love her, he was most surely never going to love her, and he doubted the prickly creature would ever let herself love anybody. Besides, just because he pitied her it didn't mean he wanted to tie himself for the rest of his life to someone who would as soon stab him with words as kiss him!

Now, isn't this a lovely mess? Kevin mused bitterly. *I don't want her, she doesn't want me, but I can't simply break off this almost-betrothal, not without offending Count Trahern.*

And that would be a most perilous thing to do. Offending such an important noble, Kevin knew, would almost certainly trap him in the midst of who knew what political tangles.

The young count let out his breath in a long sigh of frustration. Right now, he'd give anything to be back in the old days, out on the road with Lydia, Tich'ki and the others with an open world of adventure ahead. But swordplay or Bardic Magic wasn't going to help him now. He'd once fought bandits and the undead and triumphed, but there wasn't anything he could do to get himself out of this more prosaic peril. In fact, Kevin thought dourly, there was only one thing he *could* do right now. And by all the Powers, he meant to do it: go home!

Chapter VI

Gate Building

Alone in her dark little sorcery laboratory, Rualath stood a long time lost in thought, even as she had been doing again and again since boldly making her vow to Haralachan about snaring Naitachal. What was she going to do about fulfilling that vow? She couldn't afford to waste too much more time. Soon enough the Dark Elf lord would be wondering what she was about, and if she didn't have something to show him—

Wait. Panic was ridiculous, weak. Take the problem point by point. Naitachal, now . . . she could not claim to know Naitachal very well. Even though they shared clan and caste, he had always been a strange creature, keeping to himself as much as possible, never really letting himself be involved in any of the convoluted, endless tangle of *Nithathili* plots, save those necessary for his own survival. But even as a child he had attracted the attention of those whose task it was to train promising young sorcerers in the proper science of Necromancy, the potential for Power radiating around him, strong and dark.

No, Rualath corrected herself drily, it would appear

that his Power hadn't been truly Dark after all. Though at the time he had seemed most perfectly born and bred for the role of Necromancer, absorbing every harsh lesson of the art without complaint or weakness, Naitachal had most definitely perverted his talents.

"*Music.*" Rualath said that foreign word with distaste, then shook her head. How could he possibly take such deep pleasure in a random collection of sounds?

No. Never mind that. Naitachal's bizarre tastes hardly mattered. No matter how fiercely he might try to deny his heritage, he was still a fully trained Necromancer. That made him a dangerous foe—but a predictable one. Other Necromancers had challenged Rualath in the past, seeking to supplant her as Haralachan's consort. She had destroyed every one of those who'd dared challenge her. No, the difficulty would not be so much in fighting and besting Naitachal, but in finding a way to lure him back to the Darkness in which he could be conquered.

Oh, indeed. And how was she going to find such a way? With an impatient hiss, Rualath knelt and released the magical clasps of chest after chest, crouching to rummage yet again through the scrolls that represented long years of study and experimentation.

But at last she sat back in helpless frustration. Nothing! There was still nothing she could use! If Naitachal was still of the Darkness, there would have been half a hundred strategies she could have used to snare him. But what could lure him now? What had he become, this impossibility of Darkness turned Light? How did he think? What would he, what *could* he want?

Ae, but she could hardly come before Haralachan with an inane, "I've failed." That would be as good as offering him a sacrificial knife and lying meekly down on the altar. No, no, there had to be another solution.

All right, then. Think. If the finished, set magics she'd previously created were useless, perhaps one of her experimental, untested spells might serve, instead. But . . . which?

With a sudden snarl of impatience, Rualath got to her feet, straightening her robes with brusque hands. If her mind refused to help her here, perhaps a change of scene—and just possibly a brief hunt should some prey, animal or servant, cross her path—would clear her thoughts.

Rualath silently prowled the chill, dark caverns of her lord's realm, seeing no one, hearing no one. But then she stopped with a soft, startled hiss, staring into utter blackness that even *Nithathil* sight could not pierce, her every magical sense alert and on guard. Another was here, another stood silent in the darkness. Why? A threat? Rualath drew defensive Power to her, ready to cast.

"I am alone." A shrouded figure moved slightly forward, just enough for Rualath to see it assume the posture of Courteous Submission to an Equal: arms out from sides to show no weapons hidden, palms held parallel to the stone floor to show no spells being worked.

Ha, she knew the aura of this one. "Tanarchal. What do you want?"

If he was surprised at the ease with which she'd identified him, he showed no sign, calmly pushing back the hood of his cloak to meet her gaze. "I am overcome with admiration," he said.

"Meaning?"

"Your sorcerous skill. And strength of will. I would not have the courage to experiment with Power as you do."

"You would not have the talent," Rualath said flatly. "I ask again: what do you want?"

"What do *you* want? So much Power, so much talent . . . what do you want, Rualath?"

She raised a skeptical brow. "I am consort to our ruler, free to work whatever experiments I wish. What more could I want?"

His teeth flashed in the darkness in a predatory grin. "I hardly expect one such as you to show weakness."

"Weakness!"

Tanarchal kept his palms flat and outstretched. "Is not innocence a weakness?"

Rualath gave a sharp little laugh of contempt. "Don't attempt to condescend, Tanarchal."

"Never that. Not to someone who just might remember those who knew her before she . . . ah, but you surely have no desire to ascend the throne."

"The throne is already occupied," she reminded him reflexively, but the faintest spark of alarm shocked through her. Was this a genuine attempt at an alliance? Did Tanarchal truly mean to help her overthrow Haralachan? No *Nithathil* aided another without an ulterior motive: did Tanarchal see himself as the power behind the throne? Or . . . could he already have made some manner of alliance with Haralachan? Was this a trap? A test of her loyalty? There was never a *Nithathili* plot laid without a dozen interlacing possibilities and perils.

Haralachan is so much more powerful than this ambitious youngster, Rualath reasoned coldly. *He holds the support I do not yet command and Tanarchal never will. Ambition and inexperience are perilous companions.*

So, then. Better Haralachan's dangerous arrogance than the need to forever be watching her back without respite that would come with an alliance with Tanarchal.

"No," she said aloud. "Find another tool."

His smiled thinned ever so slightly. "A challenge?"

"Against you?" Rualath let contempt flavor her words ever so delicately. "No."

He bowed shortly, relief just barely veiled, his wary gaze never leaving her face just in case she might choose to attack without formal warning, then he backed away into shrouding blackness. Rualath stood with predatory patience for a long while till she was sure she was in no peril from his sudden ambush, then walked away with slow, studied grace, radiating total lack of concern with every step. It wasn't a complete act: since he had forgone attack here and now, there wasn't any real threat from Tanarchal; he knew as well as she that she wouldn't betray him to Haralachan. No, if Haralachan wasn't strong enough to hold off Tanarchal or any other would-be usurper without help, then he didn't deserve to keep the throne.

Ahh, yes. But if Haralachan continued to hold power, then the problem of Naitachal remained unsolved. Rualath let out her breath in a long sigh, and turned back towards her sorcery study, part of her mind forever wary against possible danger, the rest contemplating magic. There must be a solution, there must!

Haralachan slowly lowered the small, intricately cut gemstone from his eye, letting it fall back on the thin chain about his neck. So, and so . . . interesting. Interesting that Rualath should choose to cleave to him. She must have been sorely tempted for a moment; he was very much aware of her ambition, just as he was aware that she knew only too well that with him rested political might.

For now, whispered a sly corner of his mind, and Haralachan's lips tightened ever so slightly. Yes. For now. For now and for as long as he wished to hold that power. Tanarchal? Now and again a Tanarchal arose, more willfulness than sense. Others before him had come and gone. And Tanarchal, in turn, would someday serve his lord and the Darkness in the hunt or on the altar. In the meantime, Haralachan would let him live, for the possibility of that future entertainment.

Rualath, though. There was a deeper threat—but also the greater promise of excitement: long *Nithathili* lives soon led into boredom without the thrill that came from such potential danger from such intimate companions. Haralachan smiled languorously, coldly. If she failed him now, in the matter of Naitachal, he would, of course, take her life. If she succeeded, why then, she became all the more dangerous to his security—and all the more exciting.

Entering her study, Rualath barred the door with a commanding wave of her hand, then, safely alone, fell back against a wall. Ignoring the coldness of the stone stealing through her, she stood grimly hunting through her mind, remembering every sorcerous test she'd ever made, finding and analyzing and rejecting concept after concept, until . . . until . . .

Hai, yes! The answer hit her so suddenly Rualath straightened as though she'd been slapped, nearly cried out in startled triumph. Yes, oh yes, indeed! Pausing only long enough to will her thoughts to proper coolness, she sent a mental call.

"*Yes,*" came Haralachan's cool answer. "*What?*"

"*I have an intriguing little tale to tell you.*"

"*Well? What?*"

"Dealing with our wandering traitor. May I join you?"

"In the audience cavern, yes. Now."

He broke the mental contact so brusquely Rualath bared her teeth in a silent snarl. Oh, she'd truly named him arrogant! How dare he summon her as though she were nothing more than an erring slave? And forcing her to meet him in such a public place—Haralachan was most surely making certain she didn't dare fail him, not with potential witnesses certain to be all about.

"I will not fail," Rualath promised softly. "And may the day come when you regret that fact."

Her walk smooth and deliberate as a predator's stalk, she returned to where Haralachan sat at ease on his obsidian throne and paused a moment to study him. Ah, what an image he presented. His long legs were outstretched and crossed at the ankle, the lazy pose contrasting sharply with the darkness half hiding his lean form and the waves of cold, casual Power radiating from him.

Save the tricks, Rualath thought wryly. *I've seen them all before.*

"Well, my dear consort?" Haralachan asked with delicate irony, looking at her over steepled fingers. "What have you?"

Rualath smiled slowly. "As I hinted, I have an intriguing little solution to our . . . problem."

"Naitachal, you mean. What?"

"Ah, then you are interested, my lord?"

His eyes flickered with impatience, glinting red in the dim light above the elegant hands, but Haralachan's coldly perfect face remained impassive as stone. "Speak."

"I call my magical creation simply a Gate Spell."

"There have been other Gates."

Rualath narrowly kept from frowning at the casual scorn in his voice. "Of course there have," she replied smoothly, "but none quite like this."

"Ah? How so?"

"This Gate," Rualath purred, "shall be a sorcerous doorway, yes, but it shall," *if the magic works correctly,* she added wryly to herself, "be keyed specifically to Naitachal. It will be designed to snare him the moment he passes through the Gate, or even too near to it, and pull him, helpless as a slave, straight into our arms." She paused with a slight smile, just barely keeping it from turning into a triumphant grin. "Does that intrigue you, my lord?"

Even though his face still showed not the slightest trace of emotion, Rualath saw the mingled relief and caution glint in his eyes. *Yes, my lord,* she purred silently, *respect me. Fear me, even.*

Oh, granted, the Gate Spell was still very much in the experimental stage, with a good deal of potential for its going wrong or failing altogether. Rualath admitted to herself that she hadn't yet been able to send a rat through the Gate she had created in tests without the whole thing shattering uselessly. But showing herself as fallible in any way before Haralachan would be worse than inane: it would be suicidal.

And that, Rualath told herself, *I most certainly am not. As far as Haralachan may know, my spells never fail.*

"Yes," Haralachan said at last. "It does intrigue me. Go, my good Rualath. Begin your spell. The traitor shall be ours at last."

Yes, he shall, my melodramatic consort. But when he is snared, Rualath thought with an inner smile, *the glory of that snaring, when none else in all your realm could catch him, shall all be mine.*

Chapter VII

Pilgrimage

"How dare you!" Count Trahern thundered at his daughter where they stood alone on the castle ramparts. "How dare you act like that to such an important guest!"

"He brought it on himself!" Gwenlyn countered fiercely.

"Don't argue with me! How dare you act like such a—a—a— Bah! I can't even find the words!"

"Like a spoiled child?" Gwenlyn shouted back. "How else did you expect me to act? You've been treating me like a child!"

"Nonsense!"

"Oh, is it? Can you actually claim you gave me a chance to act like an adult anywhere along the way?"

"Of course I have, curse it!"

"You most certainly have not!" Glaring at her father, Gwenlyn continued, "All through this ridiculous non-courtship and non-betrothal I haven't had a say in anything! You've been busily trying to force me into what *you* want me to be, what *you* want me to do, as if I couldn't be trusted to make my own decisions!" *That's not quite true,* part of her mind insisted, *up till now he's always let you be your own person.* Oh, indeed. Till now. Suddenly furious at herself for feeling a ridiculous urge to weep, Gwenlyn shrieked instead, "I will not be your helpless, mindless slave!"

"You aren't a slave, you little idiot, you're my daughter! And as my daughter, you will do as I say!"

"And that is what? Are you really going to command me to marry that lout?"

"You will marry that 'lout,' as you so stupidly call him, or anyone else I order you to wed!"

"Ha! Rather than be forced into a trap like that, I would sooner stay a maid alone till the day I die!"

"That is not one of your options, girl," Count Trahern said darkly. "You are my only heir, and the family line must continue through you. Like it or not, you must marry. You *will* marry—and the man you wed will be Count Kevin!"

"It will not!"

"Dammit, Gwenlyn, stop answering back!"

"How can I keep quiet? This is my life you'd bargain away!"

Count Trahern glanced heavenward with an angry sigh. "Why?" he asked unseen forces. "Other fathers have nice, sensible, *dutiful* children. Why was I given such a sharp-tongued, sharp-willed, hopelessly stubborn creature instead?"

"I'm my father's daughter," Gwenlyn snarled.

The count lowered his head at that to glare at her. "We've been over all this ground before."

"Gods, yes! Look you, of course I know I'll have to marry. But—but can't I have *any* say in the matter?"

"I've given you too much say, there's the problem! Stop shrieking at me like a servant just for a moment and start thinking like my daughter, like the heir of a count. Count Kevin is high in the royal favor. You know it as well as I. He is far, far too valuable an ally to offend—ha, yes, and yet you've already managed to drive him away!"

"He left of his own accord." *That isn't quite true, either,* her mind insisted. *You really didn't give him much of a chance to stay.* And . . . he hadn't seemed like such a bad sort, not as bad as the others, surely; his face hadn't been a minstrel's image of handsomeness, but his eyes had been so full of life and friendliness—

Not that she'd given him much of a chance to be friendly.

"It's his own fault," Gwenlyn muttered, as much to herself as her father. "If only he hadn't tried that ridiculous masquerade, if only he'd been honest with me from the start, maybe—" She brought herself up short. "That's neither here nor there. I am not going to marry him, and there's an end to it."

"There is *not* the end to it at all!" Count Trahern caught his breath with an audible gasp. "Look you, I could have married you off long before this. You could have been wed to an old man or a cruel one long before you'd reached the age of consent. But no, I cared for your welfare, I waited till you were old enough to—yes, to have some say in the matter. Bah! I was a fool!"

"That's ridiculous! Why—"

"Don't interrupt! I let you reject suitor after suitor—"

"Because each one was worse than the next, and you know it! They didn't want a wife, not one of that glittering, empty-brained lot, they wanted a—a show-piece, a pretty creature who could breed them heirs and keep her mouth shut!"

"And keeping your mouth shut is something you've

never been able to do!" the count snapped. "I tell you, Count Kevin is known as a good, kind young man, a Bard—and I will not have you turn down someone who has the King's own ear!"

"That's the heart of it, isn't it?" Gwenlyn shouted back. "You don't care about whether or not I'd be happy, not anymore. Oh no, you're so dazzled by the thought of possible royal favor spreading your way you can't see what's right in front of your nose!"

"And what, pray tell," her father said in a dangerously low voice, "is that?"

"Don't you know? You've fallen so madly in love with the idea of having Count Kevin in the family that you refuse to see the truth: he's a—a stupid, arrogant *nobody*! And no matter what you do or say, I *will not marry him!*"

"Enough of this nonsense!" the count roared. "You *will* marry Count Kevin, you will *not* answer me back—and you are going on a little journey, right now!"

Before Gwenlyn could do more than gasp in surprise, her father grabbed her by the wrist, dragging her after him as he shouted for his servants. As they came scurrying up to bow and stare in astonishment, Count Trahern told them fiercely, "My daughter is about to leave on a pilgrimage to the retreat of Saint Verdain for a period of meditation."

It was a trip commonly made by brides-to-be. As the servants buzzed in surprise and excitement, Gwenlyn opened her mouth, shut it again, so overcome with fury and shock she couldn't say anything coherent. Her father glared at her, tightening his grip on her wrist so much the tears came to her eyes and choked off any possible protests. "You will do as I say," he whispered. "Is that understood? You will return in a more suitable frame of mind. Is *that* understood? You will return in a more suitable frame of mind—or, by all the gods, you are not to return here at all!"

The day was cool and clear, with just enough of a gentle breeze to keep off any annoying insects, and the sweet smell of spring was all around. Gwenlyn, sitting on her smooth-striding palfrey, surrounded by her father's guards, a timid maidservant on a mule beside her, was fuming. She knew that had this been any other outing—even though her father had put repulsive Captain Degalth in charge—she probably would have been enjoying herself immensely. But how could she possibly enjoy being forced into a journey she didn't want to take? A journey which was going to end in her being trapped into making a decision she didn't want to make?

How could he do this to me? How could Father virtually send me into exile?

Easily. He really had been amazingly tolerant up till now, allowing her to refuse any and all suitors. Gwenlyn admitted that freely; any other noble's daughter would never have had so much freedom. That was what had made his sudden decision that Count Kevin was the one she'd wed and no argument about it so startling. Gwenlyn shook her head in frustration. Did her father really expect her to return home nicely humbled, all ready to be married off to whomever Daddy picked?

Ha! Not a chance of that!

But at the same time, Gwenlyn uncomfortably knew there really wasn't much of an alternative. *Short of taking religious orders at St. Verdain's, of course. And I can hardly see myself as a cloistered holy woman! Gods, no, I'd have even less freedom there than I would as a wife.*

Her restlessness was communicating itself to her palfrey, which had begun pacing nervously, and for a time Gwenlyn had to turn all her attention to the horse, welcoming the distraction.

"My lady?" one of the guards asked warily. "Would you like one of us to take the reins?"

"No!" Gwenlyn snapped, and told the palfrey with hands and body to behave itself *now.* The last thing she wanted was to have even this last tiny bit of self-reliance taken from her by overly solicitous guards.

Oh, curse it all, I'm not against marriage, not to someone I could love, or at least like and respect—but can't I have a chance to live my own life at least a little first? I've never actually done *anything, not on my own, not as my own, individual self. Am I never going to have a chance to do anything interesting before I wind up going from count's daughter to count's wife?*

Am I never going to have any adventures at all?

Surrounded by the splendid spring day and the attentive guards in their blue and gold livery and glittering mail, Gwenlyn brooded.

Captain Degalth, solid, stolid, and totally without imagination, glanced uneasily sideways at his noble employer's daughter. At least the sharp-tongued creature had fallen silent—for the moment—but it was just a matter of time before she attacked again, making things miserable for him. It wasn't *his* fault Count Trahern had decided to send the little shrew off to St. Verdain's! If it had been up to him, Degalth thought angrily, he would have had her sent off gagged and bound.

A woman has no business acting like this, thinking for herself and trying to lead her own life. What garbage! Everyone knows no woman can act or think as well as a man—they just aren't up to it, the delicate things. Childbearing, that's what they're made for. And that's what my Lady Gwenlyn needs, too: a husband to keep her in line and a baby or two. That'll settle her right down.

But of course he didn't dare say anything like that to her. Even though it grated to act properly humble to a mere snip of a girl, Degalth had no intention of getting Count Trahern angry at him. Even though he secretly thought the count a fool for giving his daughter a boy's education, letting the girl get such high-and-mighty ideas as freedom and independence into her sharp-tongued head.

As though she was aware of his thoughts, Gwenlyn glanced quickly his way. Degalth grit his teeth. "Is something wrong, my lady?"

"Nothing," she snapped, "save for this whole journey," and turned just as quickly away.

Be that way, Degalth told her silently. *Keep up the shrewish behavior, my lady. And all my sympathies to Count Kevin or any other man who's unfortunate enough to be stuck with you.*

The way Degalth was right now. Suddenly he knew he couldn't bear having the hot-tempered girl on his hands one moment longer than he had to. Standing in the stirrups, Degalth studied the way ahead. If they stayed on this broad main road, they would have a perfectly safe, perfectly dull ride, and it would take several days to reach St. Verdain's. But there was another route through the forest looming up on their left. Granted, it wasn't as wide or comfortable, and technically not as safe as the main road—but it was most definitely a shortcut that would take at least two days off their journey.

Why not try it? Degalth mused. *After all, it's not really dangerous; I wouldn't deliberately take Count Trahern's daughter into peril. But there aren't any animals big enough to threaten armed men, and there haven't been any bandits in these parts for years.*

Gwenlyn was snapping at one of the guards who was trying to take the reins from her. Degalth looked at her stormy eyes and nodded.

That did it. The shorter forest route it was!

He saw Gwenlyn straighten in her saddle. "Captain Degalth, where are we going?"

"Why, to the retreat of St. Verdain, my lady!"

"Don't patronize me, Captain Degalth. Why are we leaving the main road?"

"This is a more direct route to St. Verdain's, my lady. I know it's not quite as broad or flat as the main road, but I've travelled it before, and I assure you it's quite safe and comfortable."

Gwenlyn's gaze was sharp and wary. Hell, she was going to order him back onto the main road, he knew it. But then she sighed and shrugged. "You would know that better than I. So be it."

Hastily, before she could change her mind, Degalth led the way into the forest, his horse picking its wary way down the narrow trail. It was cool in here, and dim, with isolated sparkles of sunlight; so much ancient leaf mold carpeted the ground their horses' hoofs thumped dully rather than clopping. Degalth glanced back to see how Gwenlyn was doing, and was astonished to see her actually smiling, her face for once empty of anger. As a bird darted by overhead, trilling, she looked up sharply with a little cry of delight.

She likes it in here! I bet she thinks it's all pretty birds and deer and—

A branch slapped him full in the face. Clawing free, spitting out leaves, Degalth could have sworn he heard Gwenlyn chuckle, and only barely managed to stifle a curse. The sooner he was rid of this affliction of a girl, the happier he'd be! Pulling leaves and twigs out of his helm, he signalled a faster pace to the others.

They rode on in silence for what Degalth guessed was quite a while, though it was difficult to judge time when you couldn't really see the sun. He was just beginning to wonder if they should stop to let Gwenlyn rest—though she seemed to be holding up as well as any of the men—when one of the guards forced his horse up through the bushes to Degalth's side.

"Uh, Captain," he murmured, "don't want to alarm the lady, but . . . well . . . I could swear someone's watching us."

"Nonsense. Who's going to watch us, a deer?"

"Well . . ."

"Look, there's no one living in the forest, not around here anyhow, not even a peasant."

"Bandits—"

"There have been no bandits in this region for years," Degalth snapped. "Now get back to your place and keep your mouth shut before you start scaring the lady!"

Not that a little thing like bandits are going to scare this lady, Degalth thought. *Naw, nothing short of the end of the world would bother someone like her.*

But suddenly it *was* the end of the world for him. As the arrow slammed into his chest, hitting just above the edge of his mail shirt, Degalth had time only for one quick, last, regretful, *Oh hell, looks like the guard was right.*

And then there was nothing to think about at all.

For one bewildered moment, Gwenlyn thought Captain Degalth had somehow simply managed to fall off his horse. Then she caught a quick glimpse of the arrow, the blood, while all around her, the guards were whipping out their swords and suddenly men were shouting, screaming as arrows cut them down. Her maidservant was screaming, too, a long, shrill shrieking that hurt her ears till it was abruptly cut short. Gwenlyn fought her terrified horse, just barely keeping the saddle as it bucked and plunged. The young woman turned her head this way and that, trying to find a way out, seeing only death and blood. There were wild-eyed, savage faces all around her, cutting off her escape.

Outlaws! And our guards were so—so damned complacent they weren't prepared to fight, and I—I—

As a guard slid limply from the saddle, sword falling from his hand, Gwenlyn grabbed for the hilt. The sword was heavier than she'd expected, so heavy she needed both hands to steady it, but somehow she managed to slash out at the hands reaching for her. But she couldn't hold the sword and the reins at the same time, and the palfrey, unused to battle, was wheeling and leaping wildly, throwing off her aim and balance. As Gwenlyn frantically tried to slash out again, hands clamped shut on her arms, her shoulders, pulling her over backwards off the saddle. The sword went flying as she hit the ground with enough force to drive the breath from her lungs. For a terrifying moment all she could do was gasp for air, the leering, filthy faces of her captors looming over her, and think, *This is a stupid way to die.*

But then a voice shouted, "No, you idiots! That's a lady you've got there, and she's worth a lot more undamaged. Hurry up, this place isn't going to be safe for long. Take her with us!"

As they dragged her to her feet, Gwenlyn kicked and bit and clawed frantically. But she might as well have been a child trying to hurt a giant for all the good that did. Someone threw a dirty, bloodstained cloak about her, wrapping it tightly despite her struggles, pinning her arms to her sides. Strong hands grabbed her shoulders and pulled her forward. As she was dragged helplessly off into the depths of the forest, Gwenlyn told herself wryly:

You wanted adventure, you fool. Now you've got it!

Chapter VIII

The Gate Opens

Rualath stood alone in her sorcery workroom, panting. All around her, the elements of her spellcasting littered the room: bits of feathers symbolizing air, glints of stone symbolizing earth, eerie, convoluted twists of rock and metal and sorcerous substances unknown to the outside world lying seemingly at random. Intricate, eye-hurting symbols were chalked over every available surface, and black-flamed candles burned at the five cardinal points. Two mice huddled in a small cage in one corner, test subjects; there had been four when Rualath had begun.

But for all the complicated arrangements, for all the convoluted elements of the spell, so far her efforts had ended in total failure.

The first version of the Gate Spell had caused only the slightest, most useless wavering of the air, and the first mouse had walked right through it with no effect at all, on either mouse or spell.

The second version of the Gate Spell had created a miniature whirlwind that had nearly torn apart her sorcery supplies before Rualath could dispel it and left the second mouse a lifeless, bloody mass. The sorceress thought of Naitachal suffering such a fate, dying so quickly and relatively easily before proper vengeance on a traitor could be taken, and shuddered. Should she be guilty of such failure, allowing the prey to escape, Haralachan would most surely accuse *her* of treason.

I will not fail, Rualath vowed fiercely, and refused to admit that what she really meant was: *I dare not.*

So, now. Think. She had already managed to rouse some Power; the shattered mouse had proven that. What if she altered this Rune of Transport just a touch, changing the points of orientation ever so slightly? Yes, that might prove interesting . . . and now if she shortened the distance between this candle and the outer edge of the first chalked circle to balance the change . . . yes, again. That balanced very nicely, indeed. And if she tried adding this Rune . . . yes, and added a twist to this one . . . yes, ah, yes . . .

She could hardly forget the danger of failure hanging over her. But suddenly burning with an explorer's fervor, Rualath set about her hasty rearrangements, scribbling the changes she was making on a parchment so they'd be safe till proven effective and worthy of committing to memory.

There! The new version was completed, leaving nothing left to do but activate it. Feeling her breath catch in her throat, Rualath snatched up one of the mice, gasping out the words that should, if there was any Dark Power in the world, activate the Gate Spell.

Yes, oh yes, it was happening, this time it was happening correctly! Rualath shivered, *feeling* magic stirring properly, fiercely, wild and so filled with Power it nearly dazzled her. Refusing to yield control to her creation, she watched a small shimmering form in the exact center of the innermost circle, exactly like that which formed in heated air over molten rock. *This time I shall succeed!*

Hastily, Rualath bent and placed the mouse near the shimmer. A sharp pinch made it jump forward—and reappear, without any apparent harm at all, on the far side of the outermost circle.

"It worked," Rualath breathed, and then again, more fiercely, "it worked."

Granted, there was still work to be done. The spell must be enlarged to let an elf pass; no lack of slaves for that test. Then it must be twisted and refined so it could be cast from afar . . . difficult, but she had cast other spells successfully from considerable distances. This should be no different. Most importantly, the Gate Spell must be set to specifically lure and catch Naitachal—no problem, that last, Rualath thought wildly, there surely must still be some bits of his possessions about, even if no one had yet been able to use them to snare him. Granted, the spell was still very, very experimental, granted she wasn't sure of all the possible variations its casting might create—

But it had worked, the Gate Spell worked. Not only was her life safe, but now new power, new status, would be hers as the creator of such magic, the one who had caught the traitor when all others had failed. At last the time would come when she no longer must humble herself before Haralachan but would be his true equal, even his superior!

Eyes blazing red with the force of her excitement, Rualath set about perfecting her spell.

"I will never," Naitachal exclaimed to his horse and the surrounding forest, "never, do you hear me, never understand how humans think!"

Kevin, riding beside him, both of them heading back towards his castle, stared resolutely straight ahead. "Aren't you ever going to get tired of the subject? We've been over the whole thing several times already."

"Obviously not times enough! You still aren't listening to me."

"That's right."

"Ae, *humans!*" Naitachal reached out to snatch the bridle of Kevin's horse, bringing both mounts to a stop. Slanted blue eyes glared into Kevin's own. "What is the matter with you? The woman is young, pretty in her own unique way, and decidedly intelligent."

The young count determinedly dragged his gaze away—not an easy thing when an elf was staring at you with almost sorcerous fervor. "The woman is a shrew."

"Oh, you can't tell me she doesn't have justification for being a bit sharp-tongued!"

"A bit!"

"Well, perhaps that was a little understated. But that is one of the most unhappy young people I have seen among your kind."

Kevin tried and failed to pull the bridle free from Naitachal's hand; elves could, when the fancy took them, show a supple strength far beyond human ability. With a sigh, the young count sprang from the saddle, trying to pretend that resting the horses was what he'd had in mind all along. Naitachal leaped down to join him, walking beside him, ignoring Kevin's attempt to ignore him. He looped the reins over one dark arm, the horses trailing after.

Kevin, fuming, knowing there was no way he could outwait his inhumanly patient friend, finally snatched back the reins of his own horse and admitted, "Yes. Of course I noticed the unhappiness behind her anger.

How could she not be unhappy, trapped in that rigid world of rules?"

"Oh, indeed." Kevin heard a sudden hint of hardness slip into his friend's voice and glanced his way to see the faintest hint of sorcerous red glint in Naitachal's eyes. "I know something of rigid rules," the Dark Elf said softly. "The rules that force you onto one path no matter what else you may wish. The rules that, if broken, mean death. Or worse."

Naitachal seldom gave more than reluctant hints as to what his life in the *Nithathili* caverns must have been like. Looking at the Dark Elf's carefully impassive face, Kevin wondered suddenly how it might have been if he, too, had been born into a certain race, a certain social class, forbidden to wander freely or—far, far worse—to study music, and shuddered. "I do feel sorry for her," he said defensively, "but that doesn't mean I want to tie my life to hers!"

"You could, at least, have taken some more time before rushing to that conclusion."

"I tried! She wouldn't listen to anything I had to say."

"How could she trust you? She'd already seen you change from one guise to another—for all the young woman knew she still hadn't seen the real Kevin."

Kevin glared. "Haven't you gotten weary of those 'I told you so's' yet?"

"Hardly."

"Ha." Kevin's attempt to storm away was checked by his horse stopping suddenly to grab a tasty leaf and nearly pulling him ignominiously over backwards. As he caught his balance, he saw Naitachal watching with face carefully bland, and snapped, "You can keep on with your nagging all you want. But that doesn't mean I need to listen!"

"Humans," Naitachal said conversationally to his horse. "Quite mad, the lot of them. They hunger after elves and elven magic like so many children after sweets—but let an elf try to give advice to one of them and suddenly that one turns most miraculously deaf."

"Ha," Kevin repeated. Jerking his horse's head up, he managed this time to successfully stalk away. Naitachal, chuckling, followed.

But as they walked, more or less together, the Dark Elf all at once stopped short, breath indrawn in a sharp hiss.

"Naitachal?" Kevin asked warily. "What—"

The elf curtly waved him to silence, standing as fiercely still as a questing hunting hound, eyes blazing with sorcerous force. "Magic . . ." he murmured at last. "Magic in a shape I have never known before."

Kevin bit back a groan. Elven curiosity was so much stronger than anything a human felt, strong enough at times to quite overwhelm little things such as personal safety and common sense, and right now every bit of Naitachal's curiosity was plainly aroused.

"Don't you think—" Kevin began warily, but the Dark Elf was already moving silently forward. The young count followed nervously in his wake, trying again. "Uh, Naitachal . . . don't you think you might be being just a little foolish? I mean, do we really want to investigate something that . . . well, maybe it doesn't want to be disturbed?"

"We cannot know that."

"We can't *not* know that, either! Look, if it's a type of magic you don't recognize—"

"Stay here if you are afraid," Naitachal cut in, but there wasn't any sting in the words; his voice was distracted, attention all on whatever lay before him. Without even glancing Kevin's way, he continued stalking.

"Oh, right. Let you walk blindly into peril. Of course," Kevin muttered, and followed.

But all at once Naitachal stopped, so abruptly Kevin nearly crashed right into him. "Look at that!" the Dark Elf hissed. "Look! Do you see it?"

Kevin stared. "See . . . what? It's a perfectly normal glade."

"Look!" Naitachal insisted impatiently.

"All I see that's at all unusual is a—a faint shimmering in the air. And I'm not even sure I see *that.* Naitachal, stop playing games. What am I supposed to be seeing?"

"The shimmering is exactly it! What you see is a Gate!"

"A . . . gate."

Naitachal shot him a quick glance that said, plainly as words, *oh, you ignorant human!* "A Gate, a sorcerous portal through time and space. Although . . ." he added thoughtfully, taking an intrigued step forward, "I admit I've never seen one quite like this." Kevin could almost have sworn he saw his friend's elegantly pointed ears prick forward. Fascinated as a hunting hound on a scent, the Dark Elf continued forward, eyes intent on what was clearly more than just a vague shimmering to him.

"It feels highly experimental," Naitachal commented after a moment, then stiffened. "Ae, yes, and alarmingly unstable!"

Oh, wonderful. And yet the elf showed every sign of wanting to investigate the thing more closely.

And he thinks humans *are foolish!* Kevin bit his lip nervously, wanting nothing so much as to get out of there this very moment. But he could hardly abandon his friend—foolishness or not—so he reluctantly hurried forward to grab Naitachal by the arm. "Uh, don't you think we should move back just a bit?"

But just then Naitachal cried in sudden alarm, "Rualath!"

"Who?"

"Never mind! Unstable magic, weird design—it has to be her work! Hurry, Kevin, we must get away from here before—"

"D-don't think I can . . ." Kevin murmured in misery. "Gods . . . I'm dizzy . . . suddenly so dizzy."

"Yes, of course you are. You're only human, you can't stand the sorcerous aura of a *Nithathil* Gate. Come, Kevin, hold fast. I'll help you out of range—Kevin!"

Somehow he had lost his grip on Naitachal's arm. Somehow he couldn't find the elf or the right way to move, and sky and forest were swirling crazily about him. Either the ground was stirring as well, or else he was stumbling like a man drunk beyond standing.

I c-can't move, I have to sit down, lie down . . .

But suddenly a wild shimmering of magic was all around him, bright enough for even a human to see.

The Gate! Kevin realized with a terrified flash of clarity. *I'm going to fall through it!*

He heard Naitachal shout in despair, "Kevin!" And then he was hurtling through the Gate—

—and landing with jarring force in an unfamiliar stretch of forest.

Where am I? Where's Naitachal?

Exhausted, dazed, and terrifyingly alone, Kevin made one valiant attempt to stand. But then his legs gave out under him, his senses swam sickeningly, and he collapsed.

Chapter IX

The Hunters

Lydia, once free wanderer, now commander-in-chief of Count Kevin's troops, stood in her office, a plain, stone-walled room furnished with a plain, comfortable chair and a simple table littered with military reports, and glared at the nervous soldier. "What do you *mean*, there's no sign of them! They're two grown men, Kevin and Naitachal, even if one of 'em's an elf. They can't just have disappeared!"

"Sorry, Commander. We searched, dogs and all. But there wasn't so much as a footprint to be seen, just like before, and not a hound could get a decent scent."

He had no reason to lie. Lydia sighed and waved him away. "Go get some food and drink for you and your troop. And get something for the hounds, too."

Alone, she ran a hand roughly through her curly black hair. Where were Kevin and Naitachal? When they hadn't returned after that first night, she'd sent out men to look for them, no matter how foolish D'Krikas might have thought her. But the men had come back—as had each successive troop—without so much as the slightest clue.

"Gods, I hate this sort of thing!" she said to the air.

"Playing anxious mommy again?" asked a shrill voice from overhead. Lydia glanced sharply up to see Tich'ki hanging in the air like a hovering insect, wings a glittery blur.

"You think I like it?" she snapped at the fairy. "Hell, if I'd wanted the role, I would have had kids of my own!"

Tich'ki came down to a tiptoe landing on the chairback. "Miss the old days, do you?"

"What? You mean the days of wandering about without a place to call home? Not really. No more than do you. Let's face it, Tich'ki, no matter how much fun it is to wander around without any ties to anyone, it's really good to have a home, friends."

"And responsibilities."

"Blast it, yes. In the old days, I didn't have to be responsible for anyone but myself!" Lydia shrugged. "Even nowadays it's not too bad. The guards I head up are usually smart enough to take care of themselves; they wouldn't have gotten hired otherwise."

"But then there's Kevin."

"Yeah, right," Lydia muttered. "Then there's Kevin. Where the hell *is* he?"

Tich'ki shrugged. "Who knows? He's a human. Never can tell what one of your folks are going to do. Thought that Dark Elf had more sense than to get lost, though."

"I hope they're *only* lost!" Lydia stared at the fairy, who took wing in alarm. "Come on, Tich'ki, you can't tell me you're not worried, too."

"Why should I be? They're big boys, both of them. They can take care of themselves."

"Uh-huh. Unless Naitachal's gone back to his bad old ways."

"As a Necromancer, you mean? Not a chance. He's

much too happy as a Bard to do something so stupid." But then Tich'ki paused, hanging almost motionless in the air, only her busy wings blurring with iridescent color. "Unless . . ." she began thoughtfully.

"Unless what?"

"Unless maybe his kin is after him?"

"Oh, great," Lydia groaned. "Just what I needed, something else to worry about!"

Tich'ki darted down to tousle her hair, grinning at Lydia's annoyed swipe as she quickly whirred back up out of reach. "Forget it, Lydia. If they haven't been able to snare Naitachal in the past four years, they're not going to catch him now."

"Sure. Of course. Then where is he? And where is Kevin?" Lydia started pacing, then stopped short. "Oh hell, I give up! I don't care what anybody says: I'm going after them."

"Just like that, huh? What about your duties here?"

Lydia stared up at the fairy. "Since when have you developed a sense of responsibility?"

Tich'ki shrugged, plainly embarrassed. "I like it here." Then she swooped sharply down to pinch Lydia's arm. "But don't think that makes me soft!"

"Not a chance of that," the woman muttered, rubbing her arm. "Yeah, I guess I should stay here and 'mind the shop,' as the saying goes. But, dammit, Tich'ki, someone's got to get Kevin back here." *Besides, it's been too long since I've actually had an adventure. . . . No, never mind that. It's Kevin you've got to think about, only him.*

Hurrying to the doorway, Lydia yelled for a guard. "Get Captain Sandroc in here now!" As soon as that grizzled veteran entered, Lydia began snapping out orders: "I want you to get together a troop of guards with forest experience, five to ten of 'em, and I want 'em ready to march out in two turns of the hourglass."

Sandroc must have wondered what his commander-in-chief was up to, but he saluted smartly enough and hurried to obey without question. And in an admirably short time he was back, saluting again. "The men are ready to march at your orders."

"Fine." *Nothing like an old soldier for efficiency.* Lydia had taken advantage of the brief interval to slip into her old leather armor. It was admittedly getting rather on the worn and battered side but it fit her body so comfortably she hadn't even considered replacing it. Sword a familiar weight at her side, bow and quiver slung over one shoulder, Lydia called to Sandroc, "You're in charge here till I return."

The soldier didn't show by the slightest quiver of a muscle that he was surprised. Weatherbeaten face totally impassive, Sandroc asked only, "Might I ask where you're going, ma'am?"

"To find Count Kevin." *And bring him home even if I have to haul him back by his ear!*

"You see?" the tracker said plaintively, glancing up from the foresty ground on which he crouched. "*Somebody* must have stopped here in this glade pretty recently, because there are still some traces of hoofprints and signs that two human bodies—or maybe one human and one elf—rested here. See how the grass is all disturbed? They were travelling fairly lightly, judging from how shallow the prints are, and at a guess I'd say they were both young and slender, or at least moved with the ease of young men."

"Yes, of course," Lydia said impatiently, leaning on the pommel of her horse's saddle. "I can see that much from up here. But can't you tell if those bodies belonged to Kevin and Naitachal?"

The man shook his head in frustration. "Sorry, ma'am, but there's no way to tell that, or even if the hoofprints were left by the horses Count Kevin took from the stable. And as to where they went . . ." The tracker shrugged. "We can follow 'em through the forest all right; the horses broke off enough branches as they passed to have left a clear trail. But we can't be sure we'd be following the right folks."

Lydia jumped down from her horse. She was a fine tracker in her own right, but after only a short while she straightened with a sigh, reluctantly admitting the man was quite right. Without magic, there wasn't any way to prove just who'd stopped here. *Wonderful to follow the trail all day and find out we'd wasted time trailing two common minstrels. You'd think Kevin would have been thoughtful enough to leave a scrap of cloak or a broken lute string or something*, she thought in disgust. "All right, I'm open to suggestions. Where could the two of them have gone?"

"Where do you think?" asked a sharp little voice from overhead. As Lydia glanced up, Tich'ki darted out from among the trees like a dragonfly. Hovering, sunlight sparkling off her wings, she shrugged. "I couldn't stand waiting at home, either."

"Oh, right. What about *your* duties?"

Tich'ki shrugged again, obviously annoyed at Lydia's prodding. "Oh, I think D'Krikas can manage without me for a short time," she said drily. "Besides, did you really think you could go off on an adventure without me?"

Aware of the soldiers staring at them, Lydia muttered, "It isn't an adventure, dammit, it's a mission. Now, where do *you* think Kevin's gone?"

The fairy swooped down to a landing on Lydia's shoulder, steadying herself, nearly weightless as a bird, by grabbing a handful of hair in one small fist. "Where do you think? The kid's a romantic, always has been; all of those Bards are. Ha, and that includes our music-loving Dark Elf pal as well."

"Oh, they wouldn't have—ow!"

Tich'ki had given her hair a painful tug. Launching herself into the air too quickly for Lydia to swat her, the fairy said over her shoulder, "You bet they have! The two of them have gone off to see our Kevin's prospective bride. Don't believe me? Follow me and I'll prove I'm right!"

Lydia hesitated a moment, wondering. If she followed Tich'ki, and this turned out to be nothing but one of the fairy's unpredictable pranks, she was going to look like a fool in front of her men. But without any other clues, there really wasn't anything else to do but follow.

To Lydia's relief, Tich'ki brought them straight to Count Trahern's castle. As the woman looked up at the massive walls, she heard the fairy whisper in her ear, "Done my bit. Your turn now."

At Lydia's signal, one of the soldiers, a fellow with a voice loud as a trumpet, called up to the castle guards to let them in. Rather to Lydia's surprise (*she* wouldn't have let strangers in so easily), at the mention of Count Kevin's name, the gates swung open as if by magic.

Well now, looks like Tich'ki was right. Kevin must have made quite an impression on these people!

Even more to Lydia's surprise, as she and her men clattered into the cobbled courtyard, a tall, richly dressed man who could be none other than Count Trahern himself came down from his keep to meet them.

As the man came closer, Lydia froze, staring at that elegant figure with its dark hair so fetchingly touched with silver and its strong, finely planed face, and heard something deep within her say softly, *Oh. My*. And a more irreverent corner of her mind chattered, *Mommy, buy me one of those!* Count Trahern didn't look like the sort of fellow who knew how to relax easily, but she was secretly delighted to spy a startled little glint in his eyes that said he, too, was pleased with what he saw.

Even if I'm in this old armor of mine and probably reek of horse. Well, well, isn't this interesting!

First things first, though. "My lady," the count said politely, even though Lydia knew there wasn't the slightest thing ladylike about her right now, "might I ask if Count Kevin has sent you?"

"Kevin!" Lydia exclaimed in shock. "No—he—I thought he was here!"

"He *was* here," Count Trahern corrected, frowning slightly, "but he left some time ago."

"And, uh, what about your daughter?"

The frown deepened. "As far as I know, my daughter is off at the shrine of Saint Verdain."

"Or . . . is she?" Lydia wondered. "Look, I'll be honest: I came here looking for Kev—ah, Count Kevin, because he never came home, neither he nor his Bard friend. And before you interrupt," she added, hastily holding up a hand, "no, we found no signs of violence anywhere between his castle and yours."

"I . . . see."

"Uh, I don't mean to bring up anything delicate, but . . . well . . . could you tell me if anything . . . happened?"

"Happened."

"Between Count Kevin and your daughter—"

"Count Kevin and Gwenlyn," the count said flatly, "disliked each other from first sight. They both made that most painfully clear."

"Oh."

"So if you are trying to imply that the two of them threw off their proper responsibilities and went running off together in some burst of childish exuberance, pray forget it."

"Unless . . ." Lydia stopped with a sigh. "Look you, Count Trahern, we're both adults. We both know there's that proverbial fine line between love and hate. I don't mean to worry you, but are you *sure* your daughter's gone to Saint Verdain's?"

"No, curse it, now I am not sure at all." Count Trahern paused a moment, then snapped at his servants, "Prepare my fastest horse. Yes, yes, the grey will do. Gather me an armed escort as well." Turning to Lydia, he bowed curtly. "My lady, I know you and your men have had little chance to rest, but I think we had best ride to the shrine ourselves, just in case."

"Just in case," Lydia agreed, trying her best to ignore Tich'ki, who was hidden in the wilderness of her hair, whispering, "Bet our boy's having a good time rolling around with the girl right now! Just like you wanna do with her daddy!"

Damn the fairy! And if she was right and that was what Kevin really was doing, getting them all terrified for nothing—well, then, damn that little Bard for an idiot, too!

"Come, Count Trahern," she said grimly, "let's ride."

Chapter X

In The Greenwood

The day was edging towards late afternoon, judging from the angle of the sunlight filtering down through the thick ceiling of leaves. Gwen, sitting rumpled and uncomfortable on the forest floor where she'd been unceremoniously dropped, watched the bandits moving about the mingy little campfire they were building and nervously told herself not to be a fool.

They look nasty, but they won't hurt you. You heard their leader: "undamaged" goods are worth more. Gwenlyn wasn't naive; she knew exactly what that "undamaged" meant. *Father will probably be furious about this whole thing; he probably won't want to let me out of his sight again till the day I'm safely married off. But that's better than being dead or . . . or anything else. Of—of course he'll ransom me. And of course none of these scum will hurt me till he does.*

But did they have the patience to wait that long? Their leader, a tall, skinny fellow who looked as though he didn't have one sound tooth in his head, wasn't exactly an awe-inspiring hero out of legend.

Gwenlyn doubted he would hold the others in line very long if they didn't agree.

And those others weren't any more heroic in appearance. Gwenlyn glanced from a thin, poxy-faced boy to an older man whose dark, narrow face was crossed by a livid white scar to a man of indeterminate age who had the nervous, cruel eyes of a predator. Catching this man staring back at her, Gwenlyn hastily looked away, and heard him chuckle. None of the others looked any more civilized; far from it. Gods, what filthy, half-starved, desperate-looking creatures these were!

And if I live long enough to hear a minstrel ever dare sing of noble outlaws again—

Bah! There was nothing of a minstrel's romances about this group: they had all the charm of scruffy wild things frantic enough from living with daily fear and want to be dangerous. They'd attack out of sheer panic.

Or out of sheer malice. That cruel-eyed fellow was watching her again, still chuckling softly, mindlessly, to himself, and Gwenlyn fought down a shudder. If only there'd been a woman or two among the group, she thought, she might feel at least a touch more at ease, because that would mean a settled band with at least a shred of civilized organization about it. But these men looked far too desperate to have even thought of forming such a band.

And would such creatures really be able to keep themselves in check? Would they really be able to wait long enough for a ransom to be paid? Would they even *want* to wait?

Oh, dear gods. Gwenlyn shrank into the shelter of her ragged cloak, fiercely refusing to let any fear show on her face but all at once more terrified than she'd ever been in her life. She was alone in the middle of the forest with these wretched creatures, totally at their mercy. There was nothing to stop them from doing whatever they wanted—

Stop that. Start panicking now and you may as well tell them to cut your throat now.

Which they'd do after they'd had their fun. Grimly Gwenlyn forced herself to come to grips with reality. The idea of a ransom was all nice and civilized, something to be arranged between noble foes, not with ragged men like these, ruthless simply because they had nothing left to lose. No, she couldn't sit around waiting for a messenger to arrive with payment. She didn't dare.

And, Gwenlyn thought with a flash of spirit, *damned if I'm going to be stupid enough to try waiting for some gallant to miraculously show up to rescue me!*

So. She had to get out of this herself. Gwenlyn swallowed drily, struggling to squash her growing panic. *Think*, she told herself fiercely. *Think, dammit! What advantages do you have?*

All right. Start with the most obvious things. Her riding clothing was good, sturdy stuff. An asset: she wasn't going to freeze. Her boots were reasonably suited for walking. Another asset. But she had no weapons, not even a belt knife, and no means of making fire. That was most certainly not good.

Wait, now. Gwenlyn, subtly moving her hands under cover of the cloak, froze suddenly, realizing for the first time that the bandits had done a sloppy job of binding her arms. And they hadn't thought to bother tying her feet. After all, they must have reasoned, where would she go while they were all wide awake to watch her?

Awake. Gwenlyn felt a little shock run through her, a little spark of memory. When she'd been a small child, missing her mother, too lonely to fall asleep, her old nurse (who, it was rumored, had a drop or two of elven blood) used to sing an odd little melody, the tiniest of magic charms, to make her sleep. It had worked every time, whether Gwenlyn had wanted to sleep or not. And one day, when Gwenlyn was a bit older, her nurse had taught her the tune and words.

I haven't needed them for years. Can I possibly remember them? And oh, can they possibly be strong enough to work on grown men?

No way to know without trying. Doing her best to ignore the bandits, more of whom seemed to be staring at her with every moment, Gwenlyn tried to put herself back into the mind of the child she'd been, listening to her nurse, hearing . . . hearing what? A trace of melody. Something like this . . . yes.

"Hey!" someone shouted. "Stop that stupid humming!"

A rough hand slapped her, hard enough to send Gwenlyn sprawling, tears of pain and shock springing to her eyes. Someone chuckled. Someone else started to laugh, then fell to coughing, harsh, ugly sounds that probably meant the onset of lung disease. Struggling back to a sitting position, Gwenlyn hastily wiped her eyes dry: dangerous to show signs of weakness to wild beasts. And obviously the bandits' idea of "unharmed" didn't include a little rough handling.

But I have the melody in my mind now. At least I . . . think I do. Now, if only I can remember the words, too!

They never had made too much sense to her; presumably they were human corruptions of elven words. But she'd better think of them, and think fast, because from the smoldering light in the bandits' eyes, they thought the idea of slapping a noblewoman about was a fine bit of fun. *"Lessen spring, fashion ring . . ."* No, no, that wasn't right! *"Lessen spring, fleshen sing . . ."* Yes, that was it, and—and—oh gods, she had the rest of the song now, too!

One of the bandits was getting to his feet, muttering something to the others that made them snicker. Seeing him starting towards her, Gwenlyn hastily began to sing. No, wait, her nurse had always sung the charm at a slow, deliberate pace. Even though every nerve was shouting at her to hurry because the bandit was coming dangerously close, Gwenlyn slowed her song as much as she dared.

And to her delighted astonishment, as she sang the nonsensical, Powerful words, she felt a small, odd *something* stir in the air between them. The bandit stopped suddenly to give an enormous yawn.

Yes, oh yes, it's working!

As Gwenlyn continued her song, the man sat down where he'd stood, blinking at her like a bewildered, sleepy owl. The other bandits were yawning and blinking, too, and as Gwenlyn, hardly daring to believe what was happening, kept singing, repeating the charm over and over, they dropped off, one by reluctant one, into slumber. Even though by now she was thoroughly sick of the silly words, Gwenlyn sang the whole song through one more time just to be on the safe side, then fell silent, staring in astonishment at the crumpled heaps of snoring men.

It—it worked! I don't believe it!

Yes, but she was no trained spellcaster, and whatever magic was in the song was slight at best. It wasn't going to hold a whole group of grown men for very long. Gwenlyn fumbled with the ropes holding her till she'd squirmed free, and scrambled to her feet, glancing quickly about the forest. Gods, she hadn't the vaguest idea of which way to go!

No time to worry about it. Already one of the bandits stirred in his sleep as though he was about to wake up. Gwenlyn turned and ran. Oh gods, they really were waking up behind her! The tiny spell had run its course already.

"She bespelled us!" a frightened voice cried.

"Never mind that!" someone else snapped. "She's getting away!"

"Let her!"

"No, you idiot! Want a witch loose in the forest to get revenge on us?"

With a roar of fear and fury, they started after her. Terrified, Gwenlyn raced on. She couldn't find a safe place to hide, not with them so close behind her. All she could do was run with all her might, and pray she wouldn't break an ankle or her neck!

How am I going to get out of this? she wondered. *Dear gods, how am I ever, ever going to escape?*

Rualath hissed in fury. But her rage was bluster; she was struggling to cover the cold terror seizing her heart.

The Gate Spell, the risky, experimental, not-tested-enough Gate Spell, had gone wrong, *wrong!* It had nearly caught its prey, but "nearly" was as useless—as dangerous!—as a clean miss. Somehow Naitachal had eluded the Gate, somehow he had escaped.

Rualath clenched the scrying crystal so fiercely the facets nearly cut into her hands. Who would have predicted a—a—*human* would interfere? When he had passed through the Gate instead, curse him to the Utter Dark, the fragile spell had shattered like a mirror. Shards of its magic were spiralling wildly out and out, fracturing into ever smaller, ever more chaotic Gates spilling throughout the forest! If the whole thing hadn't been of such vital importance to her, Rualath knew she would have been watching the disintegration in pure scientific fascination. How incredible! Those ever-changing Chaos Gates were confusing distance and direction throughout the forest in such unpredictable fashion. Anyone or anything passing through one of them would be thrown into odd, random teleportation jumps.

What do I do now? How do I explain to Haralachan that my spell failed and—

"So . . ." purred a voice in her ear, and Rualath drew in her breath in sharp shock. Haralachan! "I never thought your spell would cause such widespread effects."

Neither did I, curse you. "Intriguing, is it not?" Rualath said, thinking busily. "We have the chance to weaken an entire forest."

"What a pity that isn't what you meant to do."

Rualath glanced sharply his way. "Do you question my sorceries, my lord?"

"Not the sorceries, my lady. Merely their result. Where is the traitor?"

"Ah, that."

"Where is Naitachal, Rualath?"

Where, indeed? "It would have been far too simple to just bring him straight here," Rualath bluffed.

"Oh?"

Yes, yes, she had it now: even though Naitachal might have escaped the original Gate, it had still been set specifically for him; he must still have been weakened by it. That meant there was still a chance one of the chaotic facets of the shattered spell would drag him in. "Indeed," Rualath said smoothly. "I have snared him with the merest touch of my spell. And this way he knows he has been snared, yet has the merest illusion of freedom, the merest false hope he can escape. Soon, soon I will draw him in."

Would Haralachan accept that? He was guarding his thoughts so thoroughly she couldn't sense the faintest hint of emotion, and his face was its usual sculpted coldness. "Make it soon," the *Nithathil* leader said shortly. Glancing past her at the scrying crystal, he added, "What of the human? The fool who passed through the Gate?"

You don't realize the Gate shattered, do you? What of the human, indeed? Studying that far-off figure, straining every sorcerous sense to puzzle out who and what he was, Rualath felt a little shock of realization shoot through her, and smiled a thin, cold, pleased smile. "Don't you recognize him, my lord? That is the human Bard, the one known, I believe, as Kevin."

"The traitor's friend?" Haralachan asked incredulously. "Why, yes, it is he! And I already have a game piece in place to snare him, and Naitachal through him. Clever, Rualath, most clever."

She hadn't the vaguest idea what he meant. But Rualath was hardly about to admit it. *Well, now, isn't this interesting? Maybe my spell hasn't failed after all!*

"Come, my lord," Rualath purred, resting a long-nailed hand lightly on Haralachan's arm. "Let us watch the game together."

They're still right behind me, Gwenlyn thought in despair. *Aren't they ever going to give up? Aren't they—*

"Aie!"

It was a startled cry, because all at once the forest had *shifted* around her, tossing her stumbling out into—

Into a very different part of the forest. Before, the underbrush had been dense, the trees mostly oak. Now, impossibly, there was almost no underbrush, and pine trees towered all about.

It can't be, it can't—

But the bandits were staggering out behind her, and if they'd been determined to catch her before, now, wild with terror, they were twice as determined to destroy the "witch" they were sure was to blame for all this weirdness. With a sob, Gwenlyn hurried on and on and on, gasping, heart pounding so hard she thought it would burst, snagging her hair and clothes on branches, stubbing her toes on roots or rocks.

And, so terrifyingly unpredictable, the forest kept changing about her again and again, tossing her into swamp or thick bushes or tall-grass meadow. The last change brought her startlingly out from dense forest into an open world of rocky outcroppings. Blinking in the sudden bright sunlight, glancing back over her shoulder, Gwenlyn saw the bandits still close behind, following her now with blind determination: By now, Gwenlyn realized with a sob, she was the only unchanging fact in their lives; they were never going to let her escape.

I—I can't run any more, I just can't.

But what else could she do? To fall into the hands of men gone completely mad from fear would be to die. Yet ahead was nothing but rock and—and—

A hive! Oh yes, please, yes, that cave-like opening was just too smooth and round to be natural. It had to be the entrance to an Arachnia hive—yes, yes, thank you gods, she could see two of the nonhumans, guards as fierce as any predators, prowling back and forth. Maybe someone else might find them a terrifying sight, but Gwenlyn had grown up with the sight of Arachnia merchants visiting her father. She'd quickly learned that even though the beings might look frightening, they were quite polite, even kindly, to those who treated them with honor. As her father had always treated them.

They used to bring me honey candy. But—but that was a different hive from this. At least I think so. Will they know my father here?

It didn't matter, Gwenlyn told herself. She'd much rather take her chances among unfamiliar Arachnia than human bandits! Forcing her weary body forward, she gasped to the soldiers, "I—I am Gwenlyn, d-daughter of—of Count Trahern, and—and oh, I ask for sanctuary!"

The guards, who had frozen in postures of startled menace, their powerful, segmented arms raised, hastily turned to chitter to each other, glancing her way with sharp, insectile jerks of their heads, segmented eyes studying her. Suddenly they shot back into their fierce defensive poses as the bandits broke out of cover.

"Oh, hurry, please," Gwenlyn moaned.

"Yes," one Arachnia soldier said crisply. "We know of your father."

"Yes," said the other. "Enter. We cannot promise you sanctuary; that is for our Queen to decide. But we give you leave to speak with her."

With a sob of relief, Gwenlyn dove into the hive. The Queen might not like having a human in her hive, the Queen might not give her sanctuary—but at least for the moment she was safe!

Chapter XI

The Maid Of The Forest

Kevin groaned. Slowly he felt consciousness stealing back into him, which wasn't a totally good thing, because it was letting him feel exactly how sore his body seemed to be, as though someone had very deliberately beaten every bit of him, then dropped him down on . . .

On what? Where was he? In a moment, he'd have to open his eyes and find out, but right now it seemed far easier to just lie still and try to puzzle things out.

The last thing he remembered was staggering out into forest that hadn't looked at all like the patch he'd just left. The Gate . . . yes. He'd fallen through some sort of sorcerous Gate. But surely he couldn't possibly be lying cradled against something wonderfully soft, something wonderfully sweet-scented. . . .

What was this? Kevin came fully awake and aware—and found himself lying in the arms of the most beautiful young woman he had ever seen. For a breathless moment he simply stared, upside down, at a fine-boned, narrow face, the skin pale and flawlessly smooth, framed by long, silken golden hair. Elegantly slanted eyes, the most extraordinary, glowing shade of green, looked tenderly down at him.

"I've died," he murmured at last. "That's it. I've died and gone to the Hereafter. Never thought I'd warrant my own angel." *Ugh. You sound like a melodramatic minstrel.*

But the young woman didn't seem to mind the overblown language. Her laugh was sweet as silver bells. "I am not an angel."

No, Kevin realized with a shock, and she wasn't human, either! "You're an elf," he gasped in sudden wonder, seeing the delicately pointed ears peeking out from the mass of golden hair. He twisted free (not without a pang of regret) to look at her rightside up: the view was even nicer this way around. "You're a White Elf."

"And you," she answered with a tiny smile, "are a human."

Oh, what a lovely voice this was, soft and shy and filled with the most wonderful music! (And, a more rational part of his mind added in wild relief, to find a White Elf here, a member of a race that was the very opposite of Darkness, meant that wherever the sorcerous Gate might have thrown him, now, surely, he was safe.) "Uh, I'm Kevin," he remembered to say after a moment more of mindless staring, adding as a stunned sort of afterthought, "a Bard."

"A Bard!" she cried in delight. "I've never met a human Bard before. Oh, but I'm forgetting courtesy: my name is Amaranthia."

That was all? It was a charming name, Kevin thought, but as far as he knew (and he admitted he didn't know all that many of her race), elves always included their clan name in introductions. But this charming young woman was plainly too shy to boast. Or maybe she came from a humble clan. Well, he could understand her modesty, being of common blood himself; he wasn't going to push her about her clan or anything else, or—

Oh, stop that. You sound like a babbling idiot. But . . . she is so very fair . . . "You . . . ah . . . live around here?" *Now there's an inane thing to say! Why not ask her for her birth sign, too!*

Amaranthia didn't seem to mind. "No. And I—I don't think you do, either."

"Hardly. I got here by—well, I think what I did was pass through some sort of Gate."

Her eyes widened. "So! That would explain it. I found you lying here unconscious, surrounded by the oddest residue of magic." She shuddered most deliciously. "Dark magic."

"I didn't have anything to do with that," he assured her hastily.

"Oh, I know that. There isn't anything of Darkness about you."

For an instant her clear green eyes looked right into his own. Kevin froze, unable to look away, not really wanting to. *Eliathanis,* he thought without warning, *my poor dead friend, what would you think of a human daring to—to do whatever it is I'm doing or . . . going to do . . . with one of your own people's women?*

The White Elf would probably frown on the whole thing. Or else give Kevin a polite little smile and lecture him all about chivalry.

The last thing Kevin wanted to be right now was chivalrous. But Amaranthia was so plainly a gently-bred maiden—albeit of a magical, nonhuman race—that even though his body was screaming at him to seize her here and now, he found himself saying with a polite restraint that rather amazed him, "I'm glad you know

I'm not of the Darkness. I could never be anything that might hurt you."

Oh, gods, *you sound like a lovesick poet!*

She didn't seem to mind that, either. Blushing ever so slightly, Amaranthia lowered her gaze. "I—I've never met anyone quite like you."

Ah well, go ahead. Be sappy. She seems not to mind your silly babblings. "Nor I, you," Kevin murmured tenderly.

"I . . . no. It's too foolish."

"What is?"

"We've only just met, and in such strange surroundings, too. We don't know each other at all. And yet . . ."

"And yet?" Kevin prodded.

"And yet I think I would like the chance to—to know you a little better."

"Oh, so would I!" It was a heartfelt cry. Kevin edged towards her, as cautious as if she was a bird that would fly if he moved too quickly. Amaranthia never moved, save to shyly veil her green eyes with long golden lashes.

"I've never been so close to a human before," she murmured, the faintest of blushes coloring her fair cheeks a delicate pink once more. "Is it true what the elves say about your kind?"

If he moved just a fraction more, he would be able to put his arm around her, and then . . . "What do they say?"

She glanced innocently up at him. "That you all are very hot-blooded. Quick to mate. Like the animals."

Kevin straightened indignantly. "We are not!" he began, then stopped short because Amaranthia was giggling. "You were teasing me!"

"Forgive me. I—" But suddenly Amaranthia stiffened. "Oh, Kevin," she whispered, "I sense more hints of the Darkness. I don't like this forest."

It looked perfectly normal to Kevin. There were even the ordinary little cheeps and chirps that meant the bird life wasn't being disturbed by intruders. "What is it? What do you sense? Specifically, I mean."

She shook her head. "It's gone now. I'm probably being silly. I admit it, I'm not used to being out on my own. In fact, if my clan knew where I was, and with whom . . ." Amaranthia's voice trailed off as she studied Kevin, and her green gaze brightened. "Why don't you come back with me?"

"To your clan? Uh, is that such a good idea?"

"They—they don't really dislike humans, they just don't know your kind very well. I'm sure you could charm them over in a moment. And—and we'd have a chance to spend some better time together."

Oh, he wanted to say yes, he wanted that so very much! To Kevin's horror, he heard himself saying instead, "I'm sorry." *Oh, you idiot, what are you doing?* "I'm a count as well as a Bard." *No, no, no, don't be so stupidly honorable, not now!* "And, well, I just can't up and abandon my duties at home. I *am* sorry," *oh, I am, I am,* "but before I can even think of anything else I must find my friend, and then—"

Amaranthia straightened. "Your friend? Who is he? A human like you?"

"Uh, no," Kevin said warily, a little puzzled at her sudden sharp interest. "He's a Bard like me, but . . . ah . . . he's an elf."

"A White Elf? What clan?"

Oh. Now what? "He isn't exactly a White Elf," Kevin hedged.

"What else could he be? Kevin, what are you trying to say?"

"I . . . well . . ."

"You're *not* going to tell me he's a—a Dark Elf?"

"Well . . ."

"Oh no," she laughed, "he can't possibly be that! It would be too ridiculous, a *Nithathili* Bard."

"Ridiculous or not," Kevin admitted, "a Dark Elf is exactly what he is. But Naitachal's not evil!" he added hastily as Amaranthia scrambled to her feet in horror. "Please, don't be afraid! Neither one of us are allied with Darkness. He's no longer a Necromancer, honestly! I know it sounds weird, but Naitachal really is a Bard."

"That's impossible," Amaranthia said flatly.

Ah. He should have expected this. She had all the standard White Elf prejudices against Naitachal's kind, just as Eliathanis had originally had. "But he—"

"No!" Amaranthia said sharply. "I won't listen. No *Nithathil* has any music, everybody knows that. And they're all followers of the Darkness, every one of them. I've never heard of one who would even *think* about turning to the Light."

She was shrinking slowly away, as though she meant to run if he made one wrong move. "Oh, please," Kevin cried, "don't go!"

He tried to get to his feet—but as suddenly as that, such a wild wave of dizziness swept over him Kevin couldn't even see straight. As he fell back to one knee, struggling not to be sick or faint outright, Amaranthia gave a soft cry of dismay and knelt at his side, her arm going gently about his shoulders. "It's all right," she soothed. "Merely aftereffects of that strange, strange Gate Spell. Nothing to worry about."

"I . . . I can't . . ."

"Don't be afraid. Just lie back down. Put your head in my lap. That's right. All you need to do is rest . . . just rest a little more . . . just rest a little more . . ."

Her hand was softly stroking his brow, so gently, so

very gently. That, and the croon of her quiet voice sent Kevin spiralling helplessly off into slumber.

As Amaranthia watched Kevin sleep, her lovely face slowly lost its light, going cold and hard. The little fool! Did he really think she was so—so vapid? Did he really think she would ever be attracted to someone like him? A filthy human—and a Bard! All her people—her *former* people, Amaranthia corrected flatly—would fall all over him, begging him to play for them.

She shuddered at the thought of that music. They all, every one of the White Elves but she, swore that this thing called *music* was wonderful, one of the finest things in all the world.

How can they be such fools?

She could never understand them, never! Amaranthia knew, after long, tedious years among the White Elves, that there was nothing to this *music* they raved over but sounds—ugly, meaningless sounds, painful sounds that forever surrounded her no matter how she tried to escape them.

Music is nothing, nothing! *And anybody who claims otherwise is either a liar or—or a self-deluding idiot!*

Ae, and the life surrounding that stupid, ugly music was just as tedious: no real Power, no real excitement, just a peaceful, timid day-after-day of following only the way of that pale, insipid Light. Where was the challenge in it? Where was the fun in something that dull? In never risking everything there was or knowing the triumph of escaping disaster again and again?

Amaranthia shook her head impatiently. Not one of her clan—her *former* clan—sought adventure, not as she saw adventure. Not one of them dared try even the slightest of spells that might bring them even the smallest of steps away from that boring Light.

None, Amaranthia thought with a little thrill of delight, save she. Oh, granted, she had no intention of ever going so far that she would become truly enthralled to the Darkness. That was never going to happen; she was too wise for such a thing. But it was so exciting to see how perilously close she could come to the edge! Besides, there were those who dwelt in the Darkness who could teach her how to thrive on their wild, chaotic life, those who, most wonderfully, knew nothing of the dull Light—or that stupid, boring, painful, meaningless music!

Amaranthia snatched up the pretty blue crystal pendant she wore on a delicate golden chain. But as she held it, the pretty surface darkened to a plain muddy grey. The greyness cleared as she murmured certain twisting Words.

"Ah, Amaranthia," purred a voice.

She smiled. "My Lord Haralachan," said Amaranthia and bowed. "Have I done well?"

"Very well, Amaranthia. The human suspects nothing?"

"Nothing."

"So . . ." The image in the crystal was small, distorted by the gem's facets, but Amaranthia could still make out Haralachan's cold smile. "You know, of course, who he is."

"Yes, my lord. This human Bard, this . . . Kevin, is a friend of the traitor Naitachal. He told me this himself."

"Exactly. A friend." Haralachan said the word with careless disdain. "Bard or not, a human shall be far easier to control than a *Nithathil* Necromancer."

A Necromancer? "B-but isn't he a Bard now, too?" Amaranthia asked hesitantly, nervous about correcting the *Nithathil* Lord. "Didn't he forswear Necromancy?"

To her relief, then her alarm, she heard Haralachan's chuckle, a chill, mirthless sound. "Do you really think he has forsworn such immense Power?" the Dark Elf asked. "For what? For *music*?" Voice dripping with scorn, he used the White Elf word, there being, Amaranthia knew, no *Nithathil* equivalent. "No. No one abandons Power willingly. No matter what he claims, Naitachal is still very much a Necromancer. He can be nothing else. But that fact will not save him: I have conquered Necromancers ere this, as has my dear consort. With the traitor's human friend in our caverns, ah, then we shall surely lure Naitachal to us. And then," Haralachan added with delicate, cruel relish, "we shall see that he meets a traitor's fate." He paused, eyebrows raised. "Why, what is this, Amaranthia? Shivers? Are you afraid, Amaranthia?"

"Of course not, my lord," she lied hastily. "But, my lord, what now? What am I to do?"

"Now, my pale little one, I send out guards to help you bring Kevin into our realm. You shall wait, and do nothing else save disappear when it seems discreet. Do you understand me, my Amaranthia?"

She bowed again in seeming submission, but her heart was racing at the thrill of danger, at the knowledge that one wrong word could bring his wrath down on her. "Yes, my lord," Amaranthia murmured, and smiled in secret delight.

Chapter XII

At Sword's Point

He stirred slowly, rolling over on his back, staring blankly up at a shifting canopy of green. What was that? Leaves? Forest? Where was he? *Who* was he? If he tried to catch fast to memory it seemed that he could almost puzzle out . . .

No. It was gone. He wearily raised an arm, turning it this way and that, studying it as though he'd never seen it before, hunting for a clue. Smooth, dark skin, a long, tapering hand . . . an elegant hand, the hand of a sorcerer . . . no, why should he think that? It was a musician's hand, someone had once called it that, a perfect musician's hand, and thinking that felt better than thinking of sorcery. . . .

Music, yes . . . there was something about music. . . .

Ah, no. He couldn't hold on to that, either. But now he could feel that something was lying beside him. He reached out one hand (a musician's hand . . .) and touched strings, heard a silvery trill of sound—

A harp. It was a harp. *His* harp. He turned his head slowly, fighting dizziness, to stare at the harp, knowing it, knowing . . .

Bard. Something about . . . yes. He was a Bard. He was . . .

Ae, yes. He was Naitachal. Naitachal, and the Gate, the weird, chaotic Gate had been set for him, by . . . by Rualath.

Yes. Now he remembered. It had been impossible to fight the Gate's force; Rualath's spells had always been eerily unique. Unless you knew the shape and name of a spell, you couldn't really fight it. Instead, he had done the only thing he could and fled, just barely in time to escape being dragged through the Gate into . . . into where? The dark caverns of his kin? It seemed very likely they'd still be hunting him. Far too likely. Naitachal shuddered at the thought, but couldn't quite manage to focus any genuine concern yet. He couldn't focus on any true emotion yet. Enough of that Gate's bizarre sorcery must have brushed his mind to tear him from consciousness, and it was continuing to confuse his senses.

That must be it. He was vaguely aware of still not feeling like himself or thinking coherently; a good deal of that sorcery must still be loose within the forest. He would probably have to do something about it. Later.

Someone else was missing . . . a friend. . . . Fighting off what felt like clouds of soft mist enfolding his mind, Naitachal struggled to realize who that someone was: *Kevin. Kevin didn't move back when I did. I lost my hold on him. He must have been pulled right through the Gate.* He seemed to remember feeling the force of Kevin's alarm. *I must find out where he is. If Rualath gets her hands on him . . . I must find him first, and . . . and . . .*

Ae, no. I can't do it just yet. Can't do anything yet . . . I'm too tired yet, just too tired. . . .

Rualath. He must keep remembering that Rualath was hunting him. He mustn't . . .

But right now she obviously hadn't found him and couldn't find him, and he . . . just couldn't worry about it for the moment.

Cushioned on thick moss, fingers curled protectively about his harp, Naitachal slipped back into slumber.

Kevin woke with a start, this time with mind clear and body no longer aching. But this time he found himself lying on hard ground, one hand reflexively clutching his lute in its case. And when he raised himself up on one elbow to look around, the Bard realized he was alone, surrounded by dense, silent forest.

I couldn't have dreamed her, I know she was real— "Amaranthia?" Kevin called warily. "Are you—Amaranthia!"

A cold chuckle was his only answer. Soundlessly, the warriors stepped out of hiding, ringing him round: warriors with silver hair, dark skin, cold, slanted eyes glittering like so many sapphires—

"Dark Elves," Kevin hissed in shock.

"*Nithathili,*" one of them agreed sardonically, and the whole ring of them drew their swords as one, as smoothly as though they'd rehearsed it.

Why me? What did I do? It has to be something to do with Naitachal—He wasn't exactly about to ask them that, or anything else; you didn't dare show anything as "soft" as confusion to Dark Elves.

Particularly not Dark Elves who had, for whatever reason, chosen you as prey. Kevin turned slowly, looking for a gap in the perfect circle of swords, finding none. Ha, look at those cold, self-confident faces! Did they expect him to meekly surrender? *Oh, no,* Kevin thought fiercely, *not a chance of that!* Thanks to what bits and pieces of *Nithathil* life Naitachal had told him, he had a pretty good idea of how Dark Elves treated their captives. Better, far better, to die cleanly here and now!

But I'm not going to die, dammit, not if I can help it!

Ridiculous to try drawing his sword, not while he was lying in this awkward position. But elves wouldn't know anything about human dirty fighting. The Bard got his feet under him and lunged up, under one startled elf's sword, ramming his head into the elf's gut. As the Dark Elf doubled over, choking and gasping, Kevin raced through the opening he'd made in the circle of swords—

But the Dark Elves could react far more swiftly than any human, smoothly closing ranks, sealing him in again.

All right, Kevin thought, trapped, *we'll try this the heroic way,* and whipped out his sword. The odds were really terrible; it was only in ballads that one man defeated a dozen in single combat. But there wasn't anything else to do, save let himself be taken or die, so he attacked with desperate courage.

The Dark Elves grinned coolly, stepping back just out of range every time he lunged. The whole dozen could have hacked him down in a moment or simply swarmed over him. Instead, the idea of twelve predators against one prey was apparently rousing some sort of sadistic *Nithathili* delight, because now they were choosing to close with him in little groups of one or two, toying with him, giving him merely scratches with their blades whenever they got past his guard, never quite hurting him, simply trying to wear him down.

And they're going to do it, too, curse them!

Straight swordplay was going to get him killed. But the Dark Elves' very cruelty, Kevin realized with a little shock, just might give him an edge. A flash of memory:

Naitachal and he, back in his castle, trying out that new form of Bardic Magic swordplay. It had worked back then, or almost. What if he could work it, strange and experimental though it was, here and now? *What was it we did back then? Yes, I've got it.*

He had to settle into a definite rhythm, a definite sword dance, thrusting, parrying, cutting, parrying, this foe, that foe, a definite rhythm . . . yes and yes and yes, he had it now, a dance, a sword dance, here and there and here again . . .

Kevin wasn't quite sure what he was doing, he wasn't quite sure how to control it, he didn't even dare think too closely about what he was doing or he'd lose the rhythm—but all at once something odd was definitely happening. Elf after elf missed a chance to strike, elf after elf, eyes gone misty and confused, lunged and followed through where Kevin had been a moment ago but wasn't any longer, as though he and they were not quite sharing the same time frame. When he started a pattern, Kevin realized in astonishment, they *had* to complete it, whether he was there to be struck or not!

All right, here we go. Let's see if I can get one of them to strike this *way—ha, yes!*

As one Dark Elf sword helplessly followed the pattern, moving out of line, Kevin thrust, feeling his sword cut flesh, hearing a choked snarl of pain. He slashed wildly out before the pattern could loosen, hit another target, saw the circle of foes dissolve in confusion and dove through it before the Dark Elves could recover.

Unfortunately, they recovered all too quickly. Hearing them running right behind him, painfully aware of that faster elven reaction time, Kevin ran like a mad thing, struggling to get his sword back in its scabbard, fumbling to get the lute cord safely slung across his chest, feeling the lute whacking him in the back as he raced on, leaping logs, dashing through underbrush, heedless of thorns scoring his flesh, rocks bruising his feet. Gods, oh gods, he dared not stop, he dared not fall or even stumble, they were so close behind. If one of them had any sorcery at all, he was lost; the spell would surely cut him down and—

"Ahh!"

For one wild moment Kevin was sure a spell really had hit him. But no, he must have run right through the Gate again, or a smaller, weirder cousin, because the forest had suddenly been exchanged for open meadow, the sunlight hitting him like a blow.

Unfortunately, most of the Dark Elves had followed him through as well. Fortunately for him, though, *Nithathili* eyes were darkness-adapted. Judging from the startled cries of pain he heard, the sudden sunlight was even more of a shock for them. *Of course,* Kevin thought wildly as he staggered on. *Even Naitachal still has trouble with direct sunlight.*

No time to think of Naitachal now. Kevin's lungs were beginning to burn, his legs felt like two lead weights, but sheer desperation gave him a new burst of energy that let him open up a wide margin as his pursuers staggered and swore behind him.

But the Dark Elves were driven by their own inner demons. Glancing over his shoulder, Kevin groaned to see them coming after him once more, hoods pulled protectively over their eyes, running through the open meadow like so many sprinting deer.

Blast it. Where can I—oh, not—

—again!

He'd been hurled through another fragment of the Gate Spell, back into forest dimness so suddenly it staggered him. This time he was the one at the disadvantage because his human eyes couldn't adjust to sudden darkness quickly enough. A Dark Elf laughed. A hand clamped roughly shut on his arm, but Kevin drove his elbow back with all his force, hitting flesh, and heard a grunt. The hand lost its grip and he tore free, forcing himself on, struggling through forest so dense he felt like someone caught in a nightmare, gasping, aching, legs trembling, unable to hurry even though something monstrous was right behind.

But the Dark Elves, quicksilver swift though they were, were still in tangible bodies; they couldn't get through that tangled underbrush any faster than Kevin. His lead narrowed dangerously, but it remained a lead and maybe he—

"Aie!"

He'd slipped through another shard of Gate—and suddenly there wasn't anything beneath his feet! The forest here fell away into a sharp canyon, a river roaring far below. Sliding over the edge, Kevin twisted desperately about, grabbing blindly at whatever he could close his hand on, roots and earth, clawing his frantic way back up to solid land—

He made it. For a moment Kevin could do nothing but lie flat, clinging to nice, solid ground.

But he was being watched. With a moan, Kevin struggled back to his feet and found himself facing a wall of coldly smiling Dark Elves.

Oh, damn. They must have been watching his entire struggle, waiting with inhuman patience to see if he climbed back up or fell.

Probably enjoying it. Maybe even making bets on it, Kevin thought dourly.

For a long moment he and they simply stood staring at each other. They were, Kevin saw with a touch of relief, almost as winded as he. Elves, though they might not admit it, could get as tired out as any other living creatures, and all he and they could do right then was keep staring at each other and pant. There was hardly a need for the Dark Elves to rush into action: they had him trapped against empty space.

"Got you, human," one of them said at last, grinning.

"Like hell you have," Kevin snapped.

Only one dim hope for escape. Hastily offering up a quick prayer to Whomever was listening that the river was deep enough, he jumped out into space. Wind whistled madly by his ears, the river's roar surged up, but then suddenly—

—it wasn't, and he was landing with enough force to knock the air out of his lungs on something that wasn't water but turned out to be a mercifully thick bed of moss. Stunned with the shock of impact and of still being alive and on dry land, he struggled wildly up to look around.

Forest. Forest on all sides.

Kevin fell back with a groan. Another shard of Gate. He'd fallen through another shard of Gate. At least that last desperate leap seemed to have left his pursuers far behind. Wherever "behind" might be. Wherever "here" might be, for that matter.

For the moment, at least, he was perfectly safe.

And perfectly, totally lost.

Chapter XIII

The Rational Life

The Arachnia summoned by the guards to guide her through the maze of the hive moved swiftly forward, the seemingly awkward stiltlike legs folding and unfolding with silent, eerie grace. Gwenlyn followed in the tall, alien figure's wake, feeling hopelessly clumsy by comparison, hearing her boots echoing loudly on the smooth earthen floor. On either side, the walls were smooth, too, hard-packed earth like the floor, or so she guessed, but whitewashed and polished to a soft gleam, ornamented at unpredictable intervals with intricately worked geometric reliefs. The designs meant nothing to Gwenlyn: for all she knew, they told an epic saga of Arachnia history.

Assuming they go in for anything as dramatic as epics.

Or maybe they didn't mean anything at all. It was warm in here, but not unpleasantly so, and the air smelled ever so faintly of the spicy scent that seemed natural to the Arachnia people; Gwenlyn wondered how they kept the temperature so nicely uniform.

And why, for that matter? The adults I've seen in

my father's castle didn't seem to mind the cold. I guess the youngsters or larvae or whatever the baby Arachnia are called need more warmth.

The tunnel they'd been following crossed a whole maze of others, each precisely the same width and height. As they travelled deeper into the hive, Gwenlyn tried and failed to keep track of the maze, and soon gave it up. She'd just have to trust to the stern Arachnia code of honor to get her out of here again.

They . . . would get her out again, wouldn't they?

She and her guard were passing other Arachnia now in the maze of tunnels. Although no heads turned her way, Gwenlyn was very much aware of those great, segmented eyes watching her with cool curiosity. But not a word was raised in greeting or protest. In fact, other than the sound of her own footsteps, there wasn't much of anything to be heard save for a distant, atonal droning that Gwenlyn guessed was Arachnia music, from what she'd heard from the merchants who'd visited her father.

Eerie. Alien.

Gwenlyn refused to start looking over her shoulder. Yes, she was being constantly watched; of course she was being watched. *She* was the alien here. But of course she knew no one here meant her any harm.

Or at least she knew that with the rational part of her mind. The rest of it wasn't so confident. Gwenlyn sternly reminded herself that she never had been bothered by close places before this. And the tunnels really weren't that close; a full-grown Arachnia stood too tall for that. But a window or even a ceiling shaft letting in sunlight would have been oh so nice.

And without sunlight how do they get this—this quiet sort of light in here? I don't see—ah, yes. Light globes of some type. Magical? I guess so. And— "What is it?" she asked aloud as her guide stopped short, and was startled by the sound of her own voice.

"We have reached the first turning of the second corridor of the third way."

"I see. But what does that mean?"

"It means that this is the end of my district. Another guide will lead you now."

"Oh. Uh . . . thank you."

The two Arachnia guides chittered a moment. The second guide gestured for Gwenlyn to follow, looking, at least to her human eyes, exactly like the first: same grey cloak, same golden gorget. But that gorget bore a slightly different geometric pattern on it.

Status, I guess. Or different job title. Or something.

The guides changed three different times before Gwenlyn, footsore and weary, at last found herself stopped before a great golden curtain. "Wait here," said her latest guide, and disappeared behind the curtain. Gwenlyn, with no other way of judging the passing of time, tried to keep track by counting, but gave up somewhere between three hundred and three hundred and fifty heartbeats. After what might have been a short or a long time, the guide (or one who looked exactly like him) poked a head out from behind the curtain.

"The Queen waits beyond," he said in his precise voice. "She has given her permission. You may enter."

"Ah, th-thank you."

The curtain was drawn aside. Gwenlyn stepped into the room beyond, then froze, suddenly too overcome by panic to go any further. The royal chamber was smaller than she'd imagined—or maybe it was just that the presence within would have made any room look small.

The Arachnia Queen was . . . vast. *Not fat,* Gwenlyn

thought wildly, *but, well, abundant,* looking as though she could bear a hundred hundred young and not be weakened. She alone of her people wore no golden gorget or any other jewels. But then, she needed no artificial ornamentation: her own chitinous skin was ornament enough. Where every Arachnia Gwenlyn had ever seen had skin of a shiny grey-green, the Queen was a rainbow of iridescence. Her segmented eyes, too, shone like many-faceted gems, and it was only after a startled moment that Gwenlyn realized from the way her head was turned, slanted sharply and not quite towards the girl, that she was quite blind.

The Queen didn't seem to find it a true handicap. Whether the Queen scented her or felt her body heat, after that first moment the elegant, jewelled Arachnia face turned fully to Gwenlyn. "Enter, human child. You shall not be harmed."

Her voice was higher than those of the Arachnia merchants Gwenlyn had known, but piercingly sweet. Not sure if she was being foolish—after all, it wasn't as though the Queen could see her—she made her deepest curtsy. "Your Majesty."

"Ah, a human title." Amusement tinged the sweet voice. "Come closer, human child. Sit."

A segmented arm touched the mound of silky cushions on which the Queen reclined. "As—as you wish, Your, uh, Majesty," Gwenlyn stammered, and sat, very much aware of the Queen's scent, strong as cinnamon, and trying not to flinch as that arm touched her hair, her face with delicate care.

"So . . ." the Queen mused. "You are very young. Young as my own D'Senna, my Not-Queen."

That meant nothing to Gwenlyn. "Please, Your Majesty, I—I request sanctuary."

"From those unpleasant humans lurking near the

hive entrance. Yes, so my guards have told me. They are persistent, those humans. What can you have done to them?"

"I did nothing to *them*," Gwenlyn said indignantly, "*they* tried to kidnap me!"

"Indeed. How very unpleasant. But why do they linger? Surely they know they have failed?"

The irrepressible Arachnia logic—and curiosity. Gwenlyn hesitated. "I wish this was easy to explain, Your Majesty. But, well, strange things have been happening out there in the forest. Sorcery, I guess. There are places now that jump you to other places without warning. And the bandits—the humans following me—think it's all my fault."

"Nonsense. There is nothing of sorcery tainting you. You should have told them so at once."

"They were too busy trying to kill me," Gwenlyn said drily.

"Ah. Of course. I forget the violence that seems a part of human nature. It is long and long since I have visited the surface world." The Queen stirred slightly on her silky cushions. "No matter how foolishly sure you are to blame, the humans will eventually realize they are in error. Or at least that further waiting is futile. Till then, child, you are, of course, granted sanctuary. It would hardly be logical to turn you over to those who are ruled by illogic. D'Senna, come."

A smaller Arachnia head poked up from out of the cushions. Gwenlyn, who'd thought they were alone in the room, started. A slim figure, her skin mostly the standard Arachnia grey-green but sporting hints of iridescence here and there, sprang to her feet, bending her lanky body in an intricate bow. "Mother-Queen, what would you?"

"See that our human guest is given comfortable

lodging and food and drink fit for her species."

"Indeed, Mother-Queen. Come, human guest, if you would."

But as soon as they were outside the throne chamber, D'Senna chittered in the Arachnia version of a giggle. "You're a female human, aren't you?" At Gwenlyn's puzzled nod, the Arachnia added eagerly, "Not an adult yet. A youngling, like me."

Her cheerful chirp made Gwenlyn smile. "I guess so. Oh, but aren't you a princess? I mean, your mother's the Queen and—"

"Did you not hear her words? I am a Not-Queen. A—a too young, too extra fertile female."

Did that mean that most of the Arachnia were either males or neuter males and females? But there was no mistaking the unhappiness in D'Senna's voice, so Gwenlyn admitted, "I'm sorry, but I don't understand."

"The hive is large. There is more than enough room for our people. Were it otherwise, were we badly crowded in this space, with too many of us too closely related, then a new Queen would be trained, then driven off to lead some of our people out to find a new hive. But there is no need yet for a second Queen, nor is there likely to be for many a cycle. And I am not even a second Queen! There is an elder sister. And so," D'Senna finished with a stiff Arachnia shrug, "I have no use."

"I'm sorry," Gwenlyn said because she didn't know what else to say, and D'Senna chittered a nervous little giggle.

"I didn't mean to put my life on yours. Come, I will find you a nice place to stay."

The room was a clean, comfortable chamber, even if the bed was, in Arachnia fashion, only a pile of cushions, and there was no window. The walls were . . . white. (All the rooms in the hive seemed to be . . . white.) They were ornamented with neat, precise geometric designs. (All the hive walls were ornamented with neat, precise geometric designs.) Gwenlyn was sure the precisely worked patterns meant something to the Arachnia, but she would have given almost anything to see a tapestry, a fresco, or anything with no geometric designs and some good, honest *color* to it.

Oh, at first, Gwenlyn admitted, she had been fascinated by the orderly, quiet, clean underground Arachnia society, in which each member knew his, her, or its role perfectly. But they were all so incredibly, relentlessly literal-minded and *logical!* Head in hands, Gwenlyn mused that an Arachnia could take the simplest statement, such as "The grain is ripe," and turn it into an intellectual study of the meaning of "grain" and "ripe" and how one should properly harvest that grain to maximize efficiency and minimize loss! *I know I shouldn't complain. They've been very kind to me. But if I don't get out of here soon, I think I'm going to go crazy!*

It wasn't helping her mood that Gwenlyn had no idea how long she'd been here. The Arachnia had—of course—a perfectly logical, precise way of marking time, but it bore no resemblance to anything used by humans, and since they ate whenever they grew hungry (which, she mused, was all the time), she couldn't keep track of days by the number of meals, either.

It can't have been that long, Gwenlyn thought wryly. *My hair hasn't grown.*

"Gwenlyn?" asked a voice suddenly, and Gwenlyn brightened. At last! The only person other than herself who had some *life* about her.

"Come in, D'Senna."

The young Arachnia hurried in, folding her slender form down on the cushions beside Gwenlyn. "They're still out there. The human bandits, I mean. They seem to be making a camp for themselves in the forest, just out of reach of our entranceway guards, and they just will not stop watching for you."

"Wonderful. I've encouraged them to live a settled life."

D'Senna blinked. "That was meant as the human form of sarcasm, yes?"

Gwenlyn sighed. "It was."

"It must be very dull for you here." When Gwenlyn hesitated, not wanting to offend her host, D'Senna added impulsively, "It is for me."

"You don't want to be a Queen, do you?"

D'Senna shuddered as much as her stiff Arachnia body would permit. "Would you? Losing your sight, losing your mobility, serving only to keep our race renewed—no, no, I do not wish such a future."

"Ugh. I don't blame you. But you told me you're the second daughter. Can't you just leave?"

"Where would I go? What would I do? I have been taught much as a Queen's daughter—but there is not one thing among that learning that would help me live in the outside world."

"Now, *that* problem I truly understand. *I'm* not trained to do anything much—other than run a castle, I mean—either."

"But surely human women don't transform physically into Queens?"

Gwenlyn laughed shortly. "No. That requires a court ceremony and a crown that—ach, never mind. No, we don't get cooped up like your blind Queens. But, well, if I accepted my 'proper' noblewoman's role, I'd wind up a meek, dutiful wife and mother, unable to do anything save what my husband allowed."

"That does not sound like . . . what is the human word? . . . fun." D'Senna tilted her head to one side, studying Gwenlyn. "I'm thinking that we are, despite our different forms, not unalike."

Gwenlyn grinned. "I've been thinking the same thing!"

"Do you know what I would really like to do?" the Arachnia asked conspiratorially. "Go off and have an adventure, a real adventure, somewhere above ground. Does that sound too foolish?"

"Oh, no," Gwenlyn said yearningly. "I would love to do something heroic and exciting myself. But I can't do anything cooped up here in the hive. Not that I don't appreciate your people's hospitality, but—"

"But you want to get out of here. So do I."

"Right, but how? I certainly can't escape the way I came in, not with those bandits refusing to give up."

"No. I should think you would be a valuable prize to them, noble-daughter that you are."

"Or a valuable scapegoat," Gwenlyn muttered.

"Wait, now . . . are you serious about adventuring?"

Gwenlyn glanced at D'Senna, and could have sworn the young Arachnia was nervous. "What are you proposing?"

"I—I never quite dared to do anything about it, not alone. But this isn't the only exit from the hive. There's another one, at the far end of one of the less-used tunnels. The only difficulty is that I am not sure where it leads."

Gwenlyn thought about spending more time down here amid all this nonhuman peace and unending logic, and burst out, "Let's find out!"

They made a hurried stop at the Arachnia food storage area, filling two sacks full of dried meat and grain and two flasks of water. D'Senna paused long enough to add a pouch full of the high-energy food cubes the Arachnia carried to satisfy their never-ending need for food, then glanced at Gwenlyn. The segmented eyes could hold no human expression, but Gwenlyn could have sworn she saw them glint with excitement.

"Shall we?" D'Senna asked.

Gwenlyn bowed. "After you," she said.

The tunnel plainly hadn't been used for ages. Here and there earth had fallen from ceiling and walls, and the inevitable white paint was flaking and stained. "Are you sure this whole thing isn't going to come down on our heads?" Gwenlyn asked nervously.

"Quite sure. I am as good a tunneller as any of my folk," D'Senna said without false modesty. "This tunnel will hold. And there is the entrance."

It was a narrow little opening, barely wide enough for Gwenlyn to squirm her way through. She turned to help D'Senna work her way through. "I think I know where we are. Come on, let's—no-o-o!"

The sorcery had seized her once again, whirling Gwenlyn and D'Senna both from where they'd been, dropping them roughly in a small, dark glade.

"What . . . was that?" D'Senna asked.

Gwenlyn sighed. "I don't know. Some sort of spell. It's been affecting the whole forest."

"Never mind that for now. We have a more urgent problem." D'Senna drew herself up to her full height, a full head taller than Gwenlyn. "I don't see any sign of the hive, or of anything else I know. What about you?"

Gwenlyn shook her head. "At least we've gotten away from the bandits. But as to where we are: D'Senna, I haven't got a clue."

Chapter XIV

The Bandit King

"I will find you, Naitachal," Haralachan hissed. "I will find you, traitor, no matter how you try to hide, no matter where. I will find you. I shall see that you shall suffer the traitor's fate.

"I will find you.

"You are doomed, traitor. You cannot escape."

"I will! I—"

Naitachal came awake with a start at his own shout, sitting bolt upright, his heart racing, his innate Power gleaming about him. All around him, the disturbed forest had fallen silent, but after a moment the normal little chirrings of the night resumed, and the Dark Elf let out his breath in a relieved sigh, calming his Power back into quietude. It *had* been only a dream, not some new spell Rualath had thrown together, as she'd thrown together that cursed, chaotic Gate Spell.

That Chaos Gate, Naitachal thought wryly. There was a good name for the thing. What with the shards of its sorcery spreading unpredictably throughout the forest, teasing at his mind, confusing his thoughts, he'd had so few lucid moments lately that he was beginning to feel like some poor feverish human wandering helplessly in and out of delirium.

If only my mind would stay clearly focused long enough for me to do something! I could find my way out of reach of the spell—yes, and find Kevin as well!

Naitachal shook his head in bitter despair. If the *Nithathili* had his friend trapped in their caverns, what could he possibly do about it? Not simply leave that friend snared in Darkness, surely. And yet, and yet . . .

Suddenly he was so cold he grabbed at his dark cloak, pulling it tightly about himself. "The traitor's fate." Whatever might be done to Kevin, no matter how horrifying, how terrible, surely it would have this one mercy to it: it would be finite. Humans could not last long under even the most subtle of *Nithathil* torments. But . . . "the traitor's fate."

Naitachal shivered anew, remembering the time of being truly of the *Nithathili*, of darkness he had never shared with anyone in this world of sunlight and music, of memories so cruel they still—though he had confessed it to no one and never would—haunted his dreams.

I may have escaped that life, Naitachal mused, rubbing a hand over his eyes, *but oh, it does haunt me still. And . . . "the traitor's fate."*

A Dark Elf would not be as lucky as a human, to escape *Nithathil* torture through death. And the torment would never end.

But I can't *leave Kevin in their hands! I can't! Damn Haralachan and Rualath and the entire clan to the Darkness they so adore—if I could, I would send them all screaming down into the Pit!*

He could feel the old, dark Necromantic glory rousing within him at these hot, fierce thoughts of hatred, the Necromantic Power he had vanquished but could never really quite destroy. It was a part of him, like it or not, its strands woven so deeply into the magical part of him right from the earliest days of childhood that to banish one would surely be to banish the other.

And even if it could be done, did he really wish to banish his Necromantic skills? How wondrous to touch Haralachan, Rualath, any of his former clan who dared stand before him, how wondrous to see them scream and plead and shrivel into dust—

"No!" Naitachal gasped, sickened at himself. To fight Darkness with Darkness would be worse than suicidal, it would be deliberately turning to evil. Using Necromancy once more would be the death not just of his body but of who and what he really was.

With a wordless cry of despair, Naitachal snatched up his harp, bringing the brightest music he knew from the strings, playing on and on, feeling the glory that was music slowly stealing through him, quelling Dark Power, melting the inner chill.

At last, with a sigh, he put away the harp and got to his feet. So far, at least, his Bardic—or was it sorcerous?—will seemed to have been strong enough, even during his most unfocused, to keep the fragmented spell from drawing him into its Power. But what if his will failed? What if he wound up walking dizzily into Rualath's hands?

Stop that. You sound like a timid little human.

But what could be done? He could, Naitachal mused, try simply staying in this relatively safe spot and waiting out the spell. Judging from the way the thing was fragmenting, it was just a matter of time before it would shatter to the point of Powerlessness.

But who knew for sure what would happen with one of Rualath's weird, experimental spells? Naitachal gave a dour little laugh, thinking that even Rualath could never truly gauge their length. Waiting, he might well starve to death before the Chaos Gate ran out of strength!

Life is full of little uncertainties, isn't it?

So. That meant there wasn't anything to be done but head once more into the forest, accepting the risks. If he was lucky, he'd find a safe way. If not, he'd be heading once more into madness.

Or at least, Naitachal thought wryly, *into vagueness.*

The bandits stirred uneasily. "She's not coming out," scar-faced Grenik muttered.

Brennid, the bandit leader (leader only because no one else really wanted the job) snapped, "Don't be an idiot. She's *got* to come out sooner or later."

"Why?" Grenik asked. "She's a witch, right? And the Bugs aren't human, right?"

"So what's your point?"

"So maybe she *doesn't* have to come out. So maybe the Bugs've been tunnelling like they always do, see. And maybe this time they've tunnelled a little too deep. They're *not* human; we don't know who they're in league with. Or what."

"What, you saying they came across demons?"

"I'm not saying *nothing*. Just that a witch and demons would get along real fine. Real fine."

There was an awkward silence while they all considered that.

"If she brings demons up here," skinny young Kem muttered, "I'm not gonna be waiting for them."

"Me, neither," Grenik agreed.

Brennid thought about it for only a moment. He hadn't wanted to be here at all; the Arachnia gave him the creeps with their big, weird eyes and those nasty-looking arms. Like a bunch of big insects. The flesh-eating kind.

But he could hardly have confessed his fears to the others. Things had been going badly enough as it was, with barely enough to eat and no place warm and dry to sleep; there hadn't been anyone to rob in a fortnight, and even if there had been, none of them dared show his face in town to spend anything. *I didn't* ask *to be leader!* Brennid thought wistfully. *I didn't even* want *to be leader!*

Couldn't get out of it now. They'd turn on him in a minute if they thought he was afraid. "Naw," Brennid said as casually as he could. "It's not worth the risk. Besides, I'm tired of watching them ugly creatures watching us. Come on, let's go." Trying to cheer everyone up, he added, "Maybe find us a nice, rich, stupid merchant or two," and heard a few weak chuckles.

It's not going well, it's not going well at all. But how do I get out of this mess?

He couldn't find an answer to that, particularly not when Kem sidled up to him and whispered, "She ain't there no more."

"What?"

"S'truth. Heard two of the Bugs mutter something about her running off with one of them."

Brennid just barely stifled a groan. Just what they didn't need—a witch on the loose and maybe out for revenge on them for keeping her pent up. Wonderful.

Naitachal staggered dizzily out of yet another bout of mindlessness, too groggy to know exactly where he was or where he was going—and found himself facing the scruffiest, most disreputable humans he had ever seen. And judging from their fierce, terrified expressions, they'd recognized him as a Dark Elf—and weren't happy at what they saw.

"A sorcerer!"

"He's a pal of the demons!"

"Get him!" "Kill him!" "*Kill him!*"

Bandits . . . can't fight them . . . haven't the energy to run . . .

Seeing the weapons drawn, counting his life in seconds, hardly knowing what he was doing, Naitachal began to talk. And elven charm and Bardic Magic glittered in the words.

"Just the men I've been hoping to find."

They stopped short, blinking. "Huh?" one of them said intelligently.

"Oh, indeed. But, tsk, aren't you the sorriest looking bunch of men I've ever seen?" he scoffed as gently as though speaking to children, and saw them stare in now total astonishment, bewildered by the smooth charm of his voice. "Look at you, all rags and dirt and fright. Look at you, I say! Is this any way for men to live? Well, now, is it?"

"No," someone grunted. And, "No," they all muttered.

"No, of course it is not," Naitachal agreed smoothly. "You know that. You do, indeed. And you wish to live in finer fashion. Of course you do. You wish to live like men, not beasts."

Part of his mind was rather amazed at how smoothly the words were coming out, how musically, full of that astonishing elven charm and delicate trickery, full of that most wonderful Bardic persuasion. Ah yes, Naitachal mused, he was probably, when he had his full senses about him, going to be astonished at his own nerve. But for now it was the easiest thing to simply keep pouring out the words that were a magical barrier between him and the weapons.

"I can help you," he told them smoothly. "I and I alone can show you the way to better your lot. Hush, now. Wait. Just listen to me, listen and learn what I can do for you."

"What're you offering?" one of the ugly creatures asked, and Naitachal smiled charmingly.

"Now, what do you think?" he purred. "A happier life. A better life. A wonderful, glorious, riches-filled life."

What human could stand before that? And what human, all magickless and unsuspecting, could resist, beneath the smooth surface, the hidden message. *I am friendly,* it soothed, and the bandits, hardly knowing why, slowly lowered their arms, letting their weapons waver. *I am strange and magical and Powerful,* the Bardic Magic insisted, and the weapons fell from lax hands, one by one. He should stop now, Naitachal realized dimly, he should surely stop before it was too late and he said something far beyond what he meant.

But by now, half-drunk on Bardic Magic and elven charm and sheer weariness, he couldn't stop. Instead, Naitachal heard himself adding so very convincingly, "You need me if you are to survive. With your skills and my Power, we can—we will—form a new fellowship against whom no one can stand."

And, *You need me to survive,* the secret words whispered, *you need me to lead, you need me to lead, you need me to lead—*

Naitachal came to himself with a shock. Ae, what was he saying? What had he already said? Whatever it was, he really must have overdone it, because all at once the bandits were cheering and swarming about him, clasping his hand, patting him gingerly on the back, their eyes bright with an almost childlike enthusiasm.

"We're mean, we're tough," they chanted, "we got something no other outlaw's got: we got ourselves a Dark Elf leader!"

Ae!

"Won't have to live like wolves."

"We'll have *food!*"

"Food, hell! We'll have *riches!*"

"Riches! We'll have *respect!*"

"Yeah, yeah, we'll have *respect!* No one's gonna stop us, no one's gonna chase us off. We finally got ourselves a real leader!"

"A Dark Elf leader—yeah! Who's gonna dare challenge any band tough enough to have a Dark Elf leader? We're gonna have everything we ever wanted, everything! Right, boss?"

Good gods, Naitachal thought in dismay. *I really did overdo it. These idiots have made me their chief.*

Now, wasn't this ridiculous? Necromancer, Bard—now bandit king! And what, in the name of all the Powers, was he supposed to do with these noisy, smelly subjects?

I can't just tell them to—to shoo!

Wait, though . . . yes . . . they just might have a use after all. These unexpected allies might be less than elegant, but they were fully human. Being in their midst would confuse what was left of Rualath's spell and what new spells she might attempt to locate him. With their aid, he would have no need of solitary, perilous assaults on the caverns of his kin.

If Kevin is anywhere in this forest, or anywhere at all that he can be reached, we shall find him!

Now, all he had to do was convince the others. "A piece of cake," as the humans might say: if he could turn himself into a bandit king, the elven Bard thought wryly, he could do anything!

"Listen to me," Naitachal said, throwing up his arms dramatically. "I hold out phenomenal hope to you, a chance for wondrous reward: the count and Bard known as Kevin is lost somewhere in the forest." *And not, let us hope, in* Nithathil *caverns.* "I intend to find him, and I wish your aid."

"What's a count to us?" someone growled.

Naitachal quickly located the man who'd spoken, and shot out an arm, pointing so suddenly the bandit flinched. "What's a count to you? Freedom, man! Freedom!"

He let them mull that over for a bit, listening to their bewildered murmurs, then said briskly, "Here's the agreement: help me to find Count Kevin—and you will all win pardons!"

Now what made me say that? the Bard thought in dismay. *Ridiculous: I haven't got any sort of legal authority!*

Too late to try denying the whole thing now. And obviously the bandits didn't know he had no such authority. Naitachal, watching them in confusion, thought surely they were going to fall to their knees in worship. "Full pardons?" someone asked in genuine awe, and he nodded.

Ah well. Might as well be caught in a big trick as a small.

Look at them staring at him with those radiant eyes! The bandits had already made it clear that they thought the idea of a Dark Elf leader was exciting, but now they plainly believed he was a wonder worker as well. With a tiny pang of guilt, the elven Bard thought, *I sincerely hope Kevin doesn't make a liar of me,* then added, *I hope Kevin has a* chance *not to make a liar of me! Ah well, here we go.*

Feeling very much like a father duck being followed by an eager string of ducklings, the bemused Naitachal led his odd new allies off into the forest.

Chapter XV

Pilgrims

Lydia stood in the stirrups, staring over her horse's head in amazement at the busy throng ahead. "*That's* the shrine of Saint Verdain?"

Count Trahern, riding beside her, glanced at her, one dark brow raised. "I take it you've never been here before."

Lydia grinned at him. "Do I look like the sort of woman who'd be spending a lot of time around a shrine? Let alone a retreat for gals about to get married?"

"You," Count Trahern said with easy gallantry, "look like the sort of woman who would grace whatever place she chose to visit."

To Lydia's absolute amazement, she felt her face reddening. *Score one for you, Trahern,* she thought. *I haven't blushed in years.* "Uh . . . thank you," she said uneasily, trying to ignore Tich'ki, hidden in her hair, snickering in her ear. "One word out of you," she murmured to the fairy, head turned away so the count wouldn't see her face and think she was talking to herself, "and I swat you like a fly."

Tich'ki only snickered that much harder. Lydia did her best to ignore the fairy, and pretended to get very interested in the sights ahead.

"See that plain stone building?" Count Trahern said suddenly. "That houses the original spring. The one at which Saint Verdain is said to have drunk and left her blessing."

"Yeah. I see the pretty brass sign they've put up." *Can't* read *the thing, but I see it.* She wasn't going to admit her lack of book learning to a man who probably read a dozen books a year. "Building looks antique enough to be from back then."

"It is. And beyond it, behind that high wall, are the buildings of the retreat itself."

By standing as straight in the stirrups as she could, Lydia could just make out hints of red-tiled roofs. "Right." But the shrine of Saint Verdain was supposed to be, according to all the stories, a simple, tranquil place. Whoever had started those stories had either lived a very long time ago or been a marvel of misstatement. "And everything else?" she asked with only a touch of sarcasm. "What's all this outside the walls?"

Trahern gave her a wry little grin. "You can hardly expect a site, even a holy one, that's set at the junction of two trading routes to go unchanged over the years."

"Mmm. No." Lydia shrugged. "Looks like Saint Verdain's is worth the seeing, whether you're interested in religion—or bargains."

The count nearly choked on a laugh. "True," he admitted.

Over the years a whole town of elaborate outbuildings had grown up around the shrine, a jumble of temples and inns and as many merchants' stands as Lydia had seen crowded in a small city. Everyone seemed to be loudly hawking something to do with

Saint Verdain, no matter how remote the tie, from medals imprinted with what they claimed was the saint's true visage (*as if anyone knows what she looked like!* Lydia thought cynically) to pretty embroidered kerchiefs worked with the daisies the merchant selling them claimed was the saint's favorite flower. Eager hands pulled at reins and saddlecloths; eager hands thrust up holy medals or "true fragments of Saint Verdain's holy robe, honest."

"Then why is that one marked with a Sesteni trademark?" Lydia snapped, and heard Count Trahern chuckle. "Get back!" she added sharply, slapping at one too-enthusiastic hand. "I said, back off—hey, you! What the hell do you think you're doing?"

A well-placed kick sent the man sprawling. "Lydia!" Count Trahern exclaimed. "That's hardly the way to treat an honest merchant."

Lydia glared at the amusement in his eyes. "Honest, hell! The guy was trying to swipe your purse!"

The startled count slapped his hand down to it, giving a sharp oath when he found the strings already untied. "I didn't feel a thing," he admitted. "My apologies. Come, let's get to the retreat before someone steals the horses out from under us."

Feeling like a fish trying to swim upstream, Lydia forced her mount slowly forward, trying to keep from trampling anyone and determinedly ignoring voices urging her to "try this candy, direct from Saint Verdain's favorite candymaker," or "sample this perfume from Saint Verdain's home town, just the thing for a pretty lady."

"I'm neither," she snapped.

"You belittle yourself," Count Trahern murmured. "If you're quite finished terrorizing the populace," he added before she could react to that casual compliment, "the way to the retreat is up this passageway."

"Uh, sure." Dammit, she was blushing again! *Curse the man, is he going to constantly keep me off balance? I'm not some green little girl!*

But then, he wasn't exactly a little boy, either. Admiring his tall, straight-backed elegance out of the corner of her eye, Lydia found herself beginning to enjoy the ride. All too soon, as far as she was concerned, they had arrived at the heavy oaken door barring the entrance to the retreat. At a signal from the count, one of his men rapped sharply on the door and exchanged quick words with the grey-robed woman who answered. She frowned, blinking nearsightedly up at the count.

"Count Trahern?"

"Yes, madam." He bowed courteously in the saddle. "I have come to see my daughter Gwenlyn."

The priestess blinked again. "Gwenlyn?" she said thoughtfully. "Gwenlyn?" A long pause, then a slow shake of the head. "I'm sorry, my Lord Count. I don't recall the name. Wait here, if you would. I will see if the other sisters can help you."

With that, the priestess scurried away, letting the door close behind her. "Moves like a little grey rabbit," Lydia muttered, and heard Tich'ki titter in her ear and the count barely stifle a laugh.

"For shame, Lydia! That's no way to speak of a holy woman."

She shrugged. "Saint Verdain isn't *my* saint. And my people don't believe in hiding from the world."

He glanced her way. "No. I can see that. Fortunate for those of us who enjoy the sight of attractive women."

Lydia sighed. "Look, I know you're used to giving easy compliments. It's the sort of thing nobles do:

flatter noblewomen. But I'm not a noblewoman of any sort. And I'm not a fool, either. I know I'm no raving beauty."

"No," he agreed so frankly it made Lydia stare, taken aback. "You are something far finer than a trite beauty, my dear Lydia: you are a free, honest original."

"I—"

But what she would have said—and Lydia wasn't sure what it would have been—was cut short by the return of the priestess.

"I'm sorry, my lord. None of us have seen a girl named Gwenlyn."

Trahern sighed impatiently. "Your pardon, madam, but you can hardly be expected to remember the name of every girl who stops here, even one who comes with an armed escort. If we could just check with whomever keeps your records?"

"Forgive me, my lord," the priestess said, blinking timidly. "I fear I cannot grant you admission."

"In the names of all the gods, why not?"

"Because you're a *man*, my lord! Men are forbidden entry to the retreat."

"Yes, yes, I know that! I'm not planning to stay in there, or do anyone any harm! All I wish to do is check the records—"

"I'm sorry. The rules, you understand." As Count Trahern, eyes blazing, opened his mouth to argue, the priestess added hastily, "The, ah, woman beside you could enter, of course, if she'd give up her sword."

"The woman beside him," Lydia said shortly, "has no intention of giving up her sword."

"Please," Count Trahern murmured. "I'll hold the weapon. Just go check the records. No one in there is going to harm you."

Oh, those serious, beautiful eyes of his! Shaking her

head at her own foolishness, Lydia unstrapped her swordbelt and handed it to the count, ignoring Tich'ki's sneers of "He's so *pre-e-t-t-y,*" then swung a leg over the saddle and slid to the ground. "Lead on," she told the priestess.

It was startlingly quiet within the walls. Lydia followed the priestess down a narrow path lined by neatly pruned flowering bushes that scented the air almost too sweetly, gravel crunching beneath her boots, feeling very much out of place in all this nicely groomed tranquility.

Not so much as a blade of grass out of place. Ugh. How do they stand it in here?

She caught a few quick glimpses of other women, girls in white robes who were presumably postulants and others in more elaborate dresses who were probably brides-to-be. All of them glanced surreptitiously at Lydia, plainly astonished at seeing this warrior in their midst, making her feel even more uncomfortable.

"All the retreat's records are kept in here," the priestess said suddenly, standing before a squat stone building. "Sister Acteil?" she called inside. "Oh, Sister Acteil, there's someone here to ask about the entry records."

If the first priestess looked like a rabbit, Lydia thought wryly, the second looked like a tortoise caught blinking sleepily in the sun. Pushing back wire-rimmed spectacles, she asked Lydia, "Who is it you seek?"

"The Lady Gwenlyn, daughter to Count Trahern. She's supposed to have arrived here a few days back with an armed escort."

The tortoise blinked again. "That's odd. I don't remember anyone coming to me with any record of an escort."

Lydia felt her patience fraying, strand by strand. "But you must have *some* record of the girl!"

"Ah. Possibly. A few days back, you say. Let me check." She glanced at Lydia, and the faintest spasm of distaste crossed her face. "Wait out here."

Yeah. I'd probably get real life all over your prim little records, Lydia thought, but she waited.

And waited.

And waited, fighting the urge to go barging inside. It wouldn't do any good, blast it: even if she found the records, she wouldn't be able to read the things!

At last Sister Acteil reappeared, whispering in the first priestess's ear. The priestess stared at Lydia in dismay. "Oh, dear. Oh, dear. I fear we must tell this to the count himself."

Then what the hell did I come in here for? Lydia fumed, but she followed her little grey rabbit guide back out down the narrow, precise path to where Count Trahern waited. Swinging into the saddle once more, she accepted her swordbelt from the man.

"Well?" he asked sharply.

Fastening the belt around her waist, Lydia gestured with her chin. "They wouldn't tell me a thing. Ask *her*."

The priestess bit her lip nervously. "Ah, my Lord Count, I fear I have some disturbing news for you."

Count Trahern straightened in the saddle. "What?"

"Sister Acteil, our record keeper, checked very carefully. There is no record of anyone named Gwenlyn having arrived here."

"But—that can't be! Have her check again. There has to be some mistake. Ah, I know! Gwenlyn was angry enough: maybe she gave a false name."

"Yeah, and what about that escort of soldiers?" Lydia added. "I bet she didn't check for them!"

"The escort, yes!" the count exclaimed. "There must be some record of *their* arrival. Go check again, please!"

But the priestess was shaking her head. "I'm sorry,

my Lord Count. Sister Acteil *did* check. There is no record of any girl, noble or common, having arrived at this retreat within the past two fortnights."

"But . . ."

"I am sorry, truly. I wish I could help, but . . . there is nothing I can do. Save pray." With that, the priestess slowly closed the heavy door. Lydia heard the bolt slide shut with a dull finality that gave her a superstitious shiver.

"Hell, maybe it's not so bad," she said briskly. "Maybe I was right all along. Maybe she and Kevin did come to some sort of an understanding and run off together. I mean, they're both hot-blooded kids." *Yeah, but even so, Kevin would never be that stupid, never!* "I bet that's all there is to it. They'll show up at his castle or yours, shamefaced and ready for a nice, happily-ever-after wedding."

The count shook his head angrily. "You don't believe that any more than do I. No, Gwenlyn set off for here, and—oh gods!"

"What is it?"

"There's more than one way to reach this shrine from my lands." He stared at Lydia, stricken. "The road is the safest route, but it's also the least direct. The shortest way— No, I can't believe he'd be that stupid!"

"He? Who?"

"Captain Degalth, the one who was in charge of Gwenlyn's escort. He's not exactly a bright man, but he's always been a good soldier, a thoroughly reliable one. He *can't* have done something like that, he would never have risked my daughter's safety, never!"

Lydia reached out to grasp the man by the arm, as firmly as though he were a frightened young recruit. "Stop that," she said flatly. "You're working yourself up to hysteria. And that's not going to help your Gwenlyn."

The count took a deep, steadying breath. "No."

"Now, what are you trying to say?"

She felt him shudder beneath her hand, but his voice was deadly calm. "She has never liked Degalth. What if she and Degalth quarrelled? What if he decided to hand her over to the priestesses as quickly as possible? What if Degalth took my daughter by the shortest route—the part that runs through the densest part of the forest?" Trahern groaned. "If he's done that, I swear I'll have his head! There haven't been any bandits in that area for years, so my guards assure me. But what if they're wrong? Oh dear gods, what if they're wrong?"

"Only one way to find out," Lydia said grimly. "And that's to go look. Lead the way, man. Don't worry!" she added in as calm a voice as she could manage. "We'll find your daughter. And Count Kevin, too."

But, Lydia added to herself, *will we find them alive?*

Chapter XVI

Strangers In The Night

Kevin sank wearily to a rock, looking around at forest and yet more forest without much hope of recognizing where he was. He'd been wandering in confusion for what seemed an age, every now and then falling through those jarring bits of Gate without warning and getting thrown, apparently at random, from place to place.

At least I haven't been tossed off a cliff or into a wall. But isn't the stupid spell ever going to run down? Naitachal told me once even the strongest magic runs out of power sooner or later.

Ah, and if only I could get out of this cursed forest! If only I could find the road back to Count Trahern's castle or my own!

And what of Naitachal? Where was he? Kevin hadn't seen so much as a hint of the Dark Elf Bard since this insanity had begun. The Bard clenched his fists, refusing to even consider the possibility that Naitachal might have fallen into the hands of his *Nithathil* clan, that he might already be undergoing whatever horrifying cruelty they might have devised for someone they thought a traitor—

No, no, surely Naitachal was far too clever to be snared like that. After all, Kevin told himself sharply, hadn't the Dark Elf easily eluded his kin for four years? Granted, that was just an eyeblink of time to elves, but Naitachal surely wasn't about to get careless now.

Yes, but where is *he?*

Ah, and where was Amaranthia? A little pang of longing shot through Kevin at the thought. What, oh, what had happened to her? And what had that whole strange, wonderful episode been about?

Kevin shook his head in confusion. It had all happened so quickly, almost as though he'd been struck by a spell, while she . . . no, it didn't make sense. Easy enough for a human male to be smitten by a White Elf maid, Kevin admitted that freely. But what about Amaranthia? First she had all but sworn undying love to a human she'd never seen before and only known for a few moments (*And you, you idiot,* Kevin snapped at himself, *were all set to act like some lovesick swain out of one of your own songs!*), then she had disappeared without so much as a word of farewell, leaving him helplessly asleep—to wake surrounded by foes.

Kevin winced at the memory. They had come alarmingly close to taking him prisoner then and there! Amaranthia *must* have been aware how near they were; she was an elf, after all, with an elf's keener senses.

Maybe she was just too terrified to think, a White Elf all alone like that.

But Kevin realized he didn't really want to try defending her, not after what had happened. No matter how terrified Amaranthia might have been at the appearance of so many Dark Elves, she wouldn't have been in any danger if she'd just bothered to wake him before she ran. Abandoning him like that, while he slept—it was almost, Kevin thought uneasily, as though she *wanted* the Dark Elves to—

"Oh no," he murmured. "Oh no, not that."

It could never—she could never—it was impossible. A White Elf would *never* work with Dark Elves. A White Elf would never, ever, even think of turning to evil!

Right. Just as a Dark Elf would never, ever think of becoming a Bard. Impossible things had a way of happening, regardless.

Kevin shivered suddenly, remembering another White Elf, four years back in the city of Westerin, a dead-eyed, thoroughly debased White Elf turned gang leader, an evil White Elf who had tried to kill him. Such foulness could happen. It *had* happened that once. And . . . like it or not, maybe it had happened again. There were just too many strangenesses here: a White Elf girl all alone in the wilderness, refusing to name her clan, asking so many strange questions about Naitachal . . .

Yes, and disappearing so conveniently just before I was attacked.

Ah, yes. He really had been acting like a fool to trust her so easily! But then, Kevin argued with himself, he had still been shaken by the Gate Spell. And she really had been so very beautiful, and he was, after all, only human—

Never mind her beauty, he scolded himself. *Use your brain instead of your—your heart!* How was it that Amaranthia had known so much about the Gate Spell *being* a Gate Spell, when even Naitachal had said the form of the magic was new to him? How could she have known anything at all about it—unless she really had been on the side of Darkness?

With a groan, Kevin got to his feet. He didn't want

to believe it, but there wasn't a thing he could do about Amaranthia right now. Possible treachery or no, all he could do was wander on, eating what he could snare, resting wherever he could find a safe corner in which to hide, and hope that somehow, eventually, he would find the way out of this forested trap.

"Gwenlyn?" D'Senna clicked her beak nervously. "Are you all right?"

Gwenlyn glanced up from the log onto which she'd collapsed. "Fine," she drawled sarcastically, "I'm just fine. Tired and hungry and lost and sick to death of this—this damnable sorcery that keeps hurling us around like two dolls—but fine."

D'Senna folded her lean body down at Gwenlyn's side with the softest of sighs. "I am not happy, either," the Arachnia said softly. "I cannot find the scent of the hive again, or of any of my people, and I know nothing of this forest."

All at once contrite, Gwenlyn glanced guiltily at the Arachnia. "I'm sorry. I wasn't thinking." She reached out an impulsive hand to touch D'Senna's arm, feeling the cool sleekness of the chitinous skin. "All this must be much worse for you than it is for me, much more frightening. At least I've been out in the world before, at least a little."

"I am not afraid," D'Senna said. "Not quite. I am just . . . very confused."

"Aren't we both!" Wearily, Gwenlyn got to her feet. "I don't know what's been going on. I don't know whose spell has been causing all this nonsense. But at least we can grab some comfort out of all this."

"Yes?"

"So far no one's actually hurt either one of us."

"There is that." D'Senna unfolded to her full height

once more, over a head taller than Gwenlyn but slim as a racing hound. She chittered softly. "And to think I was discontent with my life. I would almost welcome the old boring uselessness."

"Me, too," Gwenlyn agreed, then grinned. "Almost. At least no one is telling us what we can and can't do."

"Indeed. That is a most pleasant change. Even in the middle of all this. Even if we are most thoroughly lost."

"You're the one who kept arguing that the forest was a finite thing," Gwenlyn said sharply.

"True, true. And if we simply keep moving in as straight a line as we can, sighting from tree to tree as you did before that last . . . jump . . . we must, eventually, come out to *some* place you know."

"From your mouth to the gods' ears," Gwenlyn said wryly. "Let's only hope they're listening! Come, my friend, time to move on."

Kevin froze in the twilight, listening with all his might. The birds that had been cheeping sleepily as they settled down a moment before had all suddenly gone silent. Why?

Someone's stalking me, he realized, *not Dark Elves, oh please, not them again . . .*

Kevin moved warily forward, testing, then stopped, straining to hear. *Ach, useless. Can't hear a thing. But elves wouldn't make a sound.*

They were there, though; it wasn't his imagination, not with all the small wild things remaining absolutely silent. And he could feel, with some obscure Bardic sense, the elves' presence as surely as any stalked animal knew its hunter. *All right, curse you, here we go again.*

Without warning, he burst into a run, dashing

through the forest as best he could, stumbling over roots, struggling to stay on his feet, half-blind in the ever-darkening twilight, this time hunting, praying for a shard of the Gate. All along he'd been trying to avoid the damned things; now that he wanted one, they all seemed to be avoiding him! Behind him, the Dark Elves had abandoned subtlety, racing after him.

Oh, I can't go through another one of these stupid chases, I—

With a startled yell, Kevin went plunging through a shard of Gate Spell and collided with someone who screamed as they both crashed to the forest floor. The someone got in a good kick to his shin, nearly raked his eyes with what seemed like talons, then squirmed free, struggling to his—to *her* feet like a wild thing, panting, hair a tangled dark mass, clothing ragged. Behind her, the slim figure of an Arachnia loomed, segmented arms in a pose of definite menace.

Great, Kevin thought wildly, struggling to his feet, trying to catch his breath. *Just what I needed: another treacherous woman.*

She was trying to gasp out something, but he held up a hand, listening fiercely, then let out his breath in a sigh of relief. The Dark Elves had *not* followed him through the Gate. At least for the moment. "Lady," he began, though this ragged creature didn't look anything like a lady (and he, he admitted, probably looked like a derelict), "I—"

He stopped short, looking behind the dirt, really seeing her for the first time. Judging from her astonished expression, she was doing the same. Simultaneously, they cried out in dismay: "You!"

"Count Kevin! I thought you were another bandit! What are you doing here?"

"What are *you* doing here, Lady Gwenlyn?"

"I—"

"The Gate—"

But the Arachnia suddenly chittered in excitement, "Not now, not now! Someone's coming—enemies!"

Kevin whirled, and groaned at the sight. "Oh hell. They did follow me. I'm sorry; I didn't intend to get you involved."

"That doesn't matter now," Gwenlyn said grimly. "They're here now. No place to run. Give me your dagger."

"What—"

"Give me your dagger! You've already got your sword and D'Senna has her Arachnia strength—I don't have *any* weapon!"

Kevin hastily passed her the knife, thinking it wasn't going to be much use against Dark Elf swords, vowing he wasn't going to let a gently bred human lady fall into *Nithathili* hands. As the Dark Elves, smiling coldly, their slanted eyes glinting red in the growing darkness, began to close in on them, the Bard heard Gwenlyn draw in her breath sharply.

At least she's not dissolving into hysterics.

But he hardly expected what came next. She snapped at him, "Follow my lead," and boldly charged the elves, screaming like a demon. They sprang back in instinctive shock from this fierce, shrieking mad thing, and Kevin laughed and charged with her, yelling as madly as he could himself, slashing out savagely with his sword, seeing sheer confusion flashing in the Dark Elf eyes.

They don't know what to do! Humans aren't supposed to act like this! Off to his right, the Bard glimpsed the Arachnia—D'Senna, was it?—snatching fiercely at the foe with her powerful claws, segmented eyes glittering in the darkness as she shrilled her own fierce war cries, while beside him, Gwenlyn, still screaming insanely, stabbed at any Dark Elf who wasn't quite quick enough to get himself out of the way.

But shock isn't going to hold them all off forever. No time for stupid heroics: we've got to get out of here, now!

"Run!" Kevin hissed, even while his overtaxed body was moaning silently *not again.* Grabbing Gwenlyn firmly by the arm, he charged forward into the night, nearly slamming into a tree in the darkness, tearing through bushes, very much aware that to the Dark Elves the night wasn't dark at all. D'Senna, with her long legs as swift as any human, kept up with him with ease, clamping down on his shoulder with just this side of painful force. "I do not . . . wish to be . . . left behind," she gasped, "if the spell seizes us again."

"And I . . . don't want . . . my shoulder broken!" he panted.

"Save . . . save your breath!" Gwenlyn snapped. "They're . . . right behind us, and—"

She screamed, suddenly falling, snatching frantically at Kevin. Overbalanced, he fell with her, and D'Senna with him, all three of them tumbling down towards a rumbling roar.

Oh gods, the Bard realized in sudden horror, *it's the same canyon, the same river—but not the same place! There's not going to be any lifesaving Gate to fall through this time. We're doomed!*

But D'Senna's powerful Arachnia arm closed about a protruding root. She was brought up short, as were Kevin and Gwenlyn. Pulled between D'Senna and Gwenlyn, Kevin gasped, feeling for a moment as though his shoulders had been snapped from their sockets, then had the terrible pressure released in the next as he and Gwenlyn smacked into the earthen side of the canyon, scrabbling for purchase, terrified that D'Senna would lose her grip.

"A cave!" Gwenlyn gasped. "Here, to my left, a cave."

It was hardly that, barely more than an indentation where the earth had worn away. But, edging their wary way sideways, the three fugitives managed to wedge their way inside.

"Not a sound," Kevin whispered, and they froze in a tangle of limbs, hardly daring to breathe as, far overhead, the Dark Elves hunted for them.

If they have a mage with them, we're lost.

But these were magickless warriors. Even their night-sighted eyes could see nothing of their prey. And after an agonizingly long time, during which Kevin was sure the Dark Elves were merely toying with him, waiting to pounce, he heard what could only have been *Nithathil* profanity. Someone snapped out what he prayed was, "The river must have taken them."

Then the Dark Elves were gone, moving downstream.

"Wait," he whispered.

"I can't!" Gwenlyn whispered back. "You're standing on my hand!"

"Sorry." He shifted ever so warily. "Better?"

"Wonderful."

"Shh." That was D'Senna, one lanky arm wedged around Kevin's shoulder, one long leg crooked around his own. "I am not comfortable, either. But, shh!"

After an endless agony of silent waiting, Kevin dared stick his head out of the cave, listening, wishing there was some way to use Bardic Magic without making a sound, trying to use Bardic senses to see. . . .

"They're gone."

D'Senna poked her head out beside his, looking over his shoulder. "They are."

"Then will you both *please* get off me?" Gwenlyn asked plaintively.

"Let me go first," D'Senna said. "I will cut handholds."

Moving very carefully, the Arachnia disentangled herself from the two humans. Very carefully, they followed her out, catching at the holds she dug in the earthen wall, working their weary, wary way up till at last:

"Solid ground!" Gwenlyn exclaimed, throwing herself flat.

Kevin, stretching out on his stomach, lute a familiar weight on his back, only groaned. But after a time, he felt laughter welling up in him and at last had to chuckle aloud.

"Lo, the conquering heroes enjoy their reward."

He heard Gwenlyn giggle. "The ridiculous heroes, you mean."

Kevin slowly sat up, feeling every muscle protest. "That was a beautifully clever thing you did, screaming and leaping at them like that. Total lunacy was the last thing they'd expected!"

He saw her teeth flash in a grin in the darkness. "I couldn't think of anything else to do. It *was* pretty clever of me, wasn't it?"

Kevin grinned back, and heard D'Senna chitter. He reached out a hand and tapped Gwenlyn on the shoulder. "I hereby dub thee knight."

"Sir Gwenlyn, eh? Some knight. Night*mare* is more like it. We look like three homeless vagabonds."

"A hero," Kevin quoted pompously, "is not to be measured in terms of his fine clothing—"

"But in terms of deep inner worth," Gwenlyn finished. "I know that one, too. Bennish the Wise, Second Book of Thoughtful Musings. Bet *he* never had to pounce on Dark Elves."

Kevin laughed. "There's a thought! I saw a portrait of him once."

"So did I." Gwenlyn paused thoughtfully. "Fat, wasn't he?"

"Like a mountain."

"Couldn't have pounced on anyone."

"Nary a one."

Kevin and Gwenlyn broke off, grinning at each other.

Ay me, the Bard thought with a little pang of regret, *this isn't real, this can't last.*

Of course it couldn't. What they were feeling had to be just the camaraderie of comrades in arms who've survived a battle; he'd felt this sort of thing before. All too soon it would fade away and they'd go right back to their former dislike.

But to his vast surprise, Kevin realized he wasn't looking forward to that return.

Now, what . . .

Ah well, all this was foolishness. Unless they could find a way out of the forest and away from the Dark Elves, how they felt about each other wasn't important. Unless they could finally escape the Gate Spell, none of this was going to matter.

Chapter XVII

Schemes

Haralachan prowled his realm in furious silence, wrapped in sorcerous Darkness, invisible in the natural darkness, his face a frozen mask revealing nothing of the rage within, dimly aware that his subjects were desperately staying out of his path.

Fool, fool, to have given her free rein, to have believed Rualath's boastings, to have let her cast that cursed spell!

A slave trudging along down a lonely corridor had not heard the whispered warnings. He had time enough only to sense darkness amid darkness, to make one frantic effort to get out of the way. Haralachan swept the living obstacle aside with a sorcerous blow, casual as one crushing an insect, leaving the slave in a crumpled, broken heap without truly noticing.

Oh yes, the spell almost worked—phaugh! Almost *is as useless as nothing at all. Worse!*

All his subjects knew what had happened, knew his consort had sworn to bring the traitor to him, knew how she had failed. She, and through her, he,

Haralachan the ruler, must find a way to turn this failure into triumph, and swiftly!

What if I condemned Rualath in Naitachal's place? Claimed that she had deliberately failed, that she was actually secretly in league with the traitor?

No, no, that was a truly double-edged blade. Either it meant he was too weak to notice his consort's treachery, or it was as good as openly declaring he was using her as a victim to hide his own failure.

The Darkness rend her!

Much as right now he'd love to see Rualath scream away her life on the altar for the trouble she'd caused him, Haralachan reluctantly considered and accepted the true: It was far better politically to keep his consort alive as a focus for blame.

Besides, curse it, there was still the matter of her sorcery. Yes, this spell—this particular, vital spell!—had failed, but there had been others before this that had not failed, secret spells no one could trace since they were hers alone, spells to weaken his foes and help him hold power. There was the promise of useful sorceries in the future.

Haralachan cursed softly, a chill whisper in the darkness. *Live, Rualath. For now. But if you cannot find a way to correct this perilous error of yours, if you cannot, indeed, bring Naitachal to me, then I think your usefulness to me is ended.*

Alone in her study, Rualath paced impatiently back and forth. The Gate Spell had come so close to succeeding! There must be some way she could reestablish the frustrating thing into a functioning whole! There were still enough shards of the spell spiralling through the forest that surely she could devise a method to draw the pieces back into one.

Yes, she could devise it—if only she was left alone!

Oh, yes, might as well wish for Naitachal here in my grasp as that, Rualath thought in fury. No chance for privacy with Haralachan forever after her! He hadn't yet accused her outright of treason or failure, but he had insisted on questioning her not once but thrice within the last two turns of the glass; every time she had started to gather the bits of a useful spell in her mind, Haralachan's interruption had broken in to send the spell whirring away out of her memory.

Curse him! It's almost as though he wants *me to fail—*

Was that the case? she wondered. Could it be? But why such a slippery, treacherous thing? What purpose could her failure possibly serve? Did Haralachan wish to humble her, perhaps? But such a humbling would be at the risk of losing personal honor for letting the capture of a traitor come second. Bah, no, he would never take such a risk!

And yet, and yet . . . Rualath refused to waste time considering that Haralachan simply didn't trust her; of course he didn't trust her! He wasn't *that* great a fool. At least, no matter what devious plans he might be considering, the man hadn't taken a certain drastic step: he'd not been angry or imprudent enough to take another consort.

No, Rualath mused, smiling thinly, think whatever he might of her, Haralachan still needed her, they both knew it. Or rather, more to the point, he still needed her magics—

Ae, yes, but how much longer was he going to keep needing them if her spells kept failing him?

The Gate Spell. The cursed Gate Spell. There must be some way to correct it . . . maybe a slightly altered proportion of flame to earth . . . Yes, what if she tried one gram of mica instead of two, half the intensity of fire and . . . yes . . . that might prove interesting . . . and then . . . and then . . .

"Rualath!"

She flinched as that sudden mental shout tore into her thoughts. "Not now, you idiot!"

Too late. The renovations she'd considered for her spell had fled her mind yet again before she could safely note them down. It had been one gram of mica, and . . . and . . .

"Rualath," the mental roar continued, heedless, *"I wish to see you. Now!"*

"Yes, my thrice-cursed lord," Rualath snarled, but only to herself, "at once, my thrice-idiotic lord. What else do you want, my idiotic lord? Shall I surrender my magics? Shall I give up trying to work my spells altogether? Would that please you, my cursed, idiotic, perilous lord?"

But of course she could not refuse the summons. And of course none but she would know her rage. By the time she had reached the royal cavern, Rualath knew that none could have told her inner fury from the composed mask she presented. Moving smoothly to where Haralachan stood beside his obsidian throne like a dark, silver-haired statue, the sorceress asked coolly, "My lord? What would you?"

He stared at her. "You know what I want. And you have yet to deliver him to me."

Because you keep interrupting me at my work, you great fool! "I would, my lord," Rualath said with immense restraint, "were I left alone long enough to repair the spell."

"The spell that, had you fulfilled your boasts, should not have shattered in the first place."

"The spell, my lord, that we both knew was experimental. I never denied that fact to you." *I merely failed to stress it.* "No true advance in magic can ever be made without trial and error."

"There was no room for error in this!"

"Perhaps," Rualath snapped, "there *was* no error!"

Haralachan tensed, eyes flickering dangerously red. "Choose your next words carefully, Rualath. What did you mean by that?"

Rualath *felt* the menace of his rousing Power, but *felt* her own Power stirring angrily as well. "I mean, my lord, that you have been interfering with every step of my work," she said coldly. "Perhaps, my lord, you wish to explain?"

"I? I need explain nothing."

"Ah? So dramatic? Perhaps that is because the fault is yours!"

Haralachan drew in his breath in a sharp hiss. "Do you dare accuse me?" he asked in a soft, deadly voice. "Me? Of what crime?"

"Oh, I can hardly say. Perhaps of envy. Or fear."

"Fear!"

Rualath smiled without the slightest trace of humor. "Can you swear to know no fear of me? Can you? Perhaps, my lord, you are guilty of simply wishing me to fail!"

"You will not shift your guilt to me!"

"Am I doing such? After all those interruptions, my lord, what else can I think but that you have deliberately, for whatever reason, been trying to sabotage my efforts?"

"If there is a saboteur, my lady, I think surely it must be *you!*"

"I! I am not the one so suspicious of his own consort he will not let her work the slightest trace of a spell without spying on her!"

"What I do or do not is not for you to question!

And if, perhaps, I have spied on you when it seemed politically wise, it has not been done without reason. You have been known to associate with proven foes of the Realm!"

"If by that portentous statement you mean I have spoken with fools like Tanarchal, yes, of course I have. What, would you have me pretend to ignore them instead, and have all say, 'The royal consort fears her lord's foes, the royal consort reflects his fears'? Would you give them such suspicions of your strength?"

"Smooth words, Rualath. But only words! Where is the traitor, Naitachal? You swore to bring him to me. Yet, where is he? Are you yourself a traitor to me, Rualath?"

"And do you dare to challenge me, my lord?" Rualath purred. "Is that what all this is for? Are you at last daring to offer me the true Challenge? Are you that curious to see the full scope of my Power?"

"Your vaunted Power," Haralachan said in a voice subtle with rage, "is an entertainment, nothing more than a toy to while away a long night. It has no true—"

"Does it not? Shall we learn the truth, here and now?"

"Are you so eager to die, Rualath? Or—"

"Ah . . . my lord," cut in a soft, nervous voice. Haralachan and Rualath both turned with predatory swiftness to see several of the over-servants, several steps up from slavery but still not of noble blood, standing before them, heads bowed, arms crossed at just the proper angle of submission in front of their bodies, palms defenselessly turned out in the full Gesture of Humblest Beseeching of Underling to Lord.

Rualath and Haralachan exchanged a sharp glance, and a hint of wry humor glinted beneath the rage. Were it not for that Gesture, Rualath knew, they both would have blasted the servants where they stood for the effrontery of their interruption. But the Gesture was quite properly presented, without the slightest flaw of angle or pose, and so Haralachan snapped instead, "What is it?"

"My lord, my lady, we . . . all know and fear your Power."

"You should. Continue."

"Ah . . ." The servant who'd dared to speak glanced nervously at his fellow, then continued in a voice that almost failed to shake, "But if you act upon the full Challenge now, surely one of you must fall."

"That is the whole point of full Challenge. What of it?"

"We do not have the traitor, Naitachal. If Challenge happens, my lord, if one of you falls, your royal Power, one way or another, will be halved. And . . . well, we still will not have the traitor Naitachal."

There was a long, thoughtful silence. And then Rualath dared a soft laugh. "He's a brave little creature, isn't he?"

"Indeed. But he raises an intriguing point."

"So he does. What say you, my lord? Shall we postpone our excitement?"

"So we shall. As we have just been reminded, we dare not dance the final dance till the traitor is ours." Haralachan waved the over-servants away, his face all at once icily composed, his emotions controlled with elven speed. As, Rualath knew, were her own. "So now, my consort," the Dark Elf lord said once they were alone, not the slightest of inflections coloring his voice, "counsel me. How may we yet salvage something out of this unpleasantly shattered situation?"

How, indeed?

"Kevin," she said in sudden inspiration.

"Ah, the human! The human who has so far eluded you."

"The spell," Rualath reminded him flatly, "was set for Naitachal, specifically for Naitachal. While anyone else could pass through the Gate, only his mind was to be confused. That the spell affected the human's mind as well only proves that they are linked—through friendship."

She said that last word with contempt and a touch of sheer bewilderment: how could anyone deliberately weaken himself like that? To profess a genuine *liking* for another, and not even for any sort of gain! How could even a debased traitor of a *Nithathil* sink to *friendship*—and for a *human*?

"They are friends," Rualath repeated. "A fact, my lord, we can most definitely use. And it was your warriors, my lord," she added coldly, "not my spell, who failed to snare him."

He acknowledged that with the barest dip of his head. "And what would you have me do, my consort, to solve that problem?"

"Send out more warriors. Not some foolish hunters this time, but a fully trained troop."

Haralachan raised a wry brow. "So many after one mere human? Do you think so poorly of my warriors?"

"Would I be so indiscreet, my lord? But since you hunger so for the blood of the traitor, and since we know without doubt that the human is linked with him, then why take the admittedly small risk that he might elude you? As," Rualath added delicately, "he has eluded you so far."

Haralachan's smile barely moved his lips. "So be it," he murmured. "Surely they will be able to find this human, this Kevin, easily enough—since *surely* you have had time enough to focus your so impressive Power on his aura."

That stung. "Of course I have, my lord," Rualath purred, lying gracefully, and privately wished Haralachan to the deepest, cruelest, most permanent torments of Darkness. "Kevin shall be yours. And then, my lord, the traitor Naitachal shall be yours as well." She added with cool, deliberate melodrama, "This time, my lord, we can rejoice. The traitor and his human friend shall not escape us."

Chapter XVIII

Comrades In Arms

Kevin stopped short, staring. "Gwenlyn? What's the matter?"

"I'm sorry," she said, suddenly sinking to the ground. "This is it. This is as far as I go."

D'Senna chittered anxiously, bending over her friend, then straightening to glance nervously about at the forest, then bending again. "You cannot stop now! Not here! We are in the middle of—of nothing! You cannot simply—tchk, tchk, what is the human term?—give up!"

"I'm not giving up." Gwenlyn's voice was perfectly reasonable. "I'm just not walking any more."

Kevin squatted beside her. "Ach, look, I know you're tired—"

"Not just tired," she corrected, still in that too controlled tone. "Hopeless. I just can't bear to go through another one of those stupid, useless, horrible spells that—" She broke off, blinking fiercely. "Damn. I sound like the wispy little girls I despise."

Kevin sighed, shifting to sit beside her, pulling his lute around to lie in his lap. "No, you don't. Wispy, my dear young woman, is the last thing you are." To his relief, she chuckled at that. "Frankly," the Bard continued, "I don't think I could stand much more of this being tossed about at random, either."

"Gods, what are we going to do?"

Kevin glanced about the forest with a critical eye, then gave his most nonchalant shrug. "Why, go camping, of course."

Gwenlyn and D'Senna both stared at him as though he'd gone mad. "Ah, what?"

Kevin grinned. "Just what I said: go camping."

"But . . ."

"Yes. We're going to find us a nice, sheltered spot—and I think this should do nicely—with a good source of water."

"There is a spring nearby," D'Senna cut in. "I feel the water. I could dig it free for us."

"Aha. There we are." Kevin waved a casual hand. "Lots of firewood all around for the asking. I know how to set snares, so we should have something fresh to eat."

Gwenlyn was still staring at him as though he'd gone mad, but she contributed warily, "I know which plants are safe to eat at this time of year. Oh, but what good is all this nonsense? We can't live here in the wilderness forever!"

"Ah, but we won't have to. At least," Kevin added with reluctant honesty, "I hope not."

"Uh-huh."

"Look you, I haven't gone mad. But we're never going to find our way out of the chaotic mess the spell's made of the forest. We *know* this spot is safe. We haven't been touched by the Gate for some time."

"Yes, but . . . ah." Gwenlyn's face brightened slightly. "You think the spell is going to just run down by itself?"

"With enough time, yes. At least," he corrected with

a weak smile, "I pray it will, and somewhere within our lifetime."

"Oh, aren't you the optimist." But Gwenlyn grinned suddenly. "Ah well, anything's better than walking any more! Come on, D'Senna, I'll help you dig out that spring."

But as she started to her feet, Kevin held out a restraining hand. She frowned at it. "Now what?"

"Just because we haven't fallen through the spell in a while doesn't mean it isn't lurking around here somewhere. From now on, everything we do, we do together."

Gwenlyn raised a wry brow. "Everything?"

To his disgust, Kevin felt himself reddening. "We can't afford to be squeamish, not unless we want the spell to separate us. I don't know about you, but I really don't want to be left alone again."

She shuddered. "No. Ah well, they do say togetherness is good for the soul!"

"So, tell me, D'Senna," Kevin said suddenly, "what's it like being an Arachnia?"

The three were sitting in relative comfort about a small campfire, idly watching the sparks rise into the night. Kevin had managed to catch a rabbit, by pure luck whapping it over the head before it could escape, D'Senna had decapitated a second with a neat click of her claws, and what with that and the plants Gwenlyn had found, they were feeling at least a little better about life.

"What is it like?" D'Senna mused. "Boring," she decided at last. "At least for me. I am, as Gwenlyn knows, a surplus young Queen, one who will never have her own hive—and never wants one!"

"Adventure hungry, are you?"

D'Senna clicked her beak uneasily. "Not anymore. I would very much like to find myself some place where I can live and be useful and happy."

"Like D'Krikas. He moved out of his hive, he told me, because of overcrowding."

"Yes. There are more surplus males, fertile or not, than females in a hive."

"Ah. Well. At any rate, now he's my seneschal, and he seems very happy about it. *I'm* happy about it, because frankly, I don't think I could manage the castle without him. I'm not exactly," Kevin added with a wry glance at Gwenlyn, "to the manor born." But then he straightened. "Hey now, here's a thought: D'Krikas can always use more help, even with Tich'ki around. Never mind who she is. Do you think you'd like to train as his assistant?"

D'Senna tensed. "A purpose? A true purpose in life for me? Akkk, yes! Yes!"

"Great." Kevin slumped. "Now all we have to do is get out of this mess."

But Gwenlyn was watching him oddly. "What?" he asked.

"You surprise me. I never thought you were the sort to worry about the happiness of others."

"Well, we didn't get much of a chance to know each other at all, now, did we?"

She had the good grace to blush. "No." Gwenlyn brushed back her disheveled black hair, then added frankly, "Look you, Kevin, I'm sorry for the way I acted back in my father's castle."

"It's all right. I understand."

"No, curse it, you don't. I acted like a spoiled child, and there's no excuse for that."

"You were scared. Of being trapped, I mean."

"Ha, yes. So were you."

Kevin grinned sheepishly. "Was it that evident?"

"It was."

"Uh, well, it was something very new to me. The thought of getting married, I mean. Of *having* to wed, *having* to sire an heir. I . . . never had much of a chance to sit down and think about it, not after I became count and found I had a whole castle and the lands around it as my responsibility, most certainly not before that!"

"How *did* you become count? Oh, not the official story. I've heard all that."

"What do you want to hear? That I was a brave adventurer who overcame all sorts of terrible odds to become a hero?" Kevin grinned. "It wasn't anything like that. I was a green kid, a bardling aching to *do* something, to become a full Bard, who happened to run into the right sort of friends. They kept me alive so Carlotta could be defeated."

"Oh, you say it so easily!"

"That part of it wasn't easy at all! And . . . not all our party survived. But we did put an end to her evil, hopefully forever." He paused, considering. "And on a personal level it was worth all the risk: I wound up gaining Bardhood." Kevin let his hand rest affectionately on the body of the lute.

"That's what really means something to you, isn't it?" Gwenlyn asked softly. "Not the title, not the fame. The music."

Kevin nodded. "It is, simplistic as this sounds, what I am. I won't say I don't enjoy being a count and all that goes with it. But I could not be *me* without my music."

"Gods, I envy you!" she exploded.

"What—"

"I've never done anything, gone anywhere—this," her sweep of the arm took in the night-dark forest, "is the only adventure I've ever had."

"I'd have passed on this one, thank you."

"Oh, so would I! But you miss my point. You've always been allowed to do what you wanted."

"Within limits. It was Master Aidan, the Bard who taught me, sending me off on an errand that started the whole thing."

"Yes, but you didn't have anyone saying, 'I'm sorry, but a noblewoman doesn't do such things as have adventures or go places, a noblewoman isn't supposed to do anything but stay at home and learn how to be a proper wife and mother and how to run her husband's castle so the dear man isn't bothered by mundane matters. It's a sin if she has a brain because everyone knows noblewomen aren't expected to think'!"

Gwenlyn stopped short, staring angrily into the fire. "I'm not going to keep whining," she muttered after a tense moment, "I promise you."

"It wasn't whining."

"Dammit, don't start pitying me!"

Kevin threw up his hands. "Hey, I'm on your side!"

"Ah. Right." Gwenlyn drew up her legs, arms around them, resting her chin on her knees. "I don't mean to bite, truly I don't. And I'm not stupid enough to wish myself nothing but 'a simple peasant lass.' Simple peasant lasses tend to look old and die young. It's only . . . I am so hopelessly *frustrated*!"

"I don't blame you."

She glanced sharply at him. "You mean that, don't you?"

"Of course. If I was being so stupidly restricted, I think I would start trying to tear down the castle with my bare hands."

"I've considered it." Gwenlyn cocked her head. "You know, this is the first time I've been able to say something this honest to a man. My father and I would be screaming at each other if I just mentioned 'boredom,' and the idiots who came courting me—present company excluded, of course," she added with a grin.

"Of course." He bowed from the waist, no easy thing with a lute in the way.

"Anyhow, they were more interested in making sure I would be a proper brood mare in mind and body." She uncurled suddenly, her tattered riding outfit giving Kevin an intriguing flash of bare legs. "Ach, enough. What is, as the saying goes, is."

"I would never treat a woman like a mindless brood mare," Kevin said very carefully, not quite sure why he felt it was so very necessary she know that.

She stared at him with a disconcertingly steady gaze. "No. I don't think you would."

For a moment Kevin could do nothing but look into those amazing indigo eyes. . . . Suddenly embarrassed, he straightened with a laugh. "Lydia—that's my commander-in-chief—would never allow it!"

"Your commander-in-chief is a woman?" Gwenlyn asked incredulously. "How marvelously strange! I've only seen a few warrior women, and only from a distance."

"Oh, you'd like our Lydia. Tough and free-spirited as they come—she'd probably have you learning swordplay the moment she met you and be lecturing you on your rights as a free and independent human being at the same time."

Gwenlyn giggled, a delicious little sound that seemed to shiver right through Kevin. "I think I might like that. And I bet I'd like her! And what about the friend you had with you? The mysterious harpist in the black cloak? Is he a Bard, too?"

All laughter slid away from Kevin. "Yes," he murmured, feeling the night turning chill. "His name is

Naitachal, but I . . . don't know where he is now. I can only pray he's safe."

"I take it he got caught in this stupid spell, too."

"Worse. I have the horrible feeling it was set specifically for him." Kevin hesitated uncertainly, then added, "Naitachal is a Dark Elf," and braced himself for her reaction.

But to his immense surprise, all Gwenlyn said was, "Oh, is *he* the one?"

"I beg your pardon?"

"I hadn't known he'd become a Bard. And don't give me that bewildered stare! He's in the official story of Carlotta's defeat, too, you know."

"Ah. Of course."

"How terribly difficult it must have been for him to change his entire life like that. And how wonderful that he succeeded!"

Hearing the sympathy in her voice, Kevin astonished himself by feeling a little stab of—oh, no, it couldn't possibly be jealousy—could it? "Yes, it was difficult," he said gruffly. "But he did it. I only hope his kin haven't caught him."

She stared at him in dawning horror. "The—the Dark Elves? Good gods, I hope not! Ach, Kevin, forgive me. Here I am babbling on about how frustrated I am with my life when all the time you're worried about your friend's very life!"

"It's not knowing if there's something I can do, something I'm missing, that's the worst of it."

D'Senna, who had been standing restlessly nearby, asked suddenly, "Have you tried music?"

Kevin glanced up at her. She looked very inhuman indeed in the dim light, the fire glinting weirdly off her segmented eyes and turning the hints of iridescence on her skin to small rainbows of glittering color.

"What, Bardic Magic, you mean?" he asked her. "Oh, yes. Whenever I could be sure the music wouldn't bring enemies down on my head."

"And?"

"Nothing. Wherever Naitachal is, he's beyond the range of my music."

"You could try again," Gwenlyn suggested. "Right now. Who knows? This time it just might work."

Kevin forced a light smile. "Can't refuse two lovely ladies, now, can I?"

At first, he felt incredibly awkward with Gwenlyn watching him, self-conscious as he hadn't felt since the old days of being a bardling. *You idiot, what's the matter with you? Are you a Bard or not?*

Covering his confusion as best he could, Kevin took a long, careful time tuning the lute's strings. Finally, though, he could stall no longer. Raising his lute, he began to play.

And almost from the first notes, the wonder happened, as it always did. The music began to take over, wiping out nervousness, losing him in its shape and sound. Little by little, Bardic Magic roused as he played, taking shape, calling to Naitachal, calling . . .

Nothing. Not the slightest psychic response from Naitachal. Kevin sighed softly and let the music trail away.

"I felt it," D'Senna said softly. "I felt the magic of the call shivering through me."

"So did I," Gwenlyn murmured, eyeing Kevin with new respect. "But there wasn't an answer, was there?"

Kevin shook his head. "Wherever he is, it's beyond my reach."

"Oh, but that doesn't mean anything. Remember this Gate Spell or whatever you call it. There's probably enough weird magic already loose in the forest to confuse any other spell."

Kevin stared at her, then let out a laugh of relief. "Yes, of course! Gwenlyn, thank you! It's such an obvious thing, but I missed it completely. Of course you're right. Ha, yes, with so much chaotic magic swirling about, it's no wonder Naitachal can't hear me!"

Because he was blazing with this sudden new hope, Kevin let out his emotions in music, playing this time just for Gwenlyn. Out of the corner of his eye, he saw D'Senna move off into shadow, chittering ever so softly in amusement. Now what did she find so funny? He could have sworn he heard her murmur something about "Something interesting starting . . . one of those odd soft-bodied matters."

Between me and Gwenlyn? Oh, nonsense.

Kevin deliberately picked some of the brightest, most cheerful tunes he knew, tunes that sounded as though the music was giggling to itself or dancing wildly, and was delighted to see Gwenlyn's eyes sparkle with pleasure. She liked music, yes, she did! Buoyed by her delight and by a strange new joy he couldn't quite define, Kevin played on and on.

But bit by bit, the music changed. As the Bard glanced up from time to time and saw Gwenlyn's eyes so bright, her lips ever so slightly parted in a smile, the melodies grew ever so slowly more tender, more romantic. Ah, fool, fool, why had he not noticed before this just how beautiful those bright eyes were? Why had he not noticed just how lovely she was?

The music faded and was gone. Kevin and Gwen leaned tentatively towards each other. Hardly daring to believe what was happening, he felt his lips brush hers—

"Enemies!" D'Senna shrilled. "Enemies are coming!"

Chapter XIX

Warriors

Alone in his private chambers, well-warded rooms in which every stone in every wall, the ceiling and floor, was guarded by threefold spells to which only he knew the secrets of setting or releasing, Haralachan lounged in apparent ease on a couch covered in priceless black spidersilk, his fingers steepled under his chin. But there was nothing at all restful about his thoughts.

Yes, curse her to the deepest Darkness for her cleverness, Rualath had been right. The human, the traitor's friend, this . . . Kevin . . . was almost certainly the key to capturing Naitachal. Haralachan paused to reflect once more on that bizarre weakness so foreign to proper *Nithathil* thought and action: friendship.

As best Haralachan could understand the concept, it meant something that bound you to another, uselessly, not for gain of any sort.

And when that other chances to fall, as must all weaklings, so, perforce, do you—phaugh, what a ridiculous obscenity!

But he had never been one to scorn something that might prove of use. This *friendship* was a weakness, yes, something to be scorned by any sensible Dark Elf—but a weakness that, since it affected the traitor as it did, would be most decidedly useful.

Still, it had been a definite mistake to underestimate the youngster, Kevin, mere human though he was. Common hunters should never have been sent after him. Ah, no, full warriors should have been sent instead—though of course, Haralachan thought dourly, he would never admit to having made that mistake.

But, the Dark Elf lord mused, *are even my warriors going to be sufficient?* Of course a troop of them would be more than powerful enough to capture one lone human. One *ordinary* human. But from everything he'd heard, the traitor's friend was not exactly ordinary.

Haralachan frowned thoughtfully. *The human is said to be a Bard, even as Naitachal has become. We know so little of this* music, *these strange sounds our foolish White Elf kin and the humans seem to enjoy so much.* Odd, odd, to enjoy a mere progression of tones. . . . Haralachan waved that away as just one more example of his people's superiority over others. But he wouldn't wave away the subject of Bards as well. *Yes, a Bard is said to be one skilled in performing* music. *But surely there is more to such a creature than mere showmanship? I* know *what Necromantic Power Naitachal possesses. But what of Kevin? What odd Powers might a human Bard possess? Powers of which we know nothing?*

Ridiculous to worry about what a human might or might not do. Still . . . there had been one mistake made already. There must not be—would not be—another. Perhaps, Haralachan mused, leaning his chin on his hands, he should add another weapon to his plan. One that had proven the only useful aspect of the situation so far.

Yes. It would be done.

✧ ✧ ✧

Moving as silently as she could along the quiet corridors, all her senses alert, Amaranthia shivered in delicious fright. The caverns of Lord Haralachan were so incredibly *dark*, particularly for one without *Nithathil* night-vision, and so intriguingly full of who-knew-what perils.

Adding to the strange, frightening thrill of potential danger was the knowledge that should she happen to fall afoul of one of the lord's more risky subjects—an alarmingly number of whom seemed to show quite a nasty interest in this White Elf who dared stray into their realm—only Haralachan would raise a hand to help her, and that only if the whim so moved him. Down here, there was no family clan to shield her, no one to protect her. She was totally on her own, reliant only on her own cunning and courage for survival.

"Ah, look," said a sudden voice behind her, and Amaranthia, who had thought herself quite alone, nearly screamed in shock, turning so sharply she nearly fell. A tall, elegant figure stood before her, bowing with intricate, mocking grace. "Our little White Elf cousin graces our corridors."

Ah, now she knew him. And wished he'd chosen some other corridor to prowl. But she would *not* show him any alarm. "My lord Tanarchal." Amaranthia let the words fall coldly from her lips. "Are you not far from your place?"

He raised a hand to lightly touch her long, golden hair. "My place, child, is wherever I choose to make it."

"Your place," she snapped, pulling sharply back out of his reach, "is wherever my Lord Haralachan allows it to be."

Perfect elven teeth glinted whitely in the darkness

in a smile absolutely without humor. "Such a brave little one, trying to play our games, trying to ape our ways. Never once seeing just how big a fool she is."

Amaranthia stiffened. "You go too far, my lord!"

Tanarchal chuckled. "Brave and daring, too. What, will you slap me for the insult, like some delicate human lady peeved at her human lord? No. You are surely not quite *that* foolish." He paused, studying her. "Ah, she rages. But anger will not change the truth, child. Silly little White Elf, can you not see it?"

"What *are* you talking about?"

"Simply this." His eyes glittered coldly. "Keep up your silly games. Try all you will. But no matter how much you wish it, no matter how hard you try to play the role, you will never change one fair-skinned, fair-haired bit of you. You can never be a *Nithathil*, girl."

"That's ridiculous! I don't want to be one of you!"

"Don't you?"

"No! I am *myself*, curse you! I don't—"

But Tanarchal had already turned and strolled away, contemptuously presenting his back to her as, she knew, he would never have dared do to one of his own race. And she—oh, she longed so fiercely to stab a knife through that mocking back she could all but feel the hilt of the blade in her hand.

But, no. Haralachan had warned her once against it. Tanarchal, he had hinted to her, was his prey-to-be, and no one else dared steal that prey from him.

"Amaranthia," a soft voice murmured, and she started, hand going to the magical gem on its chain about her neck almost guiltily. Glancing down at it, she asked warily, "My Lord Haralachan. What would you?"

"Come to me, Amaranthia. In my chambers."

Ae, had he been spying on her? Had he seen her

with Tanarchal? But surely then he knew she hadn't been plotting against him!

I wasn't plotting anything!

"Amaranthia. I shall not repeat myself. Come. To my chambers."

Who knew what strange, dark things might take place behind those spell-guarded walls? But one did not even dream of arguing with Haralachan. "At once, my lord," Amaranthia said, and hurried forward.

The doors opened silently at her knock. Amaranthia stepped cautiously inside, seeing next to nothing in the darkness, heart pounding, wondering for a panic-stricken moment if Haralachan had grown bored of her presence in his realm or decided she had somehow betrayed him, if he meant to casually destroy her.

"Here," said a quiet voice.

He was waiting in his small audience chamber, dimly lit by two blue-flamed candles, lounging at ease on his black silk-covered couch. "So, my pale little one," the Dark Elf lord purred, and gestured to her to approach. Amaranthia obeyed, falling submissively to her knees before him.

"My Lord Haralachan."

Head bowed in wary respect, she felt his hand touch her hair, stroking it with just a touch too much force to be pleasant. "So fearful, my pale little one." His voice was still as silken as the couch. "Have you something, perhaps, about which to be fearful?"

His hand closed with sudden, painful force on her hair, pulling her head back. Forced to look up at him, Amaranthia banned all thoughts of Tanarchal from her mind and said with all the fervor she could muster, "No, my lord! Never!"

"Hmm, now, I wonder . . ."

He was merely toying with her, Amaranthia realized

with a rush of relief, playing at cruelty as he sometimes did, without any real anger behind the words. But that didn't make the hand tangled so harshly in her hair any easier to bear. Struggling to keep the tears of pain from her eyes, Amaranthia told him as steadily as she could, "My Lord Haralachan, I have been totally faithful to you. Surely you know that. I have done everything you requested of me."

"Ah yes. My loyal little game piece." Without warning, he released her hair. But before she could pull away, one elegant finger with its sharp-pointed nail not quite gently traced down the line of her cheek and jaw, making her shiver. "You shall be rewarded, Amaranthia."

In that moment, she wasn't so sure she wanted such a thing.

But then Haralachan abandoned his languid pretense, straightening like a suddenly alert predator. "But first, my pale little one, before any hope of reward, you must perform one more service for me."

"Anything, my lord."

"Oh, indeed. Listen, my dear, and obey."

"Enemies!" D'Senna shrilled, and Kevin and Gwenlyn started. "Enemies are coming!"

"Oh my gods," Gwenlyn breathed in horror, and Kevin silently echoed her. The foes who had so suddenly stepped out of the night were not the Dark Elf hunters who had pursued him with such sadistic glee but who had been, despite the determined way they'd followed him, relatively easy to escape. No, he could see all too clearly, even in the darkness, that these were true *Nithathil* warriors, grimly purposeful, not the sort to be swayed from their mission by pleasure or rage. They were clad alike in dull black mail and lightweight helms that he suspected had been strengthened by sorcery, and they carried their swords with chill efficiency, their eyes like so many hard blue gems. To try fighting this lot with steel, one against their many, would be far worse than facing the hunters, far worse than hopeless.

But Kevin, for all his alarm, was still half caught in the spell of his music. Without stopping to think *this might not work, Dark Elves don't even* have *music,* he raised his lute and began to play.

Yes, but play what?

There weren't any specific Bardic songs to handle this situation: Kevin knew he could create light or ward off monsters with his music—but Dark Elves weren't going to cringe from that cool blue magical light and weren't mindless monsters. Desperately, he began the most soothing, mesmerizing songs he knew, willing softness on the elves, soft helplessness.

And to his immense relief, the magic gradually began to work, so subtly the warriors plainly weren't even aware of what was happening to them. The swords began to waver in their hands, their fierce eyes to glaze. A little more Bardic song, just a little more, and they would be asleep on their feet. . . .

"No, you idiots!" a woman's voice screamed. "It's *noise,* just *noise!* It has no power!"

Amaranthia! It was Amaranthia, proving without further doubt with whom she was allied, rushing forward in a blur of white silk to grab Kevin's arm, pulling his hand away from the lute strings, breaking the spell. Both he and the Dark Elves were equally stunned by the suddenness of the magic's shattering—but it was the Dark Elves who recovered first. Before Kevin could drop the lute and whip out his sword, they were swarming over him, bearing him down, pinning him helplessly against the ground.

"Run!" he yelled to Gwenlyn and D'Senna.

Then someone was hissing strange, alien words in his ear—the words all too clearly a *Nithathil* spell because all at once reality dissolved into colored sparks, then darkness.

"Kevin!" Gwenlyn screamed, but D'Senna's hand had already clamped securely about her arm. "No, wait, we can't abandon—"

"We must!"

D'Senna, young Arachnia though she was, was far stronger than any human woman. Gwenlyn, cursing, sobbing, was dragged helplessly after her like a child after its mother until at last the truth sank in and she ran along with the Arachnia. They forced their way through thick underbrush, at last taking refuge under a mass of tree roots and leaves, huddling together, trying to gasp in air without making a sound.

For a long while nothing happened. The forest seemed to settle into its normal stirrings and rustlings. At last Gwenlyn dared straighten enough to stare out into the night.

"It's all right," she said softly. "No one followed us."

D'Senna shuddered as much as her stiff Arachnia form would permit. "That is not a good thing."

Gwenlyn stared. "Did you *want* to be chased?"

"No. But that they did not even try to follow us means the *Nithathili* came here specifically to catch Kevin."

"Oh dear gods, it does. D'Senna, we can't let the Dark Elves have him, we can't!"

"No. Of course not. But . . . what can we do? They are many, and we are only two—and hardly trained warriors, either of us."

Gwenlyn sat down with a despairing sigh. "No. Hardly that. We have to find help. But—where? Oh, D'Senna, where?"

Chapter XX

Lost . . .

Count Trahern, Lydia thought, was riding with all the grim, silent determination of a ghostly horseman. In all this time that they'd been travelling back from the shrine of Saint Verdain, he hadn't said more than one word to her, to *anyone*.

Can't say I blame him. If it was my *kid who'd disappeared, I wouldn't be feeling so chatty, either. Poor guy. And what can I possibly say to him? "It's all right, your daughter's just disappeared in the middle of the wilderness without any supplies, nothing to worry about, and for all I know, Kevin's as lost and out of luck as Gwenlyn?" Ha. Wouldn't* that *be comforting!*

"Here's the head of the trail," the count said so suddenly Lydia started. "The one my daughter and her escort might have followed from my castle." He looked helplessly around. "Damn! If only we had some decent trackers with us!"

"I can follow a track pretty well," Lydia drawled. "Allow me."

He shot her an amazed glance, eyebrows raised. "You never do fail to surprise me."

"Good," she retorted. "I like keeping my men off balance."

Blast it, I didn't mean to say that. Now he'll think I'm being—Powers Above help me— coy!

"Cute," Tich'ki muttered in her ear. "Very cute. Next you'll be fluttering a fan and batting your pretty little eyelashes at him."

Lydia opened her mouth, closed it again without saying anything. If she answered the fairy, Count Trahern would almost surely think she'd gone over the edge and was talking to her hair. *Huh,* she thought angrily, *you'd love to see me make a total fool of myself, wouldn't you? Particularly if you could help.*

There were disadvantages to having a fairy for a friend. One of them being the fairy love for nasty practical jokes.

Right. I haven't forgotten that time we were riding guard for that caravan, you, me, and that very nice-looking blond fellow. Just when we finally managed to get a few moments alone, him and me and—I thought—no one else anywhere nearby, your spear just happened *to stab him right in the rump. An accident, you swore. Sure it was.*

Ah hell, the guy had been pretty brainless anyhow. And his look of sheer shock and outrage *was* kind of funny, now. But Lydia wasn't ready to stop being angry yet. *And where were you, you cursed little fairy nuisance,* she wondered hotly, *while I was wasting time in Saint Verdain's precious shrine? Trying to help me? Not a chance! You were probably off trying to pick some merchant's pocket and—*

"Lydia," Tich'ki cried sharply, all mockery gone, "watch out! Don't go any further!"

But Lydia's horse, shying at the shrill little voice, had already stepped forward. The animal suddenly stumbled, then flailed about in panic, screaming, nearly unseating her, as the world blurred wildly about them. Before she had a chance to really panic as well, her horse had caught its balance again and stood trembling, ears flat back.

Lydia looked around in sheer disbelief, seeing trees that weren't exactly the trees she'd seen a moment ago, trying desperately to regain her stunned senses. The others had fallen through . . . whatever . . . with her, and for a time the air was full of the frightened squealings of horses and the cursing of men, not all of whom had managed to stay in the saddle.

"What," Count Trahern said, struggling to soothe his own horse, "in the name of all the demons of the Seven Hells, was *that*? And where, for that matter, are we?"

"Another part of the forest, I think," Lydia told him uneasily. "Literally."

"Don't you get the point?" Tich'ki shot out of hiding, wings an iridescent blur. "That was a Gate! A sorcerous Gate!"

"A fairy!" the count exclaimed in shock, snatching for a weapon.

"A human!" Tich'ki sneered, fluttering out of reach.

"A friend," Lydia added. "More or less. Tich'ki, what do you mean, a Gate?"

"What part of 'Gate' didn't you understand?" the fairy snapped. But after a moment of watching the humans' confusion (and probably, Lydia thought, enjoying it), she relented enough to add an explanation. "Someone must have cast open a sorcerous portal a while back. You know, the sort of thing that lets you step from *here* to *there* without wasting time going in between. A Gate. Don't see them too often."

"Well, thank the gods for that," the count muttered.

"Yeah, right, whatever. Anyhow, the reason you don't see Gates too often is that they take a *lot* of Power to open and keep open. They're not very stable at the best of times. My guess is, something went wrong with this particular Gate and the whole thing shattered. And whoever set it wasn't too careful about picking up all the scattered bits of the broken spell. As for us . . ." Tich'ki shrugged expressively. "We were the lucky folks who fell through one of those bits."

"Oh. Wonderful. Trahern, do you have any idea where we are?"

If he'd noticed Lydia dropping his title, the count didn't comment on it. "I *think* I know where we are now," he murmured, standing in the stirrups for a better look around. "Mmm, yes. I do. If I'm right, and we keep due west for perhaps half a day, we should come out not too outrageously far from the trail we need. We should even end up closer to my castle. Unless . . . fairy, ah, Tich'ki, do you know if we're likely to come across any more of those broken spell bits?"

She shrugged in midair. "Not my sort of magic. I'd say the best thing to do is just keep going and see what happens. We'll know if they're around if we fall through them."

"Charming thought." Count Trahern glanced back at his men, who had all managed to remount by now and seemed reasonably under control. "Everyone all right? Yes? Then let's go on."

But he rode with weapon to hand. As did they all.

"Fat lot of good swords are going to be against sorcery," Tich'ki muttered in Lydia's ear.

"Huh. That's why you've got your own spear out? Or maybe you're going to use it as a magic detector?"

Tich'ki jabbed her in the shoulder with the spear, just hard enough to sting, and darted away before Lydia could retaliate. "Can't be too careful now, can we?" the fairy taunted. "We don't all have nice, handsome noblemen boyfriends to protect us!"

Oh, damn, now she was blushing again. *Bad as a girl with her first crush,* Lydia thought in self-disgust.

Trahern glanced her way. "If that is a friend of yours," he murmured, "I don't believe I wish to see your enemies."

"Don't have any," Lydia retorted sharply.

"Eh?"

"Living, that is."

Satisfied she'd restored at least some of her warrior honor, she rode on.

Naitachal glanced back at his faithful adherents. Still there, the scruffy lot of them, still determinedly following him. Not one of them seemed to realize—or at least be bothered by—the fact that their leader's thoughts faded in and out of reality from time to time.

More to the point, he thought drily, they seemed to believe his occasional vagueness all part of his aura of fearsome sorcerous Power. When he went fuzzy on them, they thought he was concentrating on focusing his magics or memorizing his spells or something along those lines. Bah, he really *was* beginning to feel like a duck being faithfully trailed by its ducklings.

I've had to fight off so many waves of that cursed Chaos Gate I'm surprised I still have any more brains than a duck.

But the spell's Power did seem, at last, to be dissipating. Today he had actually been able to keep more than one coherent thought in his head at a time.

For what good that served. No matter how I struggle, I can't seem to focus on Kevin's aura yet. I . . . hope that's just because of the interference from all those wandering bits of sorcery.

Someone was pulling at his sleeve. Naitachal whirled with elven speed, more angry at himself for being startled than at the human for startling him, and fixed the offender with as sorcerous a glare as he could manage. The bandit shrank back with a gasp. "Sorry."

"What is it?" Naitachal snapped. "You have disturbed my thoughts of sorcery. The reason for that disturbance had best be something of worth."

"Uh . . . well . . . we were . . . uh . . . all of us were wondering—"

"Wondering *what*, you idiots? Wondering why I don't strike you down where you stand?"

They flinched at that, and some of them, particularly the scrawny youngster, Kem, actually blanched. But the bandit who'd pulled at his sleeve continued doggedly, "Well . . . uh . . . you said we were going to find that Count Kevin."

"And so we are."

"Uh, yeah, sure. We're not arguing, see. Only . . . all we seem to be doing so far is a lot of walking, and—"

"And what?" Naitachal snapped.

But he was far from feeling as confident as the chill *Nithathil* image he was projecting. Humans were often a tricky lot, particularly those of such a desperate, low class. This was the first sign of rebellion from them; small though it was, he knew if he didn't stop it now, the fickle creatures would turn on him, his bright promises of a pardon notwithstanding.

"Are you accusing me of *lying* to you?" Naitachal asked coldly. "Are you actually daring to accuse me of *anything?*" As he spoke, Naitachal slid subtly into shadow, knowing from previous experience with humans that normal elven reflexes would cause his eyes to glint redly as they adjusted to the darkness. Judging from the sudden new terror on the bandits' faces, the effect was working very nicely. "Well?" he challenged, glaring. "Answer me! Do you dare accuse me?"

"No, no," they all stammered out in a tangle of voices, "of course not!"

He held up a stern hand, and they all fell obediently silent. "I need not depend on anything as slow as foot travel. Surely even such as you understand that. But you are human, only that. We have no steeds of any sort, nor could I magic any that would bear your kind." *Nor could I magic* any *steeds,* Naitachal added to himself with wry honesty. *Never was one for that type of magic.* "If you know of any faster way for humans on foot to travel, speak up now."

Silence.

"So." He fixed them all once more with his most sorcerous glare. "I am your leader or I am not. Which is it to be?"

They assured him in an eager babble that of course he was their leader, they were honored that he was their leader, they would never even dream of challenging him again. With a thin smile, Naitachal turned his back on them (not without an atavistic tingling between his shoulder blades; he *still* wasn't used to being able to safely turn his back on anyone, and these were hardly trusted friends) and stalked on.

One more battle won. Even if it was against these creatures. Nothing to do now but keep leading his adopted band of robber scum in as logical a path as he could manage. Eventually what was left of the Gate Spell would vanish completely and give him a chance to find Kevin.

I hope.

And, he hoped, before the bandits woke up to the fact that their new leader wasn't bringing them any closer to riches or that pardon.

Ah well, if the worst comes to the worst, I suppose I can sing them all to sleep long enough for me to make my escape. Naitachal grimly blocked sudden memories of earlier, darker days when Necromancy would have put a more definite end to any such human nuisances. He fought to ignore the sly little urge telling him that it would be so easy, just a few Words, a few quick, deadly touches to fragile human flesh—

No! He was not a Necromancer any longer! Come what may, he *refused* to be a Necromancer!

There are *advantages to being a Bard,* Naitachal thought dourly. *Unless, of course, one of the bandits turns out to be tone-deaf. From everything Master Aidan told me, Bardic Magic can't slide its musical way into the mind of someone who is totally tone-deaf.*

Naitachal shook his head in wry amusement. He had troubles enough without starting to imagine more.

"Onward, my gallant band," he said with a deliberately melodramatic sweep of arm. "Onward to glory."

Or whatever.

Chapter XXI

. . . And Found

Tich'ki came whirring back to Lydia so fast the woman heard the thrum of her wings. "Dead men up ahead," the fairy panted. "Looks like someone ran into an ambush."

"Oh gods," Count Trahern murmured. "Was there . . . a young woman among them?"

The fairy hesitated, looking uneasy for one of the few times Lydia could remember. "I don't want to scare you," she said at last. "I don't know what your daughter looks like. So I think you'd better see this for yourself before—"

But with an anguished shout, Trahern kicked his horse into a gallop, shooting past her with such force she swayed in the air. "—you go into a panic," she finished weakly.

"Come on," Lydia said grimly. "Might as well learn the truth and get it over with."

Tich'ki was right. These men definitely had been ambushed. Most of the bodies bore arrow wounds and signs they'd been dragged from their horses without having much of a chance to fight back. Count Trahern searched them wildly. "Deran, Terek, yes, yes, and here's Degalth, you damned idiot." He glanced sharply up at Tich'ki. "Where is she?"

"Over here. But I—"

Trahern was already turning over the sad little body. He stared a moment, then let out a sigh of relief. "It's not Gwenlyn. This is one of her maidservants, the poor unlucky . . ."

His voice trailed into silence. If Gwenlyn wasn't here, the odds were overwhelming that she had been carried off by the bandits. And that meant the slain maidservant might be the lucky one.

"We'll find her," Lydia said confidently into the silence. "You, and you, get out of my way."

Crouching, she studied the torn-up earth. Lots of frantically milling horses trampling about. But yes . . . these were definitely the footprints of the bandits, not the well-shod feet of a count's guards but men wearing makeshift sandals or worn-out boots. Now, if she could only find . . . hah, yes, look at this, here were the dainty prints of a woman's booted foot. Had to be Gwenlyn. Mm, yes, and judging from the disturbed earth here, she'd put up quite a good fight. Lost it, of course, one girl against all those bandits. No signs that they had . . . ah . . . harmed her.

But where did they go? They had to have left . . . ah, yes . . . here were the signs showing which way the bandits had gone, a mass of footprints, with one small, elegant footprint in their midst showing the bandits had, indeed, carried Gwenlyn off.

"This way," Lydia said shortly, still studying the ground. Light was tricky in a forest, what with swaying branches and lots of shadows, but natural light gave a truer picture for trackers than did torch flames, which flattened everything out, and she wanted to get as far as possible before sundown. "Someone take my horse. Hey, you! Stay behind me. Don't block my sight."

The trail was clear enough. Although one of the bandits had made a rudimentary effort to wipe out their footprints with a branch, he'd been nicely clumsy at it. Lydia moved smoothly along, reading *broken twigs here, clear footprint there, scrap of cloth on this branch.*

Then Tich'ki was suddenly screaming, "Sorcery! Stop!"

Lydia did stop, throwing herself frantically backwards—but the others didn't stop, not quite in time, and they pushed her with them through yet another blurring of the world to come out to a jarring landing in—

"Oh hell," Lydia said in disgust, scrambling up and brushing herself off, looking about at an unfamiliar glade, hearing an uproar of terrified horses and men behind her. "*Now* where are we?"

Count Trahern was afoot, clutching his panicky horse's bridle in a deathlike grip, his eyes wild with despair. "Why now, dammit?" he cried to no one in particular. "Why, just when we'd found the track—" With a visible effort at self-control, the count answered Lydia in a choked voice, "I don't know. Some other corner of forest. Ah gods, *why?* Now we'll never find her! Now we'll never find my little girl!"

Not knowing what else to do, Lydia put a comforting hand on his shoulder. His own hand closed firmly on hers, and just for a moment she was sure he was going to brush her fingers with his lips. But then he released her, almost brusquely. "There's no help for it," the count said grimly. "We must go forward."

"Yeah. The forest doesn't go on forever. We'll find our way back." *Eventually.*

Tich'ki, who had been ranging ahead of them, came

speeding back like a falcon, zooming down for a landing on a branch just over Lydia's head. "Weird."

"What's weird?" Lydia asked in alarm, craning her head back.

The fairy shrugged, the shivering of her wings giving away her uneasiness. "I'm not sure. Could have sworn I just sensed our Dark Elf friend—"

"Naitachal! Where?"

"Who knows? I *think* I sensed him, but I sure don't see him anyplace. He could be anywhere! With all this broken-up magic wandering about, it's really rough to figure anything out."

Lydia, all set to retort, *It usually is for you,* bit back the easy jest. Instead, she found herself glancing back at Count Trahern. "Yeah," she said softly. "It sure is."

Naitachal admitted wearily to himself that by now he was thoroughly sick of forest and forest and yet more forest. At least the spell's pull had deteriorated sufficiently for his mind to stay clear for reassuringly long stretches. And he was managing to lead the bandits in a relatively straight path.

But what good is that? Where are we going? I don't sense Kevin anywhere!

There hadn't been any more open signs of rebellion in the ranks, but he could hear the faintest discontented murmurings and *feel* their restlessness growing.

In a few moments, Naitachal knew, he was going to have to turn and confront them again. But intimidating them now, he thought with a silent sigh, would be a temporary measure at best. Sooner or later he was either going to have to show them something positive, or else give up on the whole idea of using them to help him, and simply find a way to escape the tedious, useless lot of them.

But suddenly Naitachal stopped short, staring, listening, with senses far beyond the human. Could that be . . . yes! Magical blood always called to magical blood, and he could swear he sensed none other than that quirky little Tich'ki! *Tich'ki!* he shouted mentally. And again, *Tich'ki! I'm here! Where are you?*

"I don't believe it!"

Lydia looked up at that startled cry to see Tich'ki freeze in midair, dropping a good hand before she recovered and got her wings working again. "What's the matter?"

The fairy swooped down to land on her shoulder, hanging onto her hair. "Naitachal just called to me! I don't see him anywhere, but I swear I heard him!"

"Can you cast any sort of spell? Get him here?"

Tich'ki shrugged. "Never was much of a magician. You know that. Still . . . I wonder . . . uh-huh. Worth a try."

"What?"

"Remember how I located the jewels that thief of a merchant was hiding?"

"They *were* his jewels," Lydia murmured.

"Details, mere details. Anyhow, remember what I did?"

"Nearly got me arrested, if memory serves."

"That was after! How was I to know the guard would wake up and sneeze when he did?"

"How could he help it? I told you not to use that feather to snare the keys—"

"Never mind, never mind. What I'm trying to say is that I did use a spell back then, a Finding Spell. It's not much of a spell, I admit it, not the sort of thing you want to use to find something as big as an elf. But who knows? Everything else around here has been so weird and unpredictable it just might work."

"Well? Try it."

"All right. Here we go." Tich'ki's small form went rigid on Lydia's shoulder, and the woman guessed she was trying to call to Naitachal, mind to mind. "Ahh," the fairy murmured after a moment, so softly Lydia almost didn't hear her. Glancing sideways, she saw Tich'ki's gaze go fierce and remote.

She's reached Naitachal, all right. At least I hope *it's Naitachal she's reached!*

Tich'ki was muttering odd, odd syllables in the fairy tongue. Lydia wasn't sure exactly what spell she was casting—it didn't quite sound like anything Tich'ki had ever tried before—but whatever the spell was, it was working. Or at least, Lydia thought warily, it was starting *something,* an odd prickling of the air around the fairy, a strange, small tension that was beginning to feel very annoying. Lydia sighed in relief when Tich'ki suddenly launched herself into the air, flying blindly forward. And suddenly the air before the fairy shimmered so strongly Lydia blinked, dazzled.

"Tich'ki, be careful . . ."

But as suddenly as the dropping of a veil, the shimmer was gone, revealing yet more forest beyond it, and— "Naitachal!" Lydia shouted.

Count Trahern hurried to her side. "What are you doing?" he whispered fiercely. "That's a Dark Elf!"

"Yeah, of course it is, *our* Dark Elf. Naitachal, I'd like you to meet Count Trahern."

The elf swept down in an elegant bow, his blue eyes amused. "We have, though I doubt the count realizes it, already met."

"Your pardon." Count Trahern was hardly about to

let a Dark Elf top him for courtesy. "If so, I fear I truly do not remember."

"The fault is mine." Only someone who knew Naitachal could have detected the tiny edge of mockery in his voice. "I never was actually introduced to you, after all. But I was the Bard who harped while Count Kevin sang." Ignoring Count Trahern's start, he added to Lydia, "You . . . wouldn't happen to have seen him, would you?"

"I was kind of hoping *you* had. Naitachal, what—"

But Lydia was interrupted by the count's men rushing forward to encircle and drag forward a scruffy, nervously struggling group of men. "Ah," Naitachal said mildly, "I see you've found my loyal followers."

"Followers!" Lydia snapped. "Are you crazy, Naitachal? Those have got to be bandits!"

"We all have our little faults."

But Count Trahern was stalking fiercely forward, asking them, "My daughter, damn you, where is my daughter?"

They shrank before his fury, stammering, "N-never saw her." "Don't know whatcha talking about."

But one scrawny youngster cut in, just a moment too late for his voice to be lost in the others, "We didn't hurt her."

He fell silent, horrified at what he'd just as good as confessed, and the furious count grabbed him by the neck of his filthy tunic, almost lifting him from the ground. "Where is she?" Trahern roared. "What have you done with my daughter?"

"You're choking the boy," Naitachal said quietly. "Let him go. I can learn the truth far more easily." There was just the faintest hint of dark menace in the simple words. "Come, let him go."

Reluctantly, the count complied. As Naitachal moved

softly forward, Kem's terrified glance shot his way, full of frantic pleading. "Kem. Listen to me. You will not be hurt if only you tell me exactly what you and your fellows have done. Did you, indeed, carry off this man's daughter?"

Held helpless by the sorcerous blue gaze, Kem at first could only nod. But then he croaked out, "D-didn't know who she was, only that she w-was a noblewoman."

"I see. And *did* you or your fellows harm her?"

"No! I swear it! N-not really. I mean," Kem added hastily, seeing Count Trahern tense, "she put up a fight, we mighta bruised her a bit, but there wasn't nothing serious, honest. We didn't . . . uh . . . you know, do anything deliberate-like."

"Ah." Naitachal glanced at the count. "I think you may just have earned back your life with your honesty. If you answer the next question as well, that is. Where is she?"

Kem licked his lips with a nervous tongue. "Dunno."

"What?" Count Trahern cut in savagely. "How could you not know?"

"I don't! I swear it!"

Naitachal held up a hand before Trahern could interrupt again. "What *do* you know of where she went?"

The boy shivered. "First she went down into a hive."

"An Arachnia hive, I take it."

"She'd be safe down there," the count muttered. "I've always had fair dealing with the Arachnia."

"And is she still there?" Naitachal asked the boy.

"N-no. She left. That's what I heard the Bugs saying before we ran off. She and one of them went off into the forest. And that's all I know. It's the truth!"

"So it is," Naitachal agreed after a moment's intense study of the boy. "It would appear we have not one lost soul to find but two." The elf turned with a sigh and walked back to where Lydia stood watching.

"How did you get hooked up with *that* lot?" she asked sharply.

"Not intentionally, I assure you. They were trying to kill me, I was trying to save my life, and one thing led to another. They seem to have adopted me. And by this point I can't really be easily rid of them. I—ah—promised them something, you see."

"What was it?" the count asked flatly.

"Ah well, a full pardon—"

"What!"

"—if they agreed to help me find Count Kevin. Count Trahern," the elf added coolly, "I am not about to cast off anyone who might help us find Kevin or, now, your daughter."

He held the count's glance transfixed until at last Trahern managed to tear his gaze away. "True," the count muttered. "So be it." Turning to the warily watching bandits, he said with full noble force, "I add my promise to that already given you. Anyone who helps us find my daughter Gwenlyn and Count Kevin will, indeed, be granted a full pardon. You have my word on it, and through me, the regal word as well."

The bandits cheered him, cheered Naitachal, cheered Lydia and the guards, cheered with the thorough, wholehearted enthusiasm that only men who had been given back their lives could know.

Chapter XXII

The Bard Of Darkness

Kevin blinked and blinked again, struggling to gather his stunned senses back together. A spell . . . the last thing he clearly remembered was someone casting a spell over him. . . .

Bit by bit the magic-caused confusion wore off, and Kevin realized he was being half-dragged, half-carried along by someone or ones with singularly cold, strong arms.

Wish they'd stop for a moment . . . let me get my mind working clearly again . . . He hadn't really lost consciousness, had he? Kevin had a vague memory of this half-dragging, half-carrying having gone on for some time. And he couldn't have been totally out of things, surely, not really, at any time, because somehow he had managed to cling to his lute all the way, so fiercely his fingers ached.

All the way to *where?* And if this was consciousness, why was everything so chill and dank and downright *dark?* There was just the dimmest glimmer of light and—

Oh gods. Of course it was dark. With a sudden rush

of panic, Kevin knew exactly where he was. He'd been captured by Dark Elves and was being dragged down by them to their sunless home. Helpless against their strength, Kevin did the only thing he could. Fighting an inner battle with his growing terror, he stayed limp, flatly refusing to let his captors know his fear.

And I'd bet anyone they just happen to be members of Naitachal's clan. Of course they are. They couldn't catch him, so they've settled for nabbing his human friend instead. A new thrill of horror shot through him at the thought. *Well, I—I refuse to betray him. They're not going to get Naitachal through me, come what may.*

Brave thoughts. But all the hints of dark cruelty he'd ever heard from Naitachal insisted on squirming into his mind, telling him, *You can't escape, you can't resist, you haven't a chance against so much cruelty, so much casual evil.*

No, dammit! He was *not* going to let his own thoughts defeat him!

Just then his captors realized that Kevin had fully regained his senses. With a rough shove, they started him forward under his own power. They had left him unbound, and after a quick flash of puzzled hope Kevin became only too well aware why they hadn't bothered with ropes. Even should he somehow manage to evade this lot of warriors, there were certainly other *Nithathili* nearby who'd take great delight in a game of Hunt the Human through the maze of Darkness. The Darkness that was no barrier at all to them.

Kevin tried to speak, coughed drily, tried again, finally managing to get the words out. "Do I dare ask where we're going?" Ah, good, his voice sounded reasonably steady.

Someone chuckled, an absolutely humorless sound. No one else even tried to reply.

Mind games, Kevin thought. *They're trying to work on my nerves. But I refuse to play along.*

Trying to keep himself from being a liar, he glanced about, slyly at first, then more boldly when no one stopped him. His captors were beautiful as all elves were beautiful, and grim as all warriors were grim. There was absolutely no emotion on their fine-boned faces, making them look like so many silver-haired living statues of dark stone. No surprises there.

But the caverns of this Dark Elf clan were hardly what he'd imagined. Kevin found himself almost . . . disappointed at what he saw. He had rather expected, since the *Nithathili* were, after all, elves, that their realm must reflect the elven love of beauty, no matter how warped, that it would be ornamented with depraved, utterly evil but strangely beautiful designs.

But there wasn't so much as a statue or tapestry. Everything was grimly plain, and the lack of even the slightest trace of ornamentation was somehow worse than the most detailed scenes of torment would have been: it made the Dark Elves even colder and more alien than he could have imagined.

Now I can believe they have no music.

Poor Naitachal, growing up amid all this . . . emptiness. How miserably unhappy he must have been—and how incredibly strong of mind and will to have survived with his sanity and his love of music intact.

He probably hadn't even known music existed till he reached the outside world. And then—how wonderful to finally feed a hunger he wouldn't have known till then how to satisfy! Odd, how things work out. Music was—

Music, yes, Kevin thought, suddenly warily curious. *Why* had the Dark Elves left him his lute? Surely they'd seen him work Bardic Magic on them? Surely they'd felt it hit them?

Ha, yes, he realized with a shock, *but they're totally ignorant of the whole idea of music! They've probably never heard music before, never seen it performed—how could they ever have reasoned that any power lay in the lute itself?*

Well, it didn't, of course, not really, but almost no Bard could work efficient Bardic Magic without some musical instrument adding its resonance to the spell.

The elves wouldn't have understood that. They probably thought I just was using my lute to keep my voice steady while I worked some weird spell casting. I bet they thought only the words *were important!*

And of course since no one here was going to let him get out so much as a syllable of song, they would have taken delight in tormenting the human by leaving him his—to them—powerless toy.

Well, now, they'd made their first mistake. It was up to him to see what he could do about—

"Ah!"

It was an involuntary exclamation, because they had suddenly come out into what could only be the clan's throne room. Again, there was no sign at all of any softening decoration, nothing but blank stone walls and two blank stone thrones, one set slightly higher than the other.

But the figures occupying those thrones were powerful enough to catch and hold the attention at a glance. One, a *Nithathil* man in silky black robes, lounged on the higher throne, his lean, elegant figure like that of a predator feigning rest. The other was a woman as elegant as the man, clad in a dark gown of starkly somber cut and sitting sternly erect on the lower throne.

With a jolt, Kevin recognized a definite family resemblance to Naitachal in the lords' proud, coldly beautiful faces.

I never knew he was related to royalty! Though I can understand why he wouldn't want to be associated with this *royalty.*

Where the severely elegant lines of Naitachal's face were tempered with warmth and humor, these two bore not a trace of any softening emotion. They were, in all senses of the word, Kevin thought uneasily, powerful, totally merciless, and totally cruel. And he knew in that moment that his only possible hope for survival was to bluff his way into seeming every bit as cold and ruthless as they.

"Who are you, human?" the Dark Elf lord purred, surprisingly in the human tongue, the casual cruelty in his voice all the more shocking for its beautiful accent.

As if you don't know perfectly well who I am! Kevin retorted silently. But he bowed his most coldly perfect Bardic bow and said, "My name, my lord, is Kevin; my title, count. And I must congratulate you."

A silvery brow raised in what might have been surprise or mockery. "Indeed. And what might you mean by that?"

"Why, I congratulate you for seeing what worth I may be to you—and what worth you, my lord, may be to me."

"So-o," the woman murmured, "the mouse dares challenge the owl."

"Your pardon, my lady," Kevin said smoothly, "but I am no mouse. If I have from time to time played the humble role in my life it was . . . for a reason."

The thinnest of cold smiles formed on the lord's lips. With a quick glance at his consort, he told Kevin, "Very well, human, I shall play this little guessing game of yours. But only as long as it pleases me. Once you cease to be amusing . . ." The sudden cruel glint in his eyes made the rest of that sentence unnecessary.

Oh gods. "So be it," Kevin said with a casual wave of his hand. Blessing Naitachal for having told him at least a little of Dark Elf customs, he added, "But first, may I not know your regal use-names? Constantly calling you merely 'my lord' is insulting to you. I would not do anything to lessen your honor."

If that wording—elven in form though human in language—surprised the lord, he showed no sign. "Daring little mouse, my use-name is Haralachan, as my consort's use-name is Rualath. Seek to learn more of us and that shall be the end of you."

Kevin refused to let himself flinch. "Clear enough."

"Fortunate," the elf drawled. "Why are you so eager to visit our realm? Most humans are terrified at the very thought of Darkness."

Ohh, yes. Including this one. But Bards were trained to perform for all audiences. Even potentially hostile ones. Without missing a beat, Kevin retorted, "I am not like most humans. Granted, I never thought to find myself visiting here, as you say. But now that I am here . . . my Lord Haralachan, surely you know the sweet, sweet taste of Power. It is a taste known to humans as well."

"Should the ways of humans interest me? Do you, perhaps, mean to lecture me?"

"No, no, I would never waste your time on such folly! I merely wished you to see that I, too, enjoy what Power I have been able to gather so far."

"Indeed."

I'm losing him. Got to be colder about this. "We both know how useful others can be, what fine tools they can make for one who is properly ambitious."

"A tool," Rualath said softly, eyes like those of a cat about to pounce, "such as Naitachal?"

Kevin hid his start with a fierce, "Bah! He was the finest tool of all!"

"That is not how I have heard it," Haralachan murmured. "It would seem from all I have gathered, that you and he are . . ." he paused, then finished thoughtfully, "friends."

"Come now, my lord!" Kevin forced as much scorn into his voice as he thought would sound believable. "The man is a traitor to his own kind!" *Forgive me, Naitachal.* "If he betrayed you, he might well betray me someday, too."

"Tsk. What a thought," the woman said in quiet mockery, and Kevin glanced her way. She was so very lovely with that dark skin framed by that silky, silver hair. But her eyes were every bit as cold and cruel as those of the lord, and the Bard quickly looked away.

"Human though I am," he said to both elves, "I am not foolish enough to fall into the trap of trusting anyone as potentially perilous as a traitor."

"Indeed. Then why were you in his company?"

Kevin feigned a smile, hoping it looked properly sardonic and not merely scared. "I used him, my Lord Haralachan, I used him and his magic to get me what I wanted." Waxing to his theme, he said passionately, "Maybe you don't understand such things, being of high birth as you are. But I was born a commoner, a *nobody.*"

"How sad," Haralachan said blandly.

"How tedious," Kevin corrected. "But I had no intention of staying nothing."

Quickly, watching Haralachan warily for the first signs of boredom, the Bard summarized the beginning of his career, rather sickening himself by how easily he could slant everything in the story, from getting his parents to send him to a music teacher to that teacher apprenticing him to Master Aidan, to look as though he'd used everyone he'd met, as though he'd coldly befriended then discarded one person after another. *Ugh, what a nasty bit of scum I was!* he thought wryly.

"And so," Rualath murmured, "you became a Bard. Was that not sufficient reward for a human?"

Kevin just barely kept from betraying himself with a lick of dry lips. *I can't let them know about Bardic Magic,* he suddenly knew. *I can't possibly take them all on, no matter what spell I sing.* And so, forcing himself to show absolutely no signs of fear, he began what he knew would be the most daring lie of all.

"A Bard is a mere wandering musician," Kevin said with carefully feigned distaste, "one with a fine name but no real status."

Would they accept that? Yes, they knew nothing of music, but did that mean they knew nothing of what it meant to be a Bard as well? He waited, heart racing, for the warriors who'd captured him to interrupt, to tell their Lord all about the Bardic Magic he was denying, the magic that had nearly overwhelmed them.

But to his astonishment, they said nothing. *Ha, of course not!* he realized with a flash of relief. *They would never confess they'd been overcome by a mere human! Admitting to such* weakness *would almost certainly be the end of them!*

"And so," Kevin continued boldly, "I decided heroism was the only path to take. With suitable friends to meet the risks for me, naturally."

"Naturally," Haralachan echoed smoothly. "Friends including Naitachal. You, then, were the one who introduced him to music."

Uh-oh. "Of course," Kevin said lightly. "It was just a matter of time before he discovered it by himself, and I needed his magic. As you see, I made good use of him."

"So you wormed your way up into the rank of count, eh?" Dark humor glinted in Haralachan's eyes.

Kevin shrugged. "The late, unlamented Carlotta was *so* convenient. With everyone else to keep her occupied, it was very easy to turn myself into a hero."

"A pretty tale. But all the tale-spinning that ever was will not be enough to save you if you do not tell me why a human is apparently so delighted to be here."

I'd rather be in the dankest swamp than here! "Because, my Lord Haralachan," Kevin said, leaning forward like a racing hound eager for the start, "I have larger dreams than being a mere count. Dreams that cannot be fulfilled without true Power backing me." He paused dramatically. "I seek a crown, my Lord Haralachan, or rather, I seek King Amber's crown."

"Do you, now?" Haralachan smiled lazily at Kevin. "What are your little human ambitions to me?"

What, indeed? For one terrifying, seemingly endless moment, Kevin couldn't find a convincing answer to that. Then inspiration struck. "Why, my lord, you may be supreme Lord over this realm, but can you really tell me you are content with only one realm to rule?" The faintest spark of interest in the cold eyes told Kevin he'd guessed right. "Yet as long as King Amber reigns in human lands, my lord, those lands are—" *Closed to you?* No, no, he didn't dare imply that Haralachan's power was less than total! "—too costly for you to possess."

"Costly?" Haralachan's smile thinned ever so slightly. "Do you think me as weak as one of your kind? Do you think such as I would worry about how many lives might be lost in conquest?"

"Oh, hardly!" Kevin countered hastily. "But why needlessly use up any of your resources? Were I Lord in King Amber's place, why how much more valuable to both of us might an—shall we say—alliance prove! Of course you would leave *my* lands alone. But think of all the other lands open to joint attack!"

Haralachan chuckled coldly. "Why, what an ambitious human it is! And how far-reaching that ambition!"

Oh gods, he's going to believe me!

I think.

"Then we have a pact, my Lord Haralachan? Your hospitality and help now in exchange for mine later?"

The cool blue eyes narrowed ever so slightly. *He* doesn't *believe,* Kevin thought in despair.

But ruthless ambition was plainly something the Dark Elf lord fully understood and appreciated. "Perhaps," Haralachan said smoothly. "Perhaps. For now, my daring, devious little mouse, I welcome you to my realm as a . . . guest."

But his chill smile told Kevin very clearly that "guest" wasn't quite the right word.

Chapter XXIII

Reunion

"We can't just give up," Gwenlyn said, not looking up from the rock on which she slumped.

"No, we cannot," D'Senna agreed, not looking up from where she sprawled on the ground.

"We have to do something to get out of here. Oh gods, and help Kevin. We c-can't just abandon him."

"Agreed. But what is there to be done?" the Arachnia added bitterly. "We cannot even help ourselves."

"I don't know what!" Gwenlyn bit her lip, struggling for control. "I'm just so scared for him."

"So am I."

"And I—I'm so very tired of this stupid, useless walking to nowhere I want to scream. Except," Gwenlyn added with weary honesty, "that if I started screaming now, I don't think I'd be able to stop."

"It has not been walking to nowhere," D'Senna corrected with Arachnia preciseness, "but rather, walking from patch of forest to patch of forest. I am so very tired of *trees*."

"And eating berries."

"And frogs."

"Ugh, yes. I would give anything for a real meal. And a bath. Oh, yes, a long, hot, wonderful bath . . ." Gwenlyn sighed wearily. "This is ridiculous. We're both healthy, reasonably intelligent . . . ah . . . beings. Between us, we should be able to figure out a way to escape this gods-cursed endless magical loop and rescue Kevin."

D'Senna lowered her head in the Arachnia gesture of helpless shame. "I know. I, for one, should have done better. My people are so famed for their sense of logic, yet I . . . I . . ."

Gwenlyn looked up at the sudden thoughtful change in the Arachnia's voice. "What is it?"

"I think I may have just found us a clue." D'Senna slowly unfolded to her full height. "Possibly a very useful clue. Gwenlyn, have you not noticed something odd about the spell upon this forest?"

"That it never quite goes away?"

"Yes, of course, that. But lately the jumps have not been truly random."

"Yes . . ." Gwenlyn said slowly. "There really has been a sort of pattern to them lately, hasn't there? Almost as though the spell is falling apart in . . ." She stared at D'Senna in sudden hope. "In a definite spiral! Oh, D'Senna—"

"A moment, please. If we are to make use of this clue I must see if I can calculate the precise measurements of that spiral."

"Uh, sure."

There was a pause while D'Senna stared blankly into space. All at once she exclaimed, "Ha!" so sharply Gwenlyn started. Triumphantly the Arachnia added, "I have worked out the mathematics of the spiral."

"Just like that?" Gwenlyn said in disbelief. "So quickly? Without writing anything down?"

D'Senna blinked. "I do not understand why you wonder. It was but a simple matter of calculating the width and breadth of the spiral, the speed of dissipation, and the angle of enlargement. Simple," the Arachnia repeated. "I should have thought to calculate it out long ago."

"Uh, right. But what does all that actually mean?"

"First, we have already decided that the forest is finite and that the spell is confined to the forest precincts. That is a given."

"Go on."

"So then, since the spell *is* dissipating in a spiral, my calculations tell me that, regardless of which way we are thrown by the fragments of that spell, we must keep turning sharply to one direction. To the right," she added cautiously, "I think."

"And if we do?"

"If we do, sooner or later, given the spiral and the finite nature of the forest, we *must* come out in some spot one of us recognizes."

"It's certainly better than aimlessly wandering." Gwenlyn got to her feet, stretching tired muscles. "Come on, my mathematical genius, let's try it."

"I am not a genius," D'Senna protested in confusion. "My one-generation-older nestmate, D'Lerak, can calculate in four dimensions at once."

"How nice for D'Lerak," Gwenlyn said drily. "But D'Lerak isn't here, and you, most modest D'Senna, are. Forward!"

D'Senna chittered in what Gwenlyn was sure was embarrassment. "Forward!" the Arachnia agreed.

"I'm not getting a thing," Tich'ki spat in disgust, settling with weary force onto Naitachal's shoulder. "What about you?"

The Dark Elf glanced over his shoulder at the wary, hopeful humans. Count Trahern in particular was watching him with such a fierce, desperate stare he could almost feel it burn his skin. Naitachal sighed and turned away.

"I haven't sensed the slightest trace of either Kevin or Gwenlyn," he admitted in the elven tongue. "I . . . am beginning to fear very strongly that we're not going to locate Kevin at all. Oh, I suspect he's still alive," he added at Tich'ki's alarmed start, "but . . . quite out of reach of our magics."

She gave him a sharp glance. "You really do think the *Nithathili* have him."

"I—yes."

He jumped as Tich'ki pinched his shoulder sharply. "Stop that!" she snapped. "Even if they've got him, don't you dare start panicking! We'll get him out of trouble. Always have before."

"My clan wasn't involved before."

"So what? They couldn't catch you. They couldn't do anything about your becoming a Bard and leading your own life. They're not perfect. We'll get him back."

"I pray you're right."

Tich'ki pinched him again, so hard he swatted her off his shoulder without thinking. Taking to the air in an angry buzz of wings, she snapped, "Of course I'm right, you stupid elven doubter! Now, as to finding Kevin's sweetheart—"

Naitachal couldn't help but chuckle at that. " 'Sweetheart' is hardly the word I would have used to describe her. You never saw the two of them together."

"Sparks, huh?"

"Whole eruptions. But that's not the point. I think the main reason we haven't been able to find Gwenlyn is that neither one of us is really acquainted with her aura."

"How could we be? I haven't even *seen* her. But what can we do about it? We can hardly include a human in our spells."

"Can't we?"

Tich'ki dropped a hand's breadth in shock before she resumed fluttering. "Add a human to an elf-fairy spell? The damn thing's unstable enough as it is!"

"I've noticed. All the more reason to strengthen it."

"You're crazy."

"Just desperate."

"But—but it's never been done before!"

"There is, as the human saying goes, a first time for everything."

"Sure, right, whatever, but this *isn't* the time for experimenting!"

"Someone," Naitachal said darkly, "should have told that to Rualath." Switching smoothly to the human tongue, he called, "Count Trahern, would you please come here? I will do nothing to harm you, my word on it." Placing his hand on the man's right shoulder, feeling Trahern's muscles tense though the count stood obediently still, he added, "Tich'ki, if you would kindly land on his left shoulder?"

"Idiot," she muttered in the fairy tongue.

"I speak Fairy," the elf reminded her.

"I know."

"Just do it."

With a great sigh of reluctance, Tich'ki obeyed. Placing one hand on the bewildered human's forehead, Naitachal glared at the fairy till she copied him. He took her free hand in his, the small fingers utterly dwarfed in his, to form a closed circle.

"Now, Count Trahern, I wish you to close your eyes

and think of Gwenlyn. That's right. Close your eyes . . . think of Gwenlyn . . . think only of Gwenlyn . . . there is only Gwenlyn . . ."

Once he was sure the human was entranced sufficiently to think of no one else, Naitachal, echoed by Tich'ki, began to murmur the words of the strongest Spell of Finding they both knew, repeating it over and over again. It would work, it must work—it *would work!*

There was never going to be an end to this, Gwenlyn thought, too tired for rancor. She and D'Senna were just going to keep trudging on and on forever. They had been turning right and right again through each eddy of the spell for what seemed an eternity, and the only bit of hope she could find about the whole weary business was that with each turning she could swear she sensed something starting to unravel.

Unless it's just my mind that's going, she thought dourly. *I just hope we don't land on that waterfall again.*

All at once the young woman froze, too stunned with sudden shock to move.

"Gwenlyn?" D'Senna asked sharply. "What is it?"

Gwenlyn hastily waved the Arachnia to silence, listening to—to what? Oh dear gods, what was happening? Maybe her mind *was* beginning to fail, because all at once she could feel someone pulling at her mind, calling her. *Hear my voice where you are. Come to me. Come to me, Gwenlyn.*

"Father?" she said doubtfully. It almost seemed like . . . no. Whatever it was, it wasn't his voice, it wasn't a physical call at all, just a—a feeling, a pulling, tickling at the edge of her thoughts. *Hear my voice. Come to me, this way, Gwenlyn, Gwenlyn, come to me this way, this way . . .*

"Gwenlyn!" D'Senna exclaimed in alarm. "What's wrong? Where are you going?"

"I d-don't know."

Hear my voice, Gwenlyn, come to me. . . .

"But you can't just—"

"I don't know *what's* happening!" Gwenlyn cut in frantically. "But I have to go this way."

"No!" D'Senna snatched at her and missed. "Gwenlyn, stop! That path is off the proper equations of the spiral!"

Come to me, Gwenlyn, this way. . . .

"I can't help it, D'Senna! I don't have a choice! It doesn't matter what your equations say, I *have* to go this way!"

Come to me, Gwenlyn, this way, Naitachal repeated yet again, his Power linked with that of Tich'ki, his thoughts linked with those of Count Trahern. *Come to me . . .*

Ae, this was no easy thing! By now his head was beginning to feel as though it would explode. Tich'ki was right; combining magic with a magickless human was foolish, impossible. It could never work, he would have to give up, he would never, ever be able to—

"I *feel* her!" he gasped suddenly. "Yes, yes, we have her!"

And with a sudden whirring of air, a wild-eyed, bedraggled young woman, dark hair a tangled cloud about her, a slender, equally young Arachnia beside her, staggered out of sudden shimmering air into solid reality. She took one look at Naitachal and screamed in fury, hunting frantically about for a weapon. But Naitachal and Count Trahern said as one:

"Gwenlyn!"

She froze, staring from the Dark Elf to the count.

"Father . . . ?" the young woman said hesitantly, and then, more forcefully, "Father!" and threw herself into his fierce embrace.

For a time daughter and father could do nothing but cling to each other and gasp out broken, joyous little phrases of love. But at last Gwenlyn pulled away, brushing back her mass of tangled hair with a hand that wasn't quite steady. "I crave your pardon," she said to Naitachal. "At first I mistook you for an enemy. But obviously you can't be such, not if you're with my father."

"I am no enemy," the elf assured her gently. "My name is Naitachal, and I—"

"Naitachal!" she cut in. "You're Kevin's friend!"

He blinked in surprise. "Yes, I am. But the only way you could have known that is if Kevin told you. I take it you didn't learn about me from him in your father's castle."

"Ah, no." She flushed slightly. "He probably told you how disastrous our first meeting was. But Kevin and I met again in the forest, when we were both caught in this weird, weird spell, and we . . . had a better chance to learn a little about each other."

Naitachal smiled at the sudden softness in her eyes. "And it was a more agreeable learning, I take it. But where is he now?"

The softness fled. "Oh gods, I wish I knew! We were set upon by Dark Elves—y-your pardon, but—"

"They aren't exactly my dearest friends," he assured her drily. "Go on. What happened?"

Gwenlyn shuddered suddenly, hugging her arms about herself. "W-we fought the Dark Elves as best we could. The first time, we—we managed to escape them. The second time they attacked, a different, colder group this time, we . . . weren't so lucky."

Gwenlyn bit her lip, then continued, in a voice that was almost even, "Kevin played what I guess was some form of Bardic Magic, the most soothing music I've ever heard. It began to put the elven warriors to sleep, and for a moment I thought we were going to escape again. But then . . ."

The young woman broke off, shaking her head in confusion. "I could have sworn the woman was a White Elf. But that's not possible, is it? I mean, a White Elf would never ally herself with Dark Elves . . . would she?"

Naitachal shrugged impatiently. "Anything, as you humans would put it, is possible. Go on. I take it she broke his spell?"

Gwenlyn nodded. "*I* was nearly asleep from the music. But she didn't even seem to hear it! She yelled at the Dark Elves to wake them up and pulled Kevin's hand from his lute."

"So, now. It would seem that Master Aidan is right; musical magic really doesn't work on the tone-deaf." Even—bizarre thought—on a tone-deaf White Elf. "Never mind. What happened to Kevin?"

"I don't know! In all the struggling, D'Senna—that's my Arachnia friend here—D'Senna and I had to run for our lives." She added with a fiercely repressed sob, "The last I saw of Kevin, the elves were bearing him to the ground. I think they carried him off to—to whatever Darkness they call home."

"As I feared," Naitachal murmured in despair.

"All right," Tich'ki cut in sharply, "enough of this. Yes, yes, girl, Arachnia, you're not seeing a mirage. I'm a fairy, my name's Tich'ki, I'm an ally. Got all that? Good. Now all we have to do is get Kevin out."

"From a *Nithathil* fortress?" Naitachal asked. "That is *not* going to be an easy thing to do."

"We can't *not* do it!" Lydia snapped.

"No," the elf agreed with a nod in her direction, "we are most certainly not going to leave Kevin there."

"We can't!" Gwenlyn added with such force that her father looked at her in surprise.

"So!" he murmured. "Have things changed *that* much?"

She glared at him. "What do you want me to say? That I was wrong and you were right? All right, I admit it! Look, we can argue about this some other time. Right now we have got to rescue Kevin—and whether or not you help, I will!"

"Of course I'll help," the count said firmly. "The only question is: how?" He glanced dubiously at his guards and the nervous cluster of bandits, then shook his head. "I rather doubt we have enough men here for a frontal attack."

"No!" Naitachal exclaimed. "Anything as bold as a frontal attack is only going to get every one of you humans slain."

"What about magic?" Tich'ki asked.

"No, again. Haralachan and Rualath, my clan's Lord and his consort, will surely sense anyone's attempt to work magic against them."

But Naitachal's mind wasn't really on his words any longer. No, his mention of Rualath made him think of that chaotic Gate Spell. She must have used an extraordinary amount of magical force to cast it. So much force in such experimental form . . . interesting, very interesting . . . there was something about it, something potentially useful, something lingering just at the edge of his mind . . .

"Yes," he said in sudden satisfaction, "I have it," and saw the others stare. "Don't worry. I haven't suddenly gone mad. It's just that all at once I'm finding something very intriguing about this Gate Spell, this magic that's scattered about so strangely."

"Intriguing, he calls it," Count Trahern said.

Naitachal ignored him. "It has been fracturing into weaker and weaker pieces, as I'm sure you've realized. But the original spell was amazingly Powerful. If I can only reach its source, I just might be able to gather the spell back together."

"Why in hell would you want to do that?" Lydia asked bluntly.

Naitachal gave her a grim little smile. "Because, my dear woman, if I can master the Gate Spell, I might be able to reverse it. That would save Kevin and—"

"Are you *insane?*" Tich'ki shrilled. "The only way you can do that is by coming face-to-face with the crazy *Nithathil* who cast it!"

Naitachal shrugged with feigned calm. "Believe me, I am not thrilled by the idea of facing down Rualath, either. But then, no plan is perfect."

"You *are* insane!"

"Possibly," he said. "But while I confront Rualath, she who cast the spell," he said to the others, "I will be providing the lot of you with a distraction. That will be your chance to get Kevin—and yourselves—in and safely out again."

"Yeah, sure," Lydia snapped. "I'm sure there's a nice, safe back exit just waiting for us to use it."

"Something like that," Naitachal murmured.

"Uh-huh. And what about you?"

"Trite as it sounds, I can take care of myself."

"Right," she said flatly. "Of course."

Naitachal turned to her in sudden fury. "What else would you have me do? Give up? Run away and leave Kevin to the fate they mean for me?"

"I didn't mean—"

"Have you a better plan? No? Do *any* of you have a plan? Well? Do you?"

There was a long, awkward silence. "So," the elf added, more softly, "you see. There is no other way." Forcing his face into a cold mask, Naitachal said flatly, "Enough of this. If we are to save Kevin, we dare waste no more time."

Chapter XXIV

The Guest

Kevin, fiercely pretending to be as casual as the Dark Elves around him, prayed that none of them were magically skilled enough to pick up any trace of his suppressed terror. If Haralachan or any of them realized just how fragile his act of ruthlessness was, they would be on him like wolves on a wounded stag.

No, enough of that, he told himself severely. *Remember that you are totally ruthless. You care for no one. You have no love in your heart at all.*

Right. Gods, if he got away with this, he would give up being a Bard and take to the stage!

Kevin stole a subtle glance at the Dark Elf who had been assigned as a guide to wherever Haralachan meant to put him. The fellow was, judging from his plain grey clothing, of no particular status, probably a servant (he lacked the cringing terror Kevin had seen on the faces of the out-and-out slaves), but he had every bit of the true *Nithathil* arrogance.

"Follow me, human," the elf said shortly, his annoyance at having to guide a mere human very evident in his voice. "Touch nothing. Stare at no one. Make no eye contact. And do not try to escape me. Even though I am not granted warrior weapons, there are those waiting who are, those who will eagerly hunt down any human foolish enough to run."

"I have no intention of running."

"Fortunate," the elf said, and said nothing more till they had reached a dark-painted door, blank and unornamented as everything else around them. At a touch and a murmured Word said too softly for Kevin to hear, the door opened, revealing a surprisingly spacious room within, dimly lit by lamps that burned with cold blue light.

The elf stood aside. "Enter," he told Kevin.

But Kevin wasn't quite so ready to walk into what just might be a trap. Struggling to keep his voice from quavering, he said as lightly as he could, "Looks a bit roomy for a prison."

That earned him an upward quirk of a silvery eyebrow. "Prison? Did you hear my Lord Haralachan order you to be imprisoned? No. You are not a prisoner, but a . . . guest."

Right. And you're a pretty pink butterfly. "Indeed," Kevin said noncommittally. Since he couldn't keep standing out here forever, he offered a quick prayer to Whomever might be listening, and stepped inside. The Dark Elf, disconcertingly, didn't follow but remained standing stock-still just outside. Kevin glanced back at him as the elf started to close the door, and added in sudden new panic, "Ah, wait, I don't see a handle on the inside of this door."

"Of course there is none." The elf's voice was cold with scorn. "Do you think us mere, magickless humans to need such things?"

"Hardly," Kevin said just as coldly. "Mind teaching me the door-opening spell as well?"

"It is not something humans could master."

"Try me."

"You will have no need to leave these chambers unaccompanied. The corridors of our realm are perilous for an unwary human."

"Yes, but—"

Too late. The door had already closed. With a sigh, Kevin turned to examine his new accommodations, heart pounding.

But there really wasn't anything openly menacing about this place, nothing that screamed *trap* at him. The main room contained nothing more than a table of black stone, perfectly utilitarian and totally unornamented, and a chair of black wood, uncushioned and also unornamented, set upon a smoothly polished stone floor. A beautifully arched doorway—the first thing he'd seen so far in this realm that had even the slightest trace of beauty about it—led to a second, slightly smaller room. Here Kevin found a bed, a surprisingly luxurious thing with a thick mattress and silken coverings and hangings.

Now, if only they were of something other than this unrelieved black! Don't they like any *color in this realm?*

He reached out a hand to gingerly touch the thick, smooth fabric of the hangings. Silk, he guessed. Maybe a variety of that tough, lightweight elven spidersilk he'd seen Naitachal wear when he traveled.

Practical stuff, he thought. *Wears well, doesn't stain easily. But does it all have to be so incredibly plain in here? They didn't even try to add any variety to the weave!*

He shuddered. These elves really did seem to lack any trace of poetry. No wonder none of them were musicians!

Save Naitachal— no. For safety's sake, he wouldn't let himself even think of his friend.

Testing the luxurious bed, Kevin grunted in surprise at its softness. Hardly something a humble prisoner would be allowed. Exploring on, he found a blank stone chest at the foot of the bed, presumably for belongings, and a niche containing the Dark Elf version of sanitary facilities, workable, Kevin guessed, by a preset spell that needed only a flash of will to operate. There was absolutely nothing else of note in either room.

Probably the Dark Elf idea of luxury. Simplicity of design and all that. I wish there was a window, though. Ha, whatever for? I'm probably surrounded by solid rock!

Now, wasn't that a comforting thought? At least air was filtering in from somewhere, though he didn't see any obvious vents. At least, Kevin tried to convince himself, he wouldn't have to worry about suffocating. Unless, of course, Haralachan decided to block off that air—

No. He would *not* let himself start dwelling on—on possibilities. Kevin prowled around his suite once more to take his mind off such things as treachery, this time hunting for magical or mundane spying devices, but found not a one.

Which, of course, didn't mean he wasn't being watched in some way he couldn't sense.

Ay me. So much for the entertainment aspects of the place. Now, what am I supposed to do with myself?

He waited a bit, half expecting a regal summons. He waited a bit longer for anything at all to happen. At last, for want of anything else, the Bard sat down on the hard, straight-backed chair and took his lute from its case. For a moment he could do nothing but run a caressing hand over the smooth wood, taking comfort in this one small bit of normalcy. Then, after carefully tuning the strings, taking a long time about it, he began his normal daily practice of scales. Every musician, no matter how professional, needed to keep up such a daily routine but, Kevin admitted, it was a ritual he'd been sadly neglecting of late.

His fingers slowed, then came to a stop on the strings. Ah, gods, how could he possibly keep up this pretense of calm? He was like a man balancing on the edge of a precipice! All it would take to bring him and his pretty picture of ruthlessness crashing down in ruins would be one of the warriors who'd caught him finally admitting the truth about that firsthand experience with Bardic Magic.

They . . . won't do it. If they haven't said anything yet, they won't dare say something now. I hope.

Kevin shook his head at the stupid irony of it all. Here he was a full Bard, in full possession of Bardic Magic—yet he dared not use any of his powers! He could probably sing that door open, he could probably use song-spells to control the minds of a few Dark Elves—but he would never get the chance! The slightest start of the slightest magical song would be enough to scream out the existence of his powers to all these magic-sensitive enemies around him. The only things he dared perform right now, surrounded by foes as he was, were lute practice and plain, unmagical music.

Particularly since even if I was allowed to finish a spell, I haven't a hope of controlling everyone.

Ah well, he thought with desperate humor, there was still acting. As long as he could keep Haralachan thinking this odd human would make a better ally than victim or lure for Naitachal, he would be safe. Or at least, Kevin added wryly, in a touch less peril. With any luck at all, this . . . enforced visit would turn out to be something less than horrifying and more like a long, boring stay in a not too uncomfortable prison.

Considering the alternatives, a long and boring stay might not be so bad!

Haralachan lay at ease in his silken bed, his consort beside him (at ease save, of course, for the defensive spell he kept at the ready, even while asleep, just in case; one could, naturally, never be too sure of one's consort), idly deciding what slave might be worthy of today's hunt. But he was suddenly aware of Rualath's gaze on him and asked shortly, not looking at her, "What?"

"You have the human. Kevin. The traitor's friend. What are you planning to do with him?"

Now Haralachan did turn to frown coldly at her. "Whatever it pleases me to do."

"But—"

"The trap is set, Rualath. The bait is ready. If 'friendship' is as strong a pull as our studies indicate—and our scholars had best be telling the truth about that—the traitor will not long leave his human in our hands. Have patience."

He heard her sigh all but soundlessly. "There are those who are not as patient as I, my lord. Those who may, perhaps, begin asking odd questions dealing with—"

"With what?" Haralachan's hand closed with such sudden force on the elegant curve of her shoulder that he heard her involuntary gasp of pain. "Were you about to say 'weakness'?" he asked quietly. "There is no weakness in me, my consort. None. Remember that."

After the smallest of hesitations, he felt her sag in submission. "Of course there is none, my lord."

Haralachan held her caught a moment more, savoring her helplessness and anger, just long enough to emphasize his point, then released her, swinging from the bed in one smooth movement. He glanced back at where Rualath lay propped up on one elbow, her eyes glowering. But she was not going to attack him; he *felt* her irresolution beneath the anger. He turned away with a contemptuous flourish to release the triplefold Spells of Locking on inner and outer doors with a flash of will, and snapped out a command for servants to enter and bathe and dress him.

As the humble creatures scurried in, terrified of doing even the slightest thing to displease their master, Haralachan added over his shoulder to Rualath, voice hard with meaning, "I have already planned what is needful for best making use of the human. And what is planned, my consort, shall be done."

"Oh, it shall," she agreed softly, "it shall, indeed," with just enough ambiguity in her voice to make him glance warily back at her.

But Rualath merely . . . smiled.

Some time later, Haralachan strode from his chambers in his elegant dark robes, the very image of controlled, cold-eyed royalty. But his thoughts were far from controlled.

Curse you, Rualath. I must find a way to keep you from asking such . . . uncomfortable questions.

He was not yet ready to send her to the altar. But there were times—Oh, he had surely done a convincing job of feigning cool cunning with her, pretending clever plotting, but the fact was that as yet he really hadn't decided what to do with the human at all.

How could it be otherwise? A ruler's life hardly allowed for idle time for thought. There had been spies to send forth, suspected traitors to be watched, punishments to be levied. The one thing there had not been was enough time for a chance to puzzle out the truth about the human, even though of course it was dangerous to leave any puzzle unsolved.

So. Kevin *must* be used to snare the traitor. And so the traitor would be snared. That was certain. Naitachal was almost certainly plotting how to retrieve his friend even now.

And yet, the human had shown such charmingly intriguing cynicism and arrogance, such almost *Nithathil* contempt for others. It might almost have been genuine. And if it was, he just might prove more useful as a puppet ally than a simple lure. Finding out the truth, though, would not be an easy thing.

Torture? No. One did not torment an ally—even one as lowly as a human—and then expect to be forgiven. Magic? Difficult. Oh, a spell strong enough to worm beneath the human's defenses would be simple enough to work. But one delicate enough to leave his mind unharmed was another matter. If Kevin really was as empty of human morality as he claimed, ah, what a useful tool he might make! Almost as useful as the arrogant little creature claimed.

But how could one learn the truth without destroying that tool? And how, for that matter, could one be sure the tool would not turn in his hand?

Haralachan stopped short, staring. And a thin smile came to his lips. So, now, this might prove interesting. Perhaps no spell would be needed after all!

He moved forward again, softly stalking. She was facing away from him, the little fool. For all her pretenses, she had yet not learned all the caution it was wise for such as she to learn.

"Amaranthia," Haralachan purred, and pounced

before she could turn. Oh, how satisfying her startled scream as his hands went so smoothly, so gently, about her neck, how satisfying her struggle for calm.

"M-my lord," she managed to gasp out, "I didn't hear you coming."

"No," he agreed softly, tightening the pressure ever so gently for a moment, not quite cutting off her breath, savoring her sudden terror, her realization of danger. He held her like that for a moment more, then dropped his hands to her shoulders, turning her with gentle force to face him. "You will not long survive here if you continue to act so incautiously. Never leave your back unguarded, little one, not even from me."

Her eyes, as always, intrigued him. So wide, so frightened, yet so perversely delighted in her peril they sent a little prickle of amusement through him. "I will not be so foolish again, my lord."

"I wonder. But no matter for now, my little pale one." He touched a fingertip lightly to her chin. "I wish you to try a small experiment for me. One, I think, you may even enjoy."

Quickly he told her what he meant for her to do. Amaranthia listened, nodding, till he was finished, then giggled softly. "It shall be a pleasure, indeed, my lord."

Chapter XXV

The Visitor

How long had he been stuck here in this not quite prison? Kevin knew he'd eaten twice, slept twice in that surprisingly comfortable bed and needed a shave once (scary that, having to trust his throat to a Dark Elf servant with a razor; if he stayed here much longer, Kevin decided, he'd consider growing a beard), but without a sun or any timekeeping device it wasn't easy to keep track of things.

All I know for sure, Kevin thought sardonically, *is that my stay has already been long enough—far* too *long! It was too long from the moment I got here!*

In all this time—however long or short it might have been—there hadn't been so much as another glimpse of Haralachan or that equally cold-eyed consort of his. What Dark Elves Kevin *had* seen had all treated him with such careful courtesy it was definitely meant as mockery. They had spoken almost nothing to him, but had ever so politely provided him with nourishing if bland—but apparently quite undrugged or magicked—food and allowed him the occasional chance to exercise his legs by walking about the dark, dank corridors—always "suitably escorted," of course.

Kevin mused darkly that he should be flattered they would send so many warriors to guard him. Even if each and every one of the humorless creatures was just waiting, or more probably out-and-out hoping, for the human they were watching to make some foolish, fatal mistake.

Huh. It's like taking a stroll in the middle of a pack of half-starved hunting hounds.

And what *about* Haralachan? He'd been intrigued by Kevin's apparent fearlessness, the Bard knew it. Elves were practically born curious; Naitachal had proved that fact over and over again. Kevin snorted. He wouldn't even be in this mess if Naitachal hadn't been driven by elven curiosity to investigate that cursed Gate Spell!

Then why had there been nothing from Haralachan, not the slightest message, not the faintest hint of a summons or of any interest at all?

I can't believe he's simply forgotten all about me, the foreign element in the middle of his realm. That's out of character for any *ruler, let alone a Dark Elf one!*

What, then? Was he being used, Kevin wondered uneasily, only as bait? As nothing more than a—a lure set out to snare Naitachal?

That idea doesn't really work, either. I mean, yes, they want Naitachal. But I can't accept that Haralachan would totally ignore that whole beautifully nasty story I wove for him. He was *interested in it, I know he was. And I don't care if he* is *a Dark Elf; he's still closer to the White Elves than to humans. From everything I've learned from Naitachal, from Eliathanis, from all the elves I've ever seen and spoken with, their kind, White or Dark, just do not abandon puzzles! Their curiosity won't allow them to do that.*

Or . . . could it be Haralachan had come to his own solution of this human puzzle after all? Had he, for whatever dark-souled reason, decided to simply let this troublesome, not-quite-prisoner, not-quite-guest rot?

Kevin swallowed drily. Pine away, was more like it, from lack of sunlight. How long, he wondered, *could* a human go without the sun?

And am I going to live long enough to find out?

He shuddered. At least Naitachal was still free; someone surely would have stopped by to gloat were it otherwise.

Stay away! he silently cried to his friend. *In the name of all the Powers, don't worry about me, don't even think of me—please, please, just stay away! Stay* free! *Stay free as I—I—I am not!*

Suddenly the terror Kevin had been keeping so sternly under control for what seemed an eternity was tearing free, totally beyond all bearing. Suddenly there was only darkness around him, the heavy weight of stone crushing him beneath it. He would never get out of here, never breathe free air again; he would die alone, forgotten, in this grim, terrible, sunless place, shut away forever from the green, living world—

With a desperate gasp, Kevin snatched up his lute, practically tearing it from its case in his haste, furiously trying to lose himself in music, thinking that maybe *this* was Haralachan's plan, to torment the human with idleness and endless waiting and ever-growing hopelessness to wear down his resistance.

And it's working, oh, it is working, curse him.

Gradually the shapeless storm of music settled into mannered shape. Gradually it beat back despair and won Kevin at least some measure of calm. But the terror still waited, lurking at the back of his mind. He could feel it like a weight on his spirit, waiting for his guard to lower again, waiting to drown him in the darkness.

And if the terror won out again, Kevin decided with sudden ferocity, if it finally went beyond all endurance, he *would* use Bardic Magic, no matter how hopeless the odds. He would not betray Naitachal. He would not surrender his soul. He would use Bardic Magic, and have the final grim satisfaction of going down fighting.

The door opened soundlessly, and Kevin shot to his feet in alarm. A slim, white-clad figure slipped inside, and he stared in disbelief. "Amaranthia!"

She put a nervous finger to her lips, glancing hastily back to be sure the door had completely closed behind her. "They don't know I'm here," she explained softly. "But I—I had to come."

"Oh, right. Of course," Kevin snapped. "I'll believe that. And I'm here to test out Dark Elf guest facilities. Didn't you know? We're thinking of building a travellers' inn down here. Amaranthia, what the *hell* are you doing here?"

"I told you, I had to—"

"Stop that! Stop acting the innocent! Look you, I *know* you're in league with the Dark Elves. I *know* everything you said and did back in the forest was a lie—"

"Not all."

"Liar, I say!" For a moment his hand was raised, for a moment he almost could have struck her. But she stared up at him as fearlessly as a deer cornered by wolves and gone quite past the point of terror, looking so lovely, so pathetically lovely, the breath caught in his throat, and Kevin found himself helplessly lowering his hand again. "What I can't understand," he murmured, "is *why.*"

"Why? Because I was a fool."

Kevin turned sharply away. "Oh please. I deal with enough words in my songs; I know when there's no real emotion behind them."

"That's not true!"

"Nonsense."

"It's not! I—Kevin, wait!"

He tried to brush her away, but Amaranthia followed him as he paced, slipping in front of him to face him before he could turn away again. With an uncomfortable little pang almost of guilt, he saw that her eyes were suddenly very bright with unshed tears.

"Amaranthia . . ."

"Kevin," she murmured, "I know you have no reason at all to believe anything I say, but . . . I . . . had to come here. I had to tell you h-how sorry I am . . ."

"Oh *gods!*" Kevin threw back his head with a great sigh, leaning back against a cool stone wall, staring blindly up at the smooth stone ceiling. He knew that Amaranthia was allied with the Dark Elves, he knew she was most certainly not to be trusted. He wanted to hate her. And yet . . . ah, and yet, there was something so unutterably *sad* about her now.

Maybe I'm *the fool here, not she!*

But even so, even knowing what she was, knowing how she'd betrayed him, he still couldn't hate her. He still couldn't help but ache with pity and regret for this beautiful, lost creature.

"Amaranthia," Kevin began again, then stopped, looking down at her in confusion. "I want to believe you, Amaranthia." He had fully meant to ask her to leave. Instead, staring into her lovely eyes, Kevin found himself adding instead, almost pleading, "Give me some reason to do so."

Amaranthia was silent for a long time, head drooping, golden hair falling about her face in a silky cloak. "I love you." It was the barest whisper.

"Oh—nonsense." He tried to walk away, but she stopped him, blocking his path.

"It's true." Her eyes were full of despair. "I never thought to say it, not to a human, but . . ." She rested a graceful hand softly on his arm. "I do love you."

The touch seemed to burn right through his sleeve. Kevin shivered despite himself, jerking out of her reach, and said, a little more roughly than he'd intended, "Odd words for someone who's allied herself to her people's bitterest enemies."

She cried out in pain and turned away. Kevin reached out to catch her by the shoulder, forcing her to face him, continuing relentlessly, "If you could betray them, you could betray me as well."

"No! I would never betray you!"

All at once she was in his arms, her beautiful, yearning face so temptingly close to his own. For one breathless moment Kevin could think of nothing but how much he ached to kiss her, to love her, to—

"Why?" he gasped. "Amaranthia, why did you do it?"

She drew back a little in surprise. "I—I don't understand."

Maybe, oh maybe she wasn't totally lost to the Darkness. Maybe he could still rouse some shreds of White Elf decency in her. Maybe they could both escape and be happy and—and— "Why did you turn from sunlight and music and joy?"

"I had no choice, I—"

"This place is cold and dank and sterile, beyond

anything as simple as ugliness. There's nothing to see in this realm, nowhere to go in this realm. There's nothing to do here but hate, nothing to feel here but cruelty and empty ambition." He took her face in gentle hands. "You had a life full of light and laughter, Amaranthia, a life full of beauty and freedom. Here, there is nothing. You *have* nothing!

"I ask you again: why did you do it?"

All at once something seemed to break within her. With a cry of anguish, Amaranthia tore free from his grip, gasping out a broken string of words. "No, you mustn't . . . I won't . . . it's not true! It's not true!"

"Amaranthia—"

"How dare you remind me of—no! I don't miss it, I don't!"

"Amaranthia! Wait—"

"No!"

Before he could take more than a step after her, she was gone, and the sound of her sobs was cut off by the relentless closing of the door behind her.

Kevin fell back against a wall with a gasp of frustration. So close, curse it, he'd been so very close! Why had he been so—so fierce about it? Why push her like that? Why, oh why, hadn't he been more gentle? Amaranthia had almost revealed what was left of the Light in her, he knew it! If only he'd been just a little more careful, she might actually have been convinced to help him, to help them both.

Now the chance was forever lost.

Ah well, Kevin thought ruefully. *I really did want to see if there was anything left of the true White Elf buried within her. I guess I can safely say there is. But it looks as though it's not going to do either of us any good at all.*

Chapter XXVI

Conflicts Escalate

Amaranthia stopped short in the corridor outside Kevin's chambers, choking on her sobs, struggling for self-control. To her immense relief, no one else was around to see her. To show any such weakness as weeping in public was perilous, so perilous. (Nothing like the way it was among the White Elves, her mind told her, unbidden. Among the White Elves all emotion, tears or laughter, joyous, free laughter, was seen as natural, not as a weakness—)

No! I will not think of that! I am in the Nithathil *realm now, I* want *to be in the* Nithathil *realm, and have the proper status and have power over them, true power and—and—*

"So, my little pale one," purred an all-too-familiar voice without warning, and Amaranthia almost screamed in despair.

Oh no, not now, please not now! But to her relief, her voice sounded relatively composed as she murmured, "My Lord Haralachan."

His smile was sharp as the edge of a blade. "I can see that your encounter with the human was a . . . rather strenuous one. But was it also a successful one?"

Amaranthia swallowed drily. *What can I say? How can I possibly convince him that—* "Most successful," she lied desperately, forcing a smile. "For a—a first meeting, that is."

"First?"

"Why, yes, my lord! Humans are—as of course you know," she added prudently "—a most peculiar breed, as much interested in the hunt as in the outcome."

"They are not alone in that," the Dark Elf murmured, and Amaranthia just barely bit back a panicky little cry. Oh, why had she reminded him of the hunt? Why, when she had seen a *Nithathil* hunt and thanked whatever Power there might be that she wasn't the prey?

"Ah, well, yes, of course," Amaranthia hurried on. "But with humans one cannot hold their interest by ceding too much to them too quickly. Kevin was . . . very interested in me. Very." That much, at least, was true. "But it was I who called an end to the session."

"Did you, now?"

"Y-yes. Yes." Thinking frantically, Amaranthia continued as matter-of-factly as she could, "Humans thrive more on anticipation than acquisition. This first encounter was to begin 'softening him up,' as that distasteful human phrase would have it. Now Kevin will be longing for my next visit, longing for me and for what he doesn't realize I will not grant him. Once he has been tantalized sufficiently, Kevin will say or do anything to win me. Anything, my lord," she added with downswept lashes, "that you may wish him to say or do, that is."

"Cunning, my little pale one, most cunning. If true."

Amaranthia struggled with herself to keep smiling,

terrified that the smile must look as false as if it were painted. "Now, why would I lie, my lord? I could hardly have acted any more swiftly. He isn't a complete fool, human though he is. I couldn't make things look too obvious, now, could I?"

Haralachan chuckled. "No. I would suppose not."

With a swirl of his black cloak, he was gone into the darkness. Amaranthia scurried off to her chambers. But as soon as she was alone within the barren little rooms, she collapsed in despair.

Why now? Why this face? Why a human, and in this place? In all her years (admittedly brief by elven standards), she had never felt anything even remotely resembling this strange, warm surging of—of—

Of love?

Nonsense, oh, nonsense, it can't be love, not with him, it can't be!

And why did this bizarre softness have to hit her now? The human wasn't even particularly handsome, not by her people's standards, and he was—he was *human!*

All her life, Amaranthia thought in despair, she had sneered at the White Elves' soft, Light-loving ways and their music that had brought her nothing but discomfort. All her life, she had been looking for someone who would understand, who could give her the perilous, wonderful, exciting existence she craved.

This can't *be the one! He simply can't!*

She was *not* going to endanger the status she'd managed to gain in Haralachan's eyes, not now, not for a—a human!

And yet, and yet . . .

Head buried in her hands, Amaranthia gave up all pretense of control and wept.

✧ ✧ ✧

Dark Elf lord and consort sat alone in his chambers, studying a spell scroll. Or at least pretending to study it.

"Do you believe her?" Rualath asked suddenly.

Haralachan glanced at his consort with a serenity that was most carefully schooled, then looked down at the scroll once more. "Our little White Elf, you mean?" he asked, tracing a convoluted rune with an elegant forefinger. "Not at all. Rather than her toying with the human as she told me, the odds are far more likely that the human, too, refused to believe her and, for all her undeniable charms, threw her out. They may be close to the animals, those humans, but they are not totally without intelligence."

"She has failed you. Why do you let her go unpunished?"

"Why, Rualath!" Haralachan said, glancing up again with cold delight. "One would almost think you jealous!"

"Of *that?*" she asked succinctly. "Come now, my lord, you insult me. I am merely expressing my curiosity. Why *do* you let the White Elf go unpunished?"

His smile thinned ever so slightly. "She amuses me," Haralachan said with rare honesty. "And such continual entertainment is, as you know, all too rare for such as we. She amuses me with her hopes and fears and those ridiculously desperate attempts to be truly one of us." He shrugged. "The time will come when she ceases to amuse me. Then and only then I shall rid myself of her. Leave the matter at that, my consort."

Rualath's raised brow said volumes. But then she, too, glanced down at the scroll as though finding it fascinating. "Obviously the girl could hardly have been part of your plans for the human. Now, my lord, will you not share those with me?"

Haralachan, well aware that he was being delicately baited, ached to simply snap out a refusal. But displaying such foolish anger would leave him the loser in this little game they were playing. Instead, he paused thoughtfully, considering. And rather to his surprise, the perfect idea came to hand.

So, now! This might actually work. At the least, Haralachan mused, it would put the burden back on Rualath's shoulders. With the subtlest of smiles, he told her, "Yes. Of course. Listen, my consort. Listen and perhaps this time you may be more successful in your magics."

To his delight, she actually flinched. But as Haralachan murmured his newly formed plans to her, his pleasure at catching her off-guard slowly faded. What good was all this nonsense about the human if the traitor, if Naitachal, did not come to save his friend? *He* was at the heart of this, not the human.

Bah, he *must* come here. All the *Nithathili* scholars swore that friendship ties were so incredibly strong Naitachal simply could not endure leaving the human in this cage.

And yet . . . what if the scholars were wrong? They had never actually felt the pull of friendship, after all. And Naitachal, no matter what new perversions he might have learned from the humans, was still of *Nithathil* blood, with all the cold will for self-preservation that implied. What if he flatly refused to risk his life for another?

Then every one of those scholars shall die screaming their regret for failing me, Haralachan thought fiercely.

But that would not wipe out the stain to his own honor.

There must not be another failure, Haralachan mused. *Let the traitor come to us, and quickly!*

Tich'ki landed heavily—for her—on Naitachal's shoulder, panting faintly. "Lot of weird magic still out there, isn't there?" she asked, wiping her brow with a hand.

No answer. Tich'ki tried again.

"Be a lot easier if we had more horses to go around. All those men on foot are slowing us down."

No answer.

"Keeping on the right path is *not* easy, is it? Not even with the two of us working on it."

Still no answer. Tich'ki sighed loudly.

"That sorceress of yours certainly knows how to set a spell."

"It failed."

"Ha, he speaks! Sure, it failed, but look how long the bits of it keep hanging around!"

"Mm."

Tich'ki twisted about to stare into his face. "Hello? Anyone in there?"

He waved her away absently. "Stop that, Tich'ki."

"You're still working on it, aren't you? That's it, isn't it? You're still trying to figure out the shape and root of that spell."

"Mm."

"Naitachal! Come on, you big fool of an elf, I'm just trying to keep you from doing something stupid!"

"Are you?"

She grabbed hold of a lock of silvery hair with both small hands, forcing him to look at her. "I don't want to see you die on some Dark Elf altar. Got that? You've got to give up on this—this idiocity!"

"No."

"But—"

"Hush. Let me work."

She threw up her hands in disgust. "Sure. Anything you say. I give up." As the fairy launched herself into the air again, she yelled to the whole party, "Suicidal. Never suspected it before. The man is downright suicidal."

A suicidal elf, Count Trahern thought. *Just what this farce needed.*

He glanced about at his men as he rode, and barely bit back a laugh. His men: a handful of soldiers, a warrior woman (maybe the most competent of the lot and certainly, a hot-blooded corner of his mind insisted, the most attractive), an Arachnia, and a filthy, raggle-taggle group of bandits, wild-eyed as so many fearful animals, who would probably run at the first hint of danger. Now that he thought about it, there did seem to be fewer bandits than before.

Wonderful. They've already started slipping away. And I don't doubt that more are going to follow.

No great loss, surely, except for the old saw about there being safety in numbers.

What an elegant army. Fit for a minstrel's song. If the minstrel were half-blind from drink, maybe.

At least he had Gwenlyn with him once more, after all the doubt and terror, Gwenlyn safe and unharmed. The count glanced over at his daughter, who was riding double behind Lydia, and his sardonic gaze softened. Ah, look at the girl, so fierce, so ragged, so very determined. He had wanted to send her safely home, but Gwenlyn had pointed out, unfortunately quite correctly, that he could hardly spare sufficient men to give her a large enough escort. She must be incredibly weary by now, poor thing, particularly after all the hardships she'd undergone, but the count couldn't find the slightest sign of flagging will in her. Every scrap of Gwenlyn's energy must be focused on this one perilous mission.

Love, he thought in wonder. *That's what must be driving her. It must be love, even if she hasn't accepted it yet. I never thought I would see the day, but here we are—my fiery, stubborn, strong-willed daughter is finally in love.*

And with a man who, praise all the Powers, was the perfect suitor for her, not only one who seemed genuinely kind and witty but one who had the ear of the king himself. Ah yes, a perfect suitor in every degree.

Or, the count remembered with a jolt, someone who should be the perfect suitor, were there any justice. Unfortunately, Kevin was instead a man who had been imprisoned by the cruelest, most inhuman of foes.

Ah gods, Trahern thought with a sudden shudder, *even if we do, by some most miraculous of chances, manage to rescue him—what are we going to recover?*

Gwenlyn felt her father's gaze on her yet again, and frowned slightly. She could almost prefer their old, quarrelsome relationship to this new gentleness. Did he think she'd been turned into some fragile little thing by her ordeal? On the contrary! With a tiny touch of pride, Gwenlyn knew the forest had toughened her, gotten rid of the softness that came with a privileged life. Oh, not as thoroughly as the warrior woman she sat behind; Lydia was all lithe power, strong, Gwenlyn didn't doubt, as any man when it came to combat. She was also undeniably female and plainly enjoyed that fact, and Gwenlyn glanced at her father again, this time with a speculative eye. There was something in the way he and Lydia kept exchanging sly glances, something decidedly interesting. . . .

Do they even know *they're flirting? Father's been out of practice so long!*

And does he think that I—that Kevin—that we—

He did, to judge from those tender looks he kept shooting her. He thought she was doing all this for love of Kevin. Well, it wasn't love, not yet, not quite. It was—she wasn't quite sure what it was yet.

But damned if she was going to abandon him to evil before they'd even had a chance to learn the truth!

"Lydia," Gwenlyn said suddenly, "will you teach me to fight?"

She heard the woman chuckle. "What, in just a couple of days?"

"I don't mean anything professional, I know that's not possible in a short time. But, well, there must be *some* self-defensive tricks you can teach me before we . . . get to where we're going."

Lydia glanced back over her shoulder. "Worried about him, too, aren't you? Hey, don't ruffle your feathers at me, kid! I've been in that sorta situation before, where you don't know if you want to marry the guy or just pull him down into the clover with you."

Gwenlyn could feel her face reddening. "But can you—"

"Yeah, kid. Sure." Lydia's voice was sympathetic. "I'll teach you what I can. I only hope you don't have to use it."

Naitachal kept his face rigidly impassive, the hood of his cloak pulled sternly forward. Yes, he was concentrating almost entirely on the spell fragments, puzzling over the *feel* of them, trying to tease out the psychic shape of each and solve the question of the whole. He really didn't want to carry on a conversation with Tich'ki or anyone else, though he could have done so had it been truly necessary. Not being a human, he didn't need to turn all his thoughts to any one task—save outright spell casting, perhaps—to succeed at it. Even while concentrating on the Gate fragments, there was still more than enough room in his consciousness for . . . other things to slip into his mind.

Things such as fear.

He would not have admitted it to Tich'ki or Lydia or anyone else, but with each step that brought him closer to that final, fateful confrontation, the terror grew. Worse, the old Naitachal, the true *Nithathil* who still hid deep within him for all his forswearing of that bitter, former way of life, whispered to him that *none of this is needed. He is a human, nothing more, you need not risk your life for him, for any human.*

He is my friend, Naitachal countered silently. *I will not let him die for me.*

But the inner whispers continued no matter how fiercely he sought to block them:

Remember how it was when you were among your clanfolk.

Remember the harshness, the lack of love or trust or laughter. Remember the punishments.

Remember the altar and the screaming of the sacrifice or the failure, remember the darkness and the coldness and the pain echoing throughout the caverns.

There will be that pain for you if they take you, that endless pain, that endless torment, there will be no escape for you, there will be endless torment for a human's sake.

He is my friend, Naitachal repeated, *and whatever fate may wait, I will not abandon him.*

Haunted by the past, he grimly pushed on.

Chapter XXVII

Alarms And Attacks

Rualath sat hunched over her sorcerous scrolls, pausing only long enough to impatiently braid her long silver hair out of her way, then returned to studying each twisting rune, each notation she'd added, hunting for a specific spell that would accomplish all that Haralachan had ordered.

No. That spell was far too dangerous; she cared nothing at all for the safety of the human, but Haralachan had forbidden her to actually harm him. Drugging the human's food or drink would have been an easy way out, but again, Haralachan had forbidden her to do anything that might permanently injure Kevin's mind.

This spell, then? No, again. It was so lightweight the human would never believe it. He would probably laugh at the thing!

Ae, you wouldn't set me a simple task, would you, my lord?

But then again, Rualath admitted with a touch of pride, her abilities were also far from simple. Any lesser sorcerous task would have been an insult.

So. Rualath bent over her scrolls again, hunting something subtle, something effective, something terrifying yet basically harmless. . . .

All at once she straightened with a thin smile, one finger tapping the chosen spell. Ah yes, what an interesting thing! Just enough Power to be effective, not so much it would drive the human mad—not for a long time, at any rate.

Bending over the scroll once more, Rualath began to chant the Words of the spell, softly at first, then more loudly and ever more loudly still, feeling the Power gathering, chanting the Words over and over and—

Yes! Yes! With a gasp, Rualath hurled the Power away—straight at the human, Kevin.

Kevin stirred restlessly in his sleep. He had been dreaming of wandering peacefully in the woods, hearing the sweet chirpings of the birds, trying to turn the bits of their songs into music. But the chirpings were subtly changing to whispers he couldn't quite understand no matter how much he strained, the sense of them not quite perceivable yet filling him with such a feeling of growing menace that the Bard awoke with a gasp, staring blankly up at the black silk canopy, a darker mass in the room's darkness, his heart pounding fiercely.

A dream, he told himself. *That's all it was. There's no one else in the room, no one menacing me. It was just a foul dream.*

After a time, his racing heartbeat slowed to normal. Kevin sat up, rubbing a weary hand over his eyes. No wonder he was starting to have nightmares, trapped in *this* place!

Ah well, he wasn't going to be able to get back to sleep, not after that dream. Besides, he wasn't really sleepy any longer. Since there wasn't anything like night and day down here, it really didn't matter if he arbitrarily declared this to be early morning.

Yawning, Kevin got to his feet, stretching luxuriously. The dim blue magical lamps would light as soon as he started moving around with sufficient vigor; he'd learned by now that they always did. Kevin stretched again—

And froze in the middle of it.

What was that? There had been the softest, most furtive of sounds coming from the outer room. Heart racing all over again, Kevin fumbled around for a weapon in the darkness, trying not to make any noise or enough movement to trigger the lights and reveal him to the foe, but came up only with his lute. Ah no, he wasn't ready to give away the secret of his Bardic Magic, not yet. And he could hardly use the lute to hit someone! Carefully putting the instrument down on the bed, he warily stalked forward. The dim lights suddenly flared into life at his movement, but there wasn't anyone to see. And yet someone was—

Behind him! Something cold and dank wrapped itself about his throat with terrifying strength, dragging Kevin over backwards, struggling wildly to fight back, his flailing arms finding nothing but empty air as the coldness tightened, tightened . . . the blood was surging in his ears, he couldn't breathe, couldn't see, couldn't even—

It was gone. So suddenly he staggered and fell to the cold stone floor, the Something was gone and he could breathe freely again.

For a long time, Kevin sprawled where he had fallen, too busy with drawing air back into his lungs to worry about anything else. Surprisingly, after that near strangulation, it didn't hurt at all to breathe. He raised a shaking hand to his throat, expecting to find bruises.

But to his bewilderment, there wasn't so much as the slightest soreness there, either. As soon as he could manage his quivering legs, Kevin scrambled up, looking wildly about.

Nothing had been disturbed. There wasn't the slightest sign anyone but he had ever been in here.

A . . . *dream?* he wondered doubtfully. After all, some of them could seem pretty realistic. Maybe waking and hearing the noise, and feeling that weird, impossible attack had all been part of the same dream.

And I don't believe that for a moment.

A genuine attack? Then why break it off just when he was about to pass out? Someone's idea of a jest? From all he'd seen so far, the Dark Elves didn't have much of a sense of humor, or at least not something humans could recognize as a sense of humor, but for all he knew, something this sadistic might be just their idea of a hilarious prank.

Kevin sank to the bed, pulling the lute into his arms. For a moment his hands hesitated over the strings.

Oh, right. What was he going to do? Reveal his only weapon prematurely? Waste Bardic Magic warding off something that wasn't there? Kevin bit his lip, wondering, then settled for playing simple, Powerless exercises instead.

Gradually the quiet discipline of the scales calmed his nerves. Kevin bent over the lute in earnest, playing every song he could remember that had to do with sunlight and joy and life. And just then, the only magic in his music was the pure glory of music itself.

Kevin sat wearily on the edge of his bed, his hand rubbing eyes that felt full of sand. This was getting ridiculous! Every time he had managed to fall asleep, his dreams had taken a dark turn, sometimes becoming merely depressing, sometimes downright terrifying. At least there hadn't been anything as bizarre as that maybe-dreamed attack on him by the Whatever-It-Had-Been.

There doesn't have to be anything that dramatic. If I don't get one good, unbroken stretch of sleep . . .

The worst part of it was that he knew enough Bardic Magic songs to ensure a peaceful night's rest—but using any of them would scream out *spellcaster* to anyone with psychic hearing.

Ah well, the longer he spent worrying about it, the less likely sweet sleep would become. This time he wouldn't let himself even think of the possibility of foul dreams.

Right. It's like the story of the man who's not supposed to think of the right wing of the eagle. Just try *not thinking of something if you want it to really haunt you.*

Kevin sighed and lay back once more, staring grimly up at nothing till at last he slipped into sleep once more.

Kevin started awake, surrounded by blackness, feeling it pressing down on him on all sides, smothering him, crushing him. Where was he? What was this—

"Why, what is it, human?" a sneering voice asked, and Kevin nearly cried out in shock, gasping out a confused, "I—"

But suddenly reality came flooding back over him and Kevin knew where he was, and why. He had been walking the endless dark corridors for what little exercise was allowed him, with his usual armed guard in attendance, and—and for a moment he actually must have been hypnotized by the smooth, unchanging expanse of walls on all sides into falling asleep on his feet. Not an unlikely thing to happen, Kevin thought bitterly, considering the lack of solid sleep he'd had lately.

"I was lost in thought," he said feebly, and did his best to ignore the contempt fairly radiating from the guards.

That was a stupid thing, the Bard scolded himself as they walked on. *They think you their inferior as it is just because you're human. Why not finish the job and scream out, "I'm a weakling! Destroy me!" while you're at it?*

Grimly alert, Kevin stalked on, surrounded by his disdainful escort. At least there was *some* variation now, a few jagged places in walls and ceiling. The Dark Elves weren't perfect after all! And the jaggedness showed a hint of the natural world that was wonderfully comforting after all the sterile perfection. Kevin nearly stubbed his toe on a rock, but almost welcomed the pain that at least reminded him there *was* a world outside. A sudden groaning made him glance sharply up—and gasp in horror.

"Look out! The ceiling's cracking!"

He sprang back into a tangle of warriors, nearly knocking some of them over. They cursed at him, shoving him rudely forward again.

"No! Don't you see the whole thing's about to fall on us? We've got to—"

Someone shook him, hard. "Look, fool. Look!"

"But—"

"*Look!* Do you see the slightest crack anywhere up there? Well, human? Do you?"

Kevin looked. The ceiling was totally smooth, smooth as the walls. There wasn't so much as a pebble out of place.

"But I . . . stubbed my toe on a rock. I felt it."

"Stubbed your toe on empty air, more likely," a

warrior muttered, and added something sharp in the elven tongue that needed no translation.

I wasn't *asleep that time, I know it. And I'm not so far gone that I'm hallucinating.* That could only mean someone really *was* working a spell on him. *But dammit, I am* not *going to be caught again!*

"Stop, you idiot!"

Suddenly hard hands were dragging him backwards, nearly pulling him off his feet. Startled, Kevin started to struggle against their bruising grip, then froze in shock.

He was standing on the lip of a narrow stone bridge over a chasm like a bottomless black pit. If the guards hadn't grabbed him when they had, he would have stepped right off the edge.

"Dear gods," he breathed.

The guards muttered something in their own tongue. Kevin didn't doubt they were calling him a fool who didn't deserve to live.

And I almost proved them right, he thought with a shudder. Someone was bespelling him, all right. But why? To wear him down? See if he betrayed himself—or, more likely, Naitachal? *So much for* guest *status, if I ever believed that stupid fiction. But who's casting the spell?* Impossible to tell that in a whole realmful of potential spellcasters. *And how do I get them to stop?*

"I wish to return to my quarters now," Kevin said with as much dignity as he could muster.

Once there, he snatched up his lute, staring at it, aching to summon his full Bardic Magic powers and—

And do what? Take on an entire realm of Dark Elves, one against who knew how many? Kevin felt new shudders rack him, knowing all too well that his endurance wasn't going to last forever. Unless he did something more than wait, and quickly, his enemies were going to wear him down to the point where he couldn't act at all.

Easy for them to do, too. All they need to do is keep me from sleeping.

But what could he possibly do in self-defense? Bitterly, Kevin realized why Haralachan had made no attempts to see the human "guest," and why all of Kevin's requests to meet with the Dark Elf lord had fallen flat; Haralachan plainly had no intention of seeing him till after he'd broken.

And I can hardly go hunting Haralachan instead.

Of course not. Even if he could somehow miraculously elude the warriors watching over him, he certainly wasn't going to be able to find Haralachan on his own, not in all that dark, perilous maze of corridors.

There was only one way out of this mess. Kevin would have to force the issue. Danger or no, he needed his music. And so, not giving himself a chance to think twice about it, the Bard raised his lute again, tuning the strings as though his life depended on it—which, he thought darkly, it did—and began to play. After a moment, once the melody was firmly established, he added his voice to it.

And this time Bardic Magic glittered in the music. All at once, with a satisfying crash, the door flew open, and astonished warriors filled the opening.

Kevin smiled at them. "Take me," he sang sweetly, "to your leader."

Chapter XXVIII

Bardic Songs

As they hurried him along down the dark corridors, servants hastily squeezing back out of their way, Kevin noted with dour humor that though the Dark Elf warriors kept him closely surrounded, watching him like so many eager predators, not one of them dared to so much as touch him.

They're afraid of me! he realized with a shock of wonder. *Why yes, that's it exactly! The door bursting open like that, so blatantly magical, startled the wits out of them, and now none of them knows what to expect of me.*

Yet now here he was singing and playing away lustily as he walked, obviously doing *something* magical—but they couldn't figure out what it was!

Without warning, one of the warriors, bolder or more foolhardy than the others, made a sudden snatch for the lute, and Kevin dodged just in time, hastily improvising a new song, putting as much raw Bardic magic into it as he could force so that the elves would sense *something* magical happening:

"The lute of a Bard is sharp as bone,
Hard as stone,
Mine alone.
The lute of a Bard is fierce as flame,
Barbed as shame . . ."

Came, lame, tame . . . what rhyme makes sense and—ah.

"Dangerous fame,
Not yours to tame."

Bad line, that. But he couldn't do anything about changing it now. Besides, this wasn't a poetry contest! Kevin sang hastily on:

"All folks save Bards who touch a string,
Shall feel the sting
Its song can bring.
All folk save Bards shall moan and sigh
Yet never die
Although they cry
For ending of their fearful pain,
Again, again,
A harsh refrain."

Could be better. Has to do. Now how do I end the thing? Ah . . . yes, I've got it.

"The Bard alone may wield its song,
Its Power song,
So fierce and strong.
The Bard alone may wield its song,
Its Power song,
So fierce and harsh and sharp and strong."

Terrible poetry, just terrible! he added in silent disgust.

But the Dark Elves weren't in any mood for literary criticism. The warrior who had reached for the lute snatched his hand back again as though he'd been stung, and Kevin could have sworn he saw some of those humorless dark faces actually grey a little in shock.

So, now. Respect me a little more, do you? If only your master feels the same way!

Without saying a word, the warriors hurried the Bard on to the cavern of the thrones. There sat Haralachan and Rualath, not the coolly elegant figures he'd first seen, but looking strangely ruffled, as though they'd only just received word of what was happening and had needed to rush to get here and in place before him.

That didn't make them any less perilous. Kevin felt his heart falter a moment at the cold wariness in their eyes and the hint of rising Power he sensed growing about them. But Bardic training wouldn't allow a Bard to panic in front of an audience, and even hostile ones.

All right, let's give them a decent performance.

With that, Kevin managed to smoothly switch melody and words over to a stronger, more legitimately magical song. It didn't really have a name as far as he knew, though he'd heard his old Bardic instructor, Master Aidan, casually refer to it once as a "Safety Song," one that was meant to keep a Bard's enemies confused, unable to attack him. But it had been intended for near-mindless creatures. Whether or not it would work on intelligent, magical foes as well . . .

Ha, yes, it was working, at least in part! Look at that helpless fury suddenly blazing in Haralachan's eyes!

"Take that—that *thing* away from him!" the Dark Elf lord ordered a servant, clearly struggling to get the words out.

Oh, I don't think so, Kevin thought, and switched back to his first threat-song, adding this time (since he'd had a chance to work on it in his head a bit) some downright vicious verses graphically detailing the endless agonies waiting for any Dark Elf foolish enough to so much as brush the lute's strings, improvising as he went along everything from slow corruption to instant incineration.

If they realize this song isn't fully magical, I'm in trouble. . . .

It couldn't be fully magical, not thrown together on the spot the way it was. But to Kevin's relief, his threats were just bizarre enough. No one dared *not* believe them. As he continued to detail the horrors in as calm a voice as he could sing—very well aware he was making those horrors seem all the more plausible for the very lack of drama in his delivery—all the servants shrank back in outright terror, the warriors tightened their hands nervously on their weapons, and even cold-eyed Haralachan drew back a bit on his black throne.

Serves them right for not knowing anything about music; they have no way of knowing I'm bluffing!

Yes, but he couldn't keep this up forever! Kevin switched hastily back to the foe-lulling song, the genuinely magical Safety Song, before anyone could sense he hadn't actually been spellcasting.

But just then a white-clad figure moved slightly out of the shadow of that throne, and Kevin's hands nearly fumbled on the strings.

Oh gods. Amaranthia.

She alone knew about music, White Elf that she was. She alone would know there was nothing perilous about his lute. And she would also know just how easy it was to stop a musician, no matter how magical he might be: grab his arm the way she'd already done once, snap the strings—oh, the possibilities were endless.

I'm doomed, Kevin thought with calm certainty, and waited, almost resigned but still singing and playing with all his might, for her to betray him one way or another.

But Amaranthia—said nothing. The Bard stared at her in confusion as he played. Why? Why was she keeping silent? She had no reason to feel anything but anger or maybe even hatred towards him after the way he'd acted. Why was she protecting him?

Love?

No way to find out the truth, though, not right now. He didn't dare stop playing for an instant. Amaranthia met Kevin's glance only for a second, her eyes totally unreadable, then dropped her gaze and slipped back into shadow. Maybe she was only tormenting him, he thought wildly, by postponing the inevitable. Maybe that was it, maybe she meant to watch him to keep holding off everyone until he dropped dead from exhaustion.

And maybe she'd get to see just that. Gradually the triumph of holding them all at bay was wearing thin. He was only mortal, after all, and surrounded by foes, and already weary. Oh yes, thanks to Amaranthia's silence, Kevin thought in growing despair, he was safe—but that safety was going to last only as long as his voice and fingers held out.

And that wasn't going to be too long at all.

Naitachal stopped dead, staring fiercely at the rugged country ahead, *feeling* the Power radiating from the rough, mountainous terrain so strongly he was amazed the humans couldn't sense it, too—feeling, as well, his heart pounding with such sudden terror he nearly staggered. "There."

"There?" Lydia echoed. "What do you mean, 'there'?"

"That is what we seek."

"That's *it?* Your clan's hiding out somewhere in those rocks?"

"Under them, rather."

Lydia slid from her horse, shaking her head in disbelief, protesting, "But it all looks so—so *normal!*"

He glared at her. "What did you expect?"

"Well . . . I don't know! Something more—"

"More what?" Naitachal snapped, too on edge for patience. "More dramatic? A towering fortress of blackest stone, perhaps? Or some other such melodramatic garbage? Ae, and wouldn't that be a ridiculously easy target for all *Nithathili* foes!"

"But—" Lydia stopped short. "Uh, yeah, right. I guess so."

"And too," Naitachal continued, still staring at the rough landscape before him, "we—ah, they—are hardly a race to enjoy living amid sunlight." He glanced at Lydia with a quick, sardonic smile. "Besides, what lies under those rocks is only partly within this realm you humans know. Believe me, there is nothing even remotely 'normal' about the caverns of the Nightblood Clan."

Her eyes widened at his chill tone. "You realize what you're saying? The place isn't even really in our world? And you're going in *there?* And *alone?*"

Naitachal sighed soundlessly. "I thought we've already established that. Yes. I am. Alone."

"But you—we—you can't—"

"I can. I will."

"No, dammit! You can't just—you—"

"Lydia."

"Ah, hell!" she exploded helplessly, eyes suspiciously bright. "Go ahead, you idiot, kill yourself if you want to!"

"I have no intention of killing myself." *No need,* he

added dourly to himself. *The odds are rather good that Haralachan or Rualath will do it for me.*

"Glad to hear that," Tich'ki cut in sharply. "But how're you going to prevent it?"

"Why, I'm expecting that you will—"

"Will what? What *about* the rest of us? How are we supposed to get in there? Maybe I could hide in your cloak or something—"

"No."

"—but the others sure couldn't!"

"The fairy has a point," Gwenlyn added. "How *do* we get in?"

"'We!'" her father echoed in dismay. "Surely not—"

"Surely yes. Father, what else were you planning to do with me? Leave me out here with an armed guard?"

"Of course! A battle is hardly the place for—"

"You're not going to say, 'For a girl,' are you? I've already been through enough fighting and escapes to qualify as a warrior—yes, yes, not a fully trained one, far from it, but—well—"

"If you leave her out here," Lydia cut in quietly, "you'll have to divide your fighting force. It also puts her in the very real peril of being taken hostage by the elves."

Count Trahern glared at Lydia as though she'd betrayed him. But then his shoulders sagged. "Danger if I allow it, danger if I don't. The gods protect you, Gwenlyn, for I fear I cannot."

"Oh Father," Gwenlyn murmured, "all will be well, you'll see." But then her voice sharpened. "Back to the real problem: How do we get in there? We can't just walk boldly in the front door behind Naitachal."

"Hardly," the Dark Elf agreed angrily. It was the one flaw in his plan he'd not yet been able to fix. *How* are *they to get inside? And without setting off any magical traps?*

"I might be able to help," D'Senna offered suddenly. As Naitachal turned to her in surprise, she continued, a touch of embarrassment in her voice at the need to praise herself, "I am considered a—a decent tunneller among my people."

"*Are* you, now?" Naitachal grinned sharply, all at once feeling the faintest stirring of hope.

"Well, I cannot dig through solid stone, of course. But—"

"But you can handle earth, I take it? And rather swiftly if need be?"

"Yes, but—"

"What a clever young Arachnia you are! Hurry, follow me, around behind these rocks. Now, do you see there, and there?"

D'Senna froze, studying the region with her great compound eyes, sniffing the air, for all Naitachal knew actually tasting the emanations of the earth on the breeze and feeling with some Arachnia sense the depth and breadth of the hidden caverns.

"There is earth between the rocks here," she mused after a moment, her voice abstracted. "More earth than rock in places. And do not look at me in such shock. Only an Arachnia would be aware of it."

He *was* shocked at the idea of his clan's security being so easily broken. *Arrogance does lead to carelessness.* "But can you do it?"

"Tunnel into the caverns within? I think so. . . ."

"Don't *think!* Kevin's life—and my own!—depend on you. *Can you do it?*"

D'Senna hesitated a maddeningly long time. But then she dipped her head in a solemn Arachnia nod. "Yes. I could tunnel into the caverns, and fairly swiftly—as long as those within were distracted."

"As they shall be," Naitachal promised her with a savage grin. "Come, let me touch your mind . . . the smallest of spells, D'Senna, just to give you the sense of where, exactly, to tunnel . . . There, now. Do you have it? Yes? They've made a mistake, my dear kinsfolk, been too confident in their Power to guard their backs. So be it!"

Hastily he returned to the others, hastily told them his plan, refusing this time to listen to so much as a word of argument.

And then, though he ached with every terrified nerve to simply turn and flee, Naitachal, once of the Nightblood Clan, now a Bard of the Light, strode with all outward bravado into the jaws of the foe.

Chapter XXIX

The Intruder

As Naitachal stalked with apparent boldness through the cavern mouth into his once-clan's stronghold, his black cloak swirling dramatically about him, he held his terror firmly repressed behind a rigid mask of deadly calm—the face of a true *Nithathil* noble and Necromancer, one who never reveals anything of his emotions and is perilous to cross.

It was a mask he found distressingly easy to reassume.

Naitachal passed warriors, servants, slaves as he walked, and knew from their reactions that they recognized him. But not an elf of them moved to stop him. Instead, they all, regardless of rank or status, stared with the same open-mouthed disbelief.

He knew exactly what they were thinking: who would be stupid enough to be so bold? Of course the idea of self-sacrifice for another was totally alien to them.

In a way what I'm doing is for personal gain, Naitachal thought with a flash of dark humor. *It will be immensely personally satisfying if I can get Kevin and myself out of here whole in body and soul!*

Ahh, the Gate Spell . . . he could feel its aura all around him, stronger now that he was closer to its source, and if he turned a part of his consciousness to it, he should be able to continue unravelling the puzzle of its creation. . . .

If he lived that long. As he walked on, determinedly projecting that aura of absolute calm and quiet danger, the astonished crowds closed in behind him, following him, and Naitachal battled the suddenly roused *Nithathil* instinct that was screaming to him not to let anyone come up behind him.

But it was far, far more effective to ignore the followers as best he could, announcing without words, *I am so far above you I scorn you. You cannot be a threat to me.* After all, the Bard tried to convince himself, he wasn't in any mortal peril from them, not yet. At least not till they'd learned what he meant to do.

And at any rate, he really didn't need threats; his own mind was doing its best to jeopardize him. With every step further into the caverns, more and more old memories roused, no matter how Naitachal tried to quell them. He had, after all, spent little more than five years outside, safe amid the Light, such a tiny, tiny span. How could he so easily forget all the long, hopeless years that had been his life before that?

There had been only Darkness about him back then, only the hatred and cruelty and cold mistrust that was the Dark Elf's heritage. He had fought and fought with himself down through the long, bitter years to prove himself truly *Nithathil*. And yes, if he was truthful with himself, he had to admit there had been a dark satisfaction in controlling the only sorcery he'd been permitted, the magic of death. Yet even at his most powerful as full Necromancer, he had never quite succeeded in hardening his spirit.

Naitachal's mouth tightened ever so slightly in pain, the only trace of emotion he dared let himself display. Ae, he had spent so much time in these grim corridors, alone, always alone amid the cold, silent darkness, desperately trying to hide his so shameful misery, burdened by the knowledge that he lived a lie, hating the Darkness yet knowing no way to flee it.

But now he was seeing the realm for the first time with an outsider's eye, and realized with a sudden shock that what had seemed so coldly terrible when he'd been young was now simply dark and dank and . . . empty.

One of the more delightful aspects of the humans was their joy in ornamenting every artifact that came into their reach. Maybe some of the results were gaudy, but they all radiated a vitality lacking here, a clear, pure love of life. And best of all the wonders they took for granted was music, glorious music, and the unmeasurable joy of its creation! Naitachal glanced around the dark, joyless, musicless realm about him and fought down a shudder, realizing only now just how far he had come in the last few years from what he'd been.

Keep walking. Just keep walking. No one must learn of your uncertainty.

But his confident steps faltered just for a moment as a series of sounds, muted by distance but still startlingly recognizable, drifted up the corridor towards him. Music? Here?

Kevin! It could be no other.

Naitachal strode forward again with new determination, his curious, bewildered audience following. But still no one tried to stop him from striding right into the cavernous throne room, crowded with warriors and scholars and obsequious servants.

There in the midst of them all stood Kevin, singing in a voice that sounded strained and weary yet still held a shimmering of Bardic Magic. Naitachal recognized the song he sang as one of the "Safety Songs," and smiled inwardly at the human Bard's sheer nerve in trying to ward off an entire Dark Elf clan. And he was doing it, at least for the moment.

Someone stirred, catching Naitachal's attention. He looked, and froze, finding himself staring right at Haralachan and Rualath on their black thrones. *They haven't changed, not in the slightest,* he thought uneasily, remembering despite himself the hunts they had led, the hopeless victims' screaming and the blood, and himself, the ruler's kinsman, forced to be in attendance lest he, too, despite his status, wind up the hunted. He had fiercely struggled to hide his disgust no matter how cruel the hunt, even when Haralachan, smiling coldly, had compelled him to make the kill. *The captive's frantic eyes, pleading with me for mercy I dared not give lest I, too, be slain—*

No, curse it! He would not fall prey to his own memories!

Held by the music's spell, neither Haralachan nor Rualath had noticed him yet, perched there on their thrones like a pair of sardonic predators just waiting for their human quarry to make a slip.

And, judging from the weariness in Kevin's voice, that slip was going to happen at any moment.

So, now, here we go. Showtime. "Enough," Naitachal said coldly, his voice cutting across the music, and stepped forward.

The stunned Kevin's fingers fumbled on the strings, breaking the spell. Chaos erupted at the sight of the interloper, the brazen traitor. At a quick gesture from Haralachan, magical barriers slammed shut, blocking every corridor into the audience chamber. Within the now-confined space, the *Nithathili* swirled like a disturbed swarm of ants, servants and scholars milling about, getting in each other's way, blocking the warriors from drawing their weapons. Naitachal saw Kevin's lute torn from his arms by a daring soldier, and quickly held up a commanding hand. To his relief, everyone fell silent, all of them watching the Dark Elf, fiercely curious.

Ignoring Kevin completely (save for noting that the young man looked unharmed and, despite his alarm, very, very relieved to be able to stop playing), Naitachal glided silently forward. Stopping before the throne at precisely the proper distance to show respect, neither too rudely close nor too cowardly distant, he paused dramatically, keeping his face absolutely still, then gave the Triple Bow of Noble Courtesy, thankful he could remember all the intricate twists and bends to it.

There was utter silence for perhaps a dozen heartbeats' time. Then Haralachan hissed, "You *dare* come here!"

Naitachal raised a cool eyebrow. "Why, of course, my lord. Why should I not?"

"Why, you—traitor! You—"

"Traitor for a reason," Naitachal cut in smoothly, and saw the faintest hint of curiosity flicker behind the outrage. "I pray you, my lord, will you not hear my tale? I am sure it will . . . entertain you."

Haralachan's face went completely still, hiding all emotion. "It had better," he said shortly. "I give you leave to speak." *While yet you can*, went the unspoken words.

Naitachal forced a thin smile onto his lips, hoping it looked properly chill, stalling desperately as he organized his thoughts. "My Lord Haralachan," he began coolly, "when our people were accused of that ridiculous crime of kidnapping a human girl—Count

Volmar's niece, already murdered though we knew it not—who was it chose me as the emissary from our people to the humans to clear our name?"

"I did, of course! You had sufficient Necromantic skill to do the task. But I never gave you permission to try becoming one of them!"

Naitachal raised a hand in polite protest. "Why would I wish to do such a tasteless thing?"

"No games, traitor! You had no reason to linger with the humans—yet you did! You cannot deny you have quite voluntarily lived among their kind for years. You cannot deny you have—again, quite voluntarily—even taken up that—music. Become a Bard."

"Why, my lord!" Naitachal protested mildly. "What better way to win their trust?"

"The human," Haralachan's jerk of chin indicated Kevin, "already spun me a pretty tale of greed and betrayal. I do not wish to hear more storytelling fiction."

"I shall not waste your time," Naitachal retorted. "Hear me out, my lord, I pray you.

"When first I met the humans, my initial thought was disgust. They are, as we both know, noisome, nasty creatures. But they do own more land than seems strictly politic, and there is always the chance of an alliance with our cousin elves of the Light." There was the softest gasp at that; Naitachal just barely kept back a start of surprise at the sight of the slender White Elf girl hiding in shadow. *Now, what* . . . "No, my lord, I am not about to lecture you in matters you already know. But as I lingered among the humans, I realized what a wonderful position I had, not merely to turn their attention from us and what we plotted, but to learn what *they* thought and plotted."

"And so," Haralachan cut in, voice dripping with scorn, "you decided to infiltrate their ranks."

"Hardly. Do I look even remotely human, my lord? They never welcomed me. They feared me!" Naitachal let genuine anger show in his voice, remembering the prejudice he'd found even among those he'd tried to help. "They feared me with good cause."

"Yet you stayed."

"Oh, I stayed. And I learned." *What did I learn?* he thought quickly. *What tales can I weave that are more believable than those Kevin tried?* "The humans never welcomed me, it's true. But their kind are creatures of habit; give a human long enough and he will come to accept even the most bizarre of circumstances.

"And so I made sure the humans saw me every day but never once saw even the slightest of sorcerous threats. Eventually, they did come to accept me. And after I had succeeded at that lengthy, tedious chore, my lord, and I no longer feared they would turn against me or try assassinating me in my sleep, my true work began."

"Which was?" Haralachan drawled.

Naitachal allowed his eyes to show just the faintest hint of ambition but kept his face absolutely cold and still, his back absolutely straight, the Pose of True Nobility. "Which was, my lord, that I began paving the way for the Nightblood Clan, for all the *Nithathili* clans, to leave these narrow caverns and rule all the realms of elf and human."

"Impressive." The word was laced with mockery.

Do not *react,* Naitachal warned himself. *Hold to the Pose.* "No, my lord, not impressive at all. It will only be impressive when my words become solid truth.

"And how shall that be done, you ask? Listen, my lord."

With that, Naitachal launched into a hastily improvised speech of where he'd been, what he'd done, and why, spinning the story out as finely as he dared without losing Haralachan's interest, delicately developing each and every point: what each human realm was like, who ruled what, where their strengths lay, carefully glossing over only their weaknesses. As he continued building his careful web, Naitachal thought that it was all too easy to fall back into the old pattern of subtle half-lies and almost-truths, all the cruel and devious ways of speech that had once been such a necessary part of his—of any Dark Elf's—survival.

And he was doing it so well! Judging from the uneasy expression on Kevin's face (the human, Naitachal knew, understood just enough of the elven tongue to be following the gist of this), he was giving the human Bard some nervous moments. Kevin was probably starting to wonder if just maybe Naitachal meant what he was saying, particularly, Naitachal noted, when the elf spoke of the Gate Spell with sinister relish.

As if I could relish anything about that abomination—except, perhaps, its unravelling and reversal!

Ha, look at this! He really must be spinning a fine web, because the cavern was filling full with an enormous, darkly amused crowd.

But then Naitachal saw how the eyes of Haralachan and Rualath glittered dangerously, and he lost any sense of triumph. They didn't believe him after all. They didn't believe a word of what he said. But for the moment, at least, Naitachal realized, he was entertaining them, enough so that they made not the slightest move to stop him.

Probably waiting for me to hang myself, as the humans say, the Bard thought. *Hear me call to you, D'Senna. Feel me pull you. Tunnel quickly, D'Senna! I can't keep this nonsense up forever—and they are not going to listen much longer!*

Chapter XXX

Attacks

Surrounded by earth and rock, the smell of dank soil heavy in her nostrils, D'Senna tried and failed to hold back a chittering little sound of sheer weariness. Her arms ached, her claws ached, her whole *body* ached.

Oh, how could she ever have been so proud? No, no, not merely proud: how could she ever have been so incredibly *foolish* as to think she could manage all this tunnelling by herself? Yes, the humans were helping her as best they could, following closely behind her, clearing out the dirt she loosened by passing it back hand to hand in makeshift cloth scoops. But there was a limit to what they could do. The main burden, all the actual digging and digging and digging, could only fall upon her.

Gwenlyn, who was right behind her in the narrow tunnel, said suddenly, "Wait a moment." She came squirming up beside D'Senna, barely able to fit in those tight quarters, and managed to give the Arachnia a comforting pat on the arm. "Don't worry, we'll get there in time."

"How?"

"What do you mean, how? You're doing an amazing job. Look how far we've come already!"

D'Senna fought down the flash of anger that would have made her shout at her human friend, *Don't patronize me!* and contented herself with a flat "It is not enough."

"It will be!"

This time D'Senna did crane her head about to glare. But humans, with their soft, flexible faces, always had found it difficult to puzzle out the subtler Arachnia expressions. Gwenlyn only smiled with great enthusiasm and patted her again on the arm. D'Senna exhaled in a weary, angry little hiss. "Go back with the others," she said shortly. "There is only room for one of us up here."

Gwenlyn grinned. "I know. But at least by getting you angry at me, I got you to take a rest."

With that, the girl squirmed back to her place, leaving D'Senna speechless. Tchik, tchik, humans were always unpredictable, and sometimes unexpectedly kind! Ah well, what was there to do after that but tunnel on and on and on?

If only we are in time, she worried. *If only we are in time and can actually do something useful!*

As she dug, D'Senna was flooded with sudden fierce longings for her home hive. Ah, to be back there in the quiet, elegant simplicity! In the hive there would be none of this endless, exhausting labor, none of that nerve-wrenching terror of what was so lightly called "adventure."

No, in the hive, things were always serene, controlled, safe. Everything was done together; no one ever had to act alone. If she was back there, D'Senna thought with renewed longing, she would still be part of that gentle, never-changing, always safe life—

That boring life, she reminded herself sharply. *The life you couldn't wait to leave and which nearly drove you as mad as any one of these wild-minded humans.*

Besides, there were perfectly happy Arachnia out there in the world beyond the hive. Arachnia actually *doing* things with their lives. Like Kevin's own seneschal, D'Krikas.

D'Senna sighed. What a wonderful, fascinating being this D'Krikas must be! How exciting to manage the affairs of an entire castle—rather like being a Queen without having to endure all the unpleasantnesses of blind captivity. It would be an honor, indeed, to apprentice with D'Krikas. If he accepted her. And, of course, if she survived.

Which you won't, D'Senna snapped at herself, *if you don't stop acting like a soft-shelled idiot and* dig!

Just how long, Naitachal wondered, was he going to be able to keep up this ridiculous monologue? More to the point, how long was Haralachan going to let him continue? So far, the ruler had shown not the slightest sign of boredom, but that could very well be merely part of a typically Dark Elf ploy. Haralachan was a master at the sadistic *Nithathil* game of putting a victim's mind at ease, waiting with delicate care till that victim dared begin to hope—and only then attacking.

Not now, Haralachan, not yet.

Now that he had set his mind into the flow and pattern of his speech, Naitachal didn't really need to concentrate on it totally. He could continue his guiding mental call to D'Senna and allow a tiny part of his consciousness to warily search for the residue of the one specific magic he needed, sensing the source of the

Gate Spell still radiating, as he'd expected, from Rualath.

Ha, of course she still bore the traces of the spell! Cast magic always left some residue about the spellcaster, and that had been a singularly Powerful spell the woman had loosed. There was enough left to seize upon—if he ever got the chance to concentrate fully on it.

But how can I possibly do that while I have to keep up this preposterous speech?

If only he could somehow let Kevin know . . .

But even if Kevin had no way of knowing what Naitachal was trying to do, he could certainly understand from the elf's wary little sideways glance that his fellow Bard needed a chance to rest. Out of the corner of his eye, Naitachal saw the young man erupt into a frenzy of motion, risking his precious musician's hands to punch the startled Dark Elf warrior smack in the face and snatch back his lute, fingers fumbling on the strings in his haste. Wincing slightly (his tired and now probably bruised hands must be complaining) he burst into song once more. The human's very desperation put a new, bitterly sharp edge of Power on that song, and all the *Nithathili* cringed back in shock, Naitachal—acting with all his might—among them.

But even as he pretended to flinch, Naitachal flung all of his magical will towards what was left of the Gate Spell, trying in that moment when everyone else was too stunned to realize what he was doing to analyze it, trying to capture it, carefully puzzling out this twist of the spell, that turn, delicately, delicately . . .

By all the Powers! Naitachal was so astonished he nearly cried that aloud. *It's a Spiral, that's all the cursed thing is, nothing but a Basic Magical Spiral with some eccentric twists worked on it!*

Clever of Rualath: a Basic Spiral was one of the easiest foundations on which to hang a spell, but one that allowed for infinite variation. Still, even with the bizarre changes she'd worked on it, Naitachal knew he would have the shape of it caught firmly in his mind in just another moment, if only he could manage to—

But he'd been too eager. His mental touch, Naitachal realized a bare instant too late, had suddenly been noticeable. Rualath sprang to her feet with so fierce a shriek of alarm that Kevin started, his hands slipping on the strings, shattering his Bardic spell.

Ah well, Naitachal thought with elven fatalism in the sudden tense silence, *it almost worked. Here's where we die.*

With each painful bit of ground gained, the air in the tunnel grew more and more stale. D'Senna, choking on dust, knew with bitter certainty that she wasn't going to get much further. The Arachnia could survive on far less air than the humans, but they still did need to breathe! If she ran completely out of air, her body might go into involuntary hibernation—or it might shut down altogether.

I can't back out, D'Senna realized, *not with all those frightened humans behind me. I—I can only go forward.*

Closed-in places like this didn't frighten Arachnia, but someone had told her once that humans were scared of them. What if these humans panicked like a swarm of *chakchik* and jammed her into a corner where she didn't have room to dig? What if they all got stuck in here and—

D'Senna froze, listening. Behind her, the humans were complaining at her sudden stop, but she gave them a fierce hiss and they fell silent. Was it imagination, or did she really hear . . .

Yes! She could hear sounds, voices. And they were just ahead of her! *Just a little more digging,* she urged herself, *just a little more digging and you're done.*

But the earth up ahead was more firmly packed, almost rock-hard. Her claws scrabbled on it, barely able to find purchase, and D'Senna nearly shrieked aloud. So close, so very close! Would she ever be able to break through? Would they ever, ever get there in time?

No need to pretend anything now. Naitachal moved smoothly to stand back to back with Kevin.

"Sorry about this," he murmured to the human.

"Not your fault," Kevin shot back. "We gave it a good try, anyhow. At least now we have a chance to die cleanly."

"I don't intend to die."

"Well, I'm not exactly thrilled by the thought either, but we don't really have much of a—here they come."

But even as the Dark Elves started grimly towards them, a tremendous crash reverberated throughout the cavern and a great choking cloud of dust filled the air.

"D'Senna," Naitachal gasped, "bless her Arachnia claws. We're not going to die this day after all!"

As the Dark Elves closed in, Kevin had hastily slung his lute over his back in a desperate attempt to protect it, thinking that at least it might have a chance of survival even if he didn't.

But then came that astonishing crash and the dust, and Naitachal's bewildering words. Before Kevin could believe what he saw, a mad swarm of humans, some in uniform, some in outright rags, came rushing into the cavern before the dust had settled, shouting wildly. They attacked the startled Dark Elves with what looked to his astonished gaze like hysterical ferocity, fighting so suddenly and fiercely none of the *Nithathili* could muster control enough for spells. The air was heavy with shouts and the clang of blade on blade.

Did I just see—is that Gwenlyn?

It looked very much like her—a wild-haired Gwenlyn screaming like a fury. But before Kevin could see for sure, the frenzied crowd swept her aside like a chip of wood on a flood. Trying to find her again, he caught quick glances of a Dark Elf warrior and a human guard in hand-to-hand combat, several ragged humans armed with clubs whaling away at a whole crowd of Dark Elves, a woman in worn leather armor—Lydia, by the gods—handling a sword with practiced skill and almost elven grace—

Kevin dodged back in shock as a Dark Elf sword nearly spitted him. *Oh, you idiot, standing here gawking in the middle of a battle!*

He hastily retreated before the attack, dodging back again and again as the elf cut at him, not caring at the scorn in his opponent's eyes, hunting for a weapon. Who cared what a *Nithathil* thought of him? If he didn't find a weapon in the next few moments, Kevin decided he was just going to run and to the Pit with any ridiculous—

Ah! Someone had dropped a sword, a Dark Elf sword from the looks of the odd glint of the metal and curve of the hilt, but one that, Kevin's Bardic senses told him, was mercifully free of sorcery. He snatched it up with a grateful gasp, struggling to find the balance of a weapon that was both longer and lighter than those he knew, and just barely managed to parry in time, the shock of blade hitting blade nearly staggering him.

But suddenly the Dark Elf broke off the attack, his gaze shifting to a point just beyond Kevin's shoulder. The warrior's eyes widened in alarm and he hastily retreated.

"Human," said a cold voice, and Kevin whirled.

Oh, hell.

No wonder the warrior had fled. Kevin was facing none other than Haralachan himself, the very image of elegant cruelty, his smile thin and chill, his eyes glinting a predatory red in the dim, dusty light.

And in his hand he held a dull black weapon that made Kevin's own eyes widen in horror.

"So, now, human," the Dark Elf purred. "You recognize a *Nithathil* Death Sword, do you? Splendid. That will make our little game all the more interesting."

Wonderful, Kevin thought. He was facing a Dark Elf lord whose reflexes were faster than human, who'd had untold ages to perfect his duelling techniques—and who held a Necromantic weapon that could kill him with a scratch.

Ah well. Nobody ever said life was fair. Kevin raised the unfamiliar sword and saluted Haralachan with a desperate gallantry, then sprang to the attack. The Dark Elf parried his every move with ease, smiling each time the blades clashed together, his greater reach and strength pushing Kevin back each time. But Kevin wasn't worried about being driven back just yet; he was simply trying to establish a definite pattern, a definite rhythm, trying to work his steps into his still so very experimental sword dance Bardic Magic.

Experimental, maybe. But right now, like it or not, the young Bard knew it was his only chance for survival.

Chapter XXXI

War

Naitachal was only dimly aware of the fierce battle raging all about him, seeing only Rualath towering over him, standing on the royal dais as she was, feeling only her mind beating against his. She was strong, she had always been strong; her will was a full flood of sorcery like the blackest of waves crashing at his senses. To his horror, Naitachal felt his old Necromantic skills, so fiercely repressed, rising to the surface of his being in reaction.

No! I will not!

But the Darkness called to him, so temptingly, the black flood pulled at him, telling him *respond, respond.* . . . And . . . where would be the harm? This was a fellow *Nithathil,* after all, whom he battled. Why not use *Nithathil* sorcery against her?

Because, Naitachal answered himself with grim certainty, if he once started using the spells of Darkness again after he had fought so hard to subdue them, he would never be able to stop using them. He would never again be able to return to the Light.

Besides, Naitachal added with a trace of irony, *she*

knows how to deal with Necromancers. It's Bards *who are foreign to her!*

But she was strong, indeed, so strong, tearing relentlessly at the wall of his will, that he wasn't sure he could hold her off. Worse, even as he was trying to defend himself, Naitachal dared not surrender what he'd already gained of the Gate Spell. If he let go now, the backlash of the newly freed bits of Power would tear apart his mind as surely as Rualath herself would.

Powers, Powers, whatever had made him think he could survive this? Whatever had made him think he, or anyone, could manage not one but *two* magical feats at the same time? Naitachal threw more and more of his will into the psychic wall of self-defense he'd thrown up but, torn between the two forces of Rualath and the Gate Spell, he could feel his strength already starting to shred.

Unless he gained control of the whole Gate Spell, and quickly, Naitachal knew he was lost.

Amaranthia huddled in the shadow of Haralachan's throne, staring at the chaos about her in sheer terror. In all the time she had spent among the Dark Elves, she had witnessed many acts of cruelty, many acts of carefully planned violence. But she had never seen anything like this—this open warfare! All around her elves and humans were falling, dying, splashing their blood on the cold stone, trapped within the confines of the audience chamber by the magical gates Haralachan had set, and her ears ached from the clamor of blade on blade, of shouts and screams and moans. She shrank as far back against the throne as she could, wondering how she was going to survive this madness, wondering if *anyone* was going to survive.

If the humans catch me, I—I'll pretend I was a

captive here. Surely they won't hurt me then.

But what if Kevin lived through the battle? (*He must,* a traitor thought whispered, *oh he must!*) He would know the truth about her. And then—Amaranthia had heard her share of horrifying tales of human cruelty. Nothing to match anything known to the *Nithathili,* of course, but—but the dishonor of it was surely—

Amaranthia screamed as a human crashed into her, and continued to scream as he slid slowly past her to crumple lifelessly on the floor. His blood had stained the hem of her gown, but Amaranthia barely noticed. Hardly aware of what she was doing, she bent and tore the dagger from his flaccid hand. A weapon, at least she had a weapon.

Amaranthia froze in sudden disbelief, staring, knife clutched in one fist. Who was that girl, that human girl? Her aura was so clearly revealed by strong emotion, and part of that emotion was surely love. For Kevin.

No, curse her, no!

The madness all around suddenly seemed to swirl up over her. Drowned in it, Amaranthia leaped to the attack.

Gwenlyn, armed with a stave dropped by one of the bandits, fought to keep her mind clear of anything but those hasty lessons in defense Lydia had taught her. Parry this sword like *this,* whirl, crack the end of the stave over that elf's head like *that,* spin and circle and never let any weapon catch her or the stave, never stop to think of what she was doing—thrust to an unprotected throat, blow to an elven wrist—or of the deafening, deadly chaos happening all about her.

And then all at once a white-robed demon was

leaping at her, screaming. *A girl,* Gwenlyn had time to think in astonishment, *a White Elf girl—with a knife!*

Then the girl was thrusting at her. Gwenlyn, remembering Lydia's lessons, stepped quickly back out of reach and brought the stave down with all her force on the elf's fist. The White Elf screamed in pain, losing the knife, and for an instant Gwenlyn wanted to say an inane, *I'm sorry.* But the elf dove at her, ducking under the stave before she could bring it down, nearly knocking Gwenlyn off her feet.

This is crazy! Gwenlyn thought, struggling to keep the elf's hands from her neck, very well aware of elven strength. Particularly the strength of one who seemed to have gone insane.

Oh, don't be silly, Gwenlyn snapped at herself, and delivered a blow to the White Elf that sent the girl sprawling.

D'Senna stood surrounded by bloody, noisy chaos, trembling in shock. With one last great effort and a surge of triumph, she had broken through the remaining wall and gone tumbling out into the cavern in a cloud of dust, but before she could catch her breath or her dazed senses, the humans had poured out of the tunnel, racing past her like a horde of outraged warrior Arachnia. *No! They can't—they mustn't—*

She had never seen violence before, never anything as terrible as this. The hive had always been a peaceful place; she had even once overheard the Arachnia warriors complaining about the lack of foes!

Let them see this, D'Senna thought, *oh, let them see this.* She couldn't seem to move or act or do anything but stare at the sheer ferocity blazing up about her.

But even though she had been raised as the "spare"

daughter of a Queen, D'Senna still was of that royal blood. And deep within her were a Queen's strong instincts for survival. When a snarling Dark Elf lunged at her with his sword, the young Arachnia, reacting totally without thought, snapped out with her claws with flawless aim. And to her horror, she learned in that moment that those claws, powerful as they were and so useful for tunnelling, were equally useful and quite deadly when they closed on Dark Elf flesh.

But there wasn't time to think about what she'd just done, even though she wanted to chitter in panic like a mindless larva and scrub and scrub the stains from her claws. The battle was still raging about her. Unless she stayed in control of her fear and continued to defend herself, she would surely be slain. Allowing herself to die like a useless thing, D'Senna scolded, would hardly be logical. Logic was the keystone of life. Logic was the beginning and the all. Logic was the mortar that held the world together. *Logic is a pain in the posterior regions*, D'Senna thought defiantly. *But cursed if I'm going to let lack of logic kill me!*

And so, closing her mind to horror, the young Arachnia waded into the thick of the battle, a quiet, efficient, and very, very deadly predator.

"Watch your back!"

Count Trahern whirled at the sudden shout, just in time to see Lydia parry the Dark Elf sword that would have cut him down. "Back to back," she snapped before he could thank her, "quick."

Gods, how long had it been since he had needed to lift a sword in self-defense? Trahern hastily parried, thrust and missed, parried again and then again, feeling the impact of sword against sword shivering all the way up to his aching shoulders. These cursed elves were so cursedly *quick!* And so damnably strong. Yes, he tried to work out with sword and knife every day, but exercise against a friendly opponent who had no intention of hurting you was hardly the same as coming up against someone who was trying his best to kill you.

The Dark Elf he'd been fighting was suddenly jostled aside in the crush, giving Trahern a bare moment to catch his breath before another warrior closed with him. Behind him, he could feel Lydia fighting with a dancer's easy grace, and felt a pang of envy.

Ha, wait! The elf, quick though he was, had been too hasty to attack. He was letting his sword slip out of line just enough, and with a sharp cry, Trahern hastily lunged, feeling his blade cleave flesh, then nearly had the sword jerked out of his hand as his opponent fell. Grabbing the hilt with both hands, he just barely managed to pull it free in time to meet—

A breathing space. The tides of battle had surged away from Lydia and him for the moment. Panting, Trahern asked over the clamor, "Are you all right?"

"Uh-huh. You?"

"Winded. At least no more elves seem able to get in here."

"Yeah, but how the hell do we get out?"

"Naitachal will take care of that. I hope."

All around them, the battle raged on. Trahern searched, suddenly panic-stricken, for his daughter. Ah, thank you gods, there she was, out of the thick of things and apparently quite unhurt. The count noted with approval that his men were fighting with the grim efficiency of warriors too seasoned to let even the most bizarre surroundings get to them. Hardly the case with the bandits. Not at all seasoned and far past the point of simple terror, they were fighting with such wild hysteria that the Dark Elves couldn't handle them.

"Good for them!" Trahern muttered. "They're earning that pardon."

"Never mind that," Lydia said. "Here come the bad guys again." With a sudden grin, she twisted about and planted a quick, fierce kiss on his lips: "For luck!"

"For luck!" the count agreed breathlessly.

Kevin cut and parried, thrust and parried, arms aching with the strain, praying his musician's hands wouldn't be damaged, praying *he* wouldn't be damaged, struggling to establish a settled sword dance rhythm that would spark his peculiar sort of Bardic Magic. It was working at least a little; Haralachan's attack had grown just a touch slower than it might have been.

Right. Now he's moving only twice *as fast as a human.*

Hastily tossing damp hair back from his sweaty forehead, he caught a glimpse of Naitachal facing the Dark Elf woman he had named as Rualath. Haralachan's consort. The sorceress who had set the Gate Spell. Nothing dramatic seemed to be happening between them, nothing at all. But Kevin knew that tense immobility, those rigidly locked stares, could only mean some terrible magical battle was being fought.

Can't do anything to help him. Can't even do much to help myself right now.

As if this duel wasn't bad enough, Kevin had gone into it already weary—but the Dark Elf lord was not. His cold, sorcerous swordplay gradually beat down Kevin's ever more frantically improvised Bardic Magic, and the eerie black Death Sword in Haralachan's hand had begun its soft, chilling chuckle, anticipating blood. One scratch from it would be fatal to body, and for all

Kevin knew, soul. Haralachan was starting to smile, sure of victory, but Kevin refused to let himself despair, telling himself, struggling to believe it:

I still live. And, dammit, I will continue to live!

Rualath was never going to weaken, Naitachal thought wearily. Her attack was going to go on and on, and he—ah, he was already trembling with strain, struggling to hold off the relentless waves of her sorcery, struggling to capture all the bits of the Chaos Spell and make it his. The wall of his will was still holding firm, but it was beginning to crack here and there. Dark images were beginning to seep through, confusing trickles of memories, of terrible, terrible scenes from his past, of the harsh, cold things he'd been forced to do to survive. . . .

The altar and the sacrifice, and the knife clutched in his fist . . .

The noble who had challenged him turning to ash from the merest touch of his hand . . .

The slaves he had been forced to hunt to show he was a true Nithathil *noble worthy of life . . .*

The Death Magic running, cold and terrible and splendid, through his mind, giving him the strength he must have, turning him into a figure of awe and terrified respect . . .

The Death Magic that still whispered at him to use it, use it—

No! Naitachal cried silently. *I did what I did for good or ill, but what I did is* past! *I am no longer who or what I was—I* will not be *what I was!*

Grimly, Naitachal clung to the Gate Spell shards, grimly clung to the force of his will, grimly clung to his very sanity.

✧ ✧ ✧

Gwenlyn drew back, gasping. No matter what she did, she couldn't get the White Elf to surrender! And the elf was so much swifter than a human, so much stronger. Gwenlyn's body ached from kicks and slaps, and even though she knew she'd gotten in some good blows herself—Lydia, she thought with a flash of wit, would be proud of her—she just couldn't find a way to end this stupid fight. What made it worse was that all around them deadly battles were still going on, and the more attention she had to give to the elf, the less attention she could pay to keeping herself out of the reach of Dark Elf swords.

Wait, wait, what if—yes.

"Come on, you pallid little fool!" Gwenlyn taunted. "Want Kevin, do you? As if he'd want anything to do with a scrawny little traitor like you!"

By the gods, the White Elf understood the human tongue. With a scream, she rushed at Gwenlyn—

Who threw herself over backwards, bringing her knees up, kicking out, and—Ha! It worked! Gwenlyn scrambled to her feet in astonishment. It had actually worked, just as Lydia had told her! The White Elf had gone hurtling neatly over her head to crash to the floor some distance away.

But then Gwenlyn's triumphant laugh faded. Oh no . . . oh dear gods, no. . . . The sorcerers among the Dark Elves at first hadn't had a chance to gather their magical concentration thanks to the sudden human attack. But by now they had recovered enough to work their spells. As Gwenlyn watched in wide-eyed disbelief, she saw one dark hand merely touch a human shoulder—and that human withered to dust on the spot.

Gwenlyn gave a choked sob of horror, hands at her mouth. *How are we ever going to survive now?*

✧ ✧ ✧

As the Death Sword came whirring down at him, Kevin threw himself frantically to one side, hearing the blade clash against stone again and again as he fell, rolled, feeling the lute banging painfully against back and hip, and scrambled up again. For a moment his wild gaze met Gwenlyn's glance halfway across the cavern, for a moment—*like lovers in one of those mawkish ballads*, he thought—the battle around them seemed to disappear, leaving only them, staring at each other in dazed wonder. And then Kevin cried out in horror, "Amaranthia, no!"

Then Haralachan was after him once more, the Death Sword narrowly missing the side of his head, and Kevin could do nothing but simply try to stay alive.

Was I in time? he thought in anguish. *Oh gods, oh gods, was I in time?*

Gwenlyn stared in horror. That was surely the Dark Elf lord Kevin fought—and from every tale she had heard, that dull black blade was an evil Death Sword. *No, oh no—*

And, like an echo of her thought, Kevin shouted, "Amaranthia, no!"

Gwenlyn whirled at that frantic shout, just in time to meet the White Elf (Amaranthia?)—and an upraised dagger. *Idiot,* Gwenlyn found herself thinking, *you stab someone underhanded, not over.*

She dove at the elf's knees, sending them both tumbling to the floor, Amaranthia landing on her back, Gwenlyn on top. Screaming, Amaranthia stabbed up at her. Gwenlyn scrambled back to avoid the blade, tripped over someone's fallen helm, and landed flat on her back with enough force to make sparks flash across her vision. But beyond the sparks blazed Amaranthia's savage green eyes—and the gleaming blade.

As the knife came flashing down, Gwenlyn, still dizzy, shot both hands up in a desperate bid at defense. She missed Amaranthia's wrist completely. But just by luck one hand caught one of the elf's slender fingers instead.

Ha, yes!

With a ferocity that might have horrified her if she'd thought about it, Gwenlyn bent Amaranthia's finger back with all her strength. Something gave. The elf screamed in pain, losing her hold on the dagger, and Gwenlyn triumphantly snatched it as it fell. Scrambling to her feet, she raced straight for the Dark Elf lord, blade pointed at his chest.

Kevin saw Gwenlyn rush forward, saw the knife flash. But Haralachan's reflexes were swifter. He backhanded Gwenlyn with inhuman speed, avoiding the blade—and gave Kevin the barest instant of free time. If he attacked Haralachan—

No! Whatever else Naitachal was doing in his sorcerous duel, he was almost certainly trying to wrest control of the Gate Spell from Rualath. He'd need an unhampered moment for that—so Kevin hurled his sword straight at the sorceress.

Rualath screamed in shocked pain as Kevin's blade slashed her, and lost her hold on her sorcerous concentration. Freed without warning, Naitachal staggered as the full force of the suddenly released Gate Spell hit him. He couldn't hold it, he was too weary, too dizzy—

You will hold it, fool, you have to hold it! You can collapse afterwards!

The Darkness was swirling about him, crushing him, strangling him, trying to make him one with it or slay him. No, damn it, he would not die, he would not surrender, he would not turn to evil— He would not stop being *Naitachal the Bard!*

Clinging with all his might to will and consciousness, Naitachal shouted out the ugly, twisted, Powerful syllables, feeling them tear painfully at his throat, activating the Gate Spell—in reverse.

"*Get out of here!*" he shouted to the humans in their tongue. "That way! All the barriers have fallen. Get out of here, *now!*"

The sheer desperation in Naitachal's voice left no room for argument. The humans all broke off combat as cleanly as though they'd rehearsed it, catching the Dark Elves by surprise, and ran for their lives down the long, dark corridors, aiming for the dimly seen light so far ahead. With shouts of triumph, they burst out of darkness into the wonderfully free air and forest outside the caverns.

"Naitachal!" Kevin gasped, looking wildly about. "Where is he?"

"I don't know," Lydia cried. "He was somewhere behind us. Gods, if he's still in there, all alone—"

But just then Naitachal appeared in the mouth of the cavern, shouting out what were blatantly the final spell-syllables of the Gate Spell as he went.

"Down!" he shouted hoarsely to the staring humans. "Everyone down!"

He hurled himself to the ground as the reversed Gate Spell roared into effect. The world went wild: branches, earth, and rocks went flying, and the humans and D'Senna clung frantically to the ground, struggling not to be dragged off as well.

At last the sorcerous storm died away, and there was silence:

Total, terrible silence.

Chapter XXXII

After The Storm

"Naitachal?" Kevin asked, his voice sounding very small and weak against all the silence. "Naitachal!"

He struggled to his feet, staring at the mound of rubble where the cavern had been. Gods, the whole side of the mountain had come crashing down! If the elven Bard had been buried under all that, he was surely—

"Naitachal!" Kevin raced forward as a dark hand emerged from the debris. "Someone help me!"

Lydia, Trahern, even little Tich'ki joined him as he frantically dragged rocks aside. At last Kevin managed to claw the elven Bard free. "Are you hurt? Are you badly hurt?"

Coughing, gasping for breath, Naitachal could only manage to shake his head. With Kevin's aid, he managed to stagger to his feet, filthy and tattered, his torn clothing stained here and there with blood. "Not badly hurt," he rasped. "Just bruised. And weary to the point of collapse."

"Come on, we've got to get out of here before—"

But Naitachal held up a hand. "No need. First, rest."

His voice was plainly paining him. *No wonder*, Kevin thought, *after shouting out that ugly-sounding spell.* "Then I'll explain."

Much later, Naitachal stirred from the bank of moss onto which he'd fallen and slowly sat up. "How do you feel?" Kevin asked. "How's your voice?"

"Sore," the elf said hoarsely. "Me and my voice both. But functional." He touched his neck gingerly. "That spell really wasn't meant for elf or human throats. How is everyone?"

"We lost seven of Count Trahern's soldiers and maybe five of the bandits. Can't be sure about that part; I'm not sure how many ran off during the fight. But we were relatively lucky: No one who survived is really too badly hurt."

"Ah. Fortunate."

"Never mind that," Lydia cut in suddenly. "What happened," her gesture took in the entire mound of fallen rock, "back there? Where *are* all the Dark Elves?"

"Nowhere near." Naitachal staggered to his feet, looking at where the caverns had been, his face gone suddenly quite blank.

"Naitachal?" Kevin asked warily. "Are you all right?"

The elven Bard shuddered. "Dazed a bit, that's all. It just struck me. I no longer have a clan. I am now quite clanless."

"What—"

"Wait. What I did, Kevin, was capture the Gate Spell—and as I'm sure you've figured out, it was an extremely Powerful spell—then cast it in reverse."

If a Gate Spell opened magical doorways, then a Gate Spell cast in reverse would surely— "Clever. And did it . . . ?"

Naitachal shrugged, a little too casually to be convincing. "There was more than enough Power in the thing to seal off the Nightblood caverns from the rest of this realm. Possibly forever."

"But that's a good thing!"

"Oh, rationally I know that." But Naitachal's eyes were still bleak. "We are used to our clans, my people. I know it sounds odd, but . . . I will need some time to get used to the idea of being clanless." He paused. "Bizarre, isn't it? In a manner of speaking, I've been more or less clanless ever since I chose to turn to the Light."

"Naitachal . . ."

"Don't worry, my friend. I'm hardly about to pine away for lack of clan like a forlorn woodsprite. And I most assuredly am not sorry at the thought of never seeing Haralachan or Rualath again, may they forever vent their spite on each other."

"Then you really are safe from them. You . . . *are*, aren't you?"

Naitachal smiled slightly. "There are still Dark Elves around, of course, and I don't doubt one or more of them will try to attack me for being what I am. But my own—my *former* clan will never bother me again."

"And Amaranthia?" Kevin asked suddenly. "Is she . . . ?"

"Sealed away with the others? Oh, indeed."

"Ah."

Naitachal glanced at him, silvery eyebrow raised. "Now, don't tell me you feel sorry for her."

"How can I not? She was such a—a sad creature."

"A creature who willingly chose her own path. I cannot find it in me to pity such a one."

"Neither can I," Gwenlyn cut in. "Not after she did her best to cut me into pieces."

Kevin stared at her in dismay. "That's right, I saw her try— She didn't—"

"Hurt me? Not really. Thanks to Lydia. She didn't have much time to do it in, but she taught me a little bit about fighting." Gwenlyn grinned at Kevin. "So watch your step with me, my friend."

He had to laugh at that. "I will. But where *is* Lydia? She was here a moment ago."

"And where, for that matter, is my father?"

Naitachal chuckled. "I wouldn't worry about either one of them."

"This is ridiculous," Count Trahern murmured, and without further ado, took Lydia in his arms and kissed her with all the pent-up fervor in him.

"Sure is," Lydia agreed, coming up for air some time later, and kissed him back so fiercely for a while neither of them could think about anything at all.

But at last Lydia reluctantly pulled away. "Helluva place for anything more. Someone's bound to stumble over us."

"True." Count Trahern was finding it difficult to catch his breath. "Unfortunately."

"Besides, this isn't really going to work, is it?"

"You and me, you mean?" Trahern sighed. "I'd like to give some gallant, easy answer, but I . . . don't see how it can. We'd make a terrible couple."

"Different worlds and all that."

"Exactly."

"I'm not going to give up being what I am."

"And I can hardly stop being a count."

"But I'm not ready to just say good-bye and mean forever, either."

"Gods, no," Trahern said emphatically. "Ach, what a mess. What are we going to do about it?"

Lydia grinned. "Stop being so dense, Trahern."

"Dense!" he echoed, stung.

"Hell, man, think! Your land's not so far from Kevin's, now, is it?"

Trahern suddenly mirrored her grin. "Not far at all. We might make a terrible couple, but there's nothing wrong with a little . . . ah . . . back-and-forth visiting, is there?"

"Nothing wrong at all," Lydia agreed, and linked her arm in his. "Come, my gallant, let's go find the others."

Kevin glanced at D'Senna, who was standing forlornly a little bit apart from the others, and went over to give her arm a pat. "Hey, don't look so lost! I haven't forgotten about you. Are you still interested in apprenticing with D'Krikas in my castle?"

She quivered with sudden excitement. "Yes. If—if you really mean it."

"Of course I mean it! None of us would be here if it wasn't for you. I owe you that apprenticeship!"

As the Arachnia chittered happily to herself, Kevin felt Gwenlyn tap him on the arm. "We need to talk," she told him.

"Ah . . . yes. We most certainly do."

While the amused Naitachal got the attention of the others on a pretext of checking names, Kevin and Gwenlyn slipped off into the forest together. For a long while they walked side by side in silence. And something seemed to break within Kevin as he looked at Gwenlyn. Tired, ragged, dirty though she undeniably was, she had never seemed so wonderfully alive to him, so heartstoppingly lovely.

And because he realized with sudden stunning finality that he loved her—prickles and temper and all—Kevin knew what must, of honor, be done, although he could have wept at the thought of it.

"Gwenlyn," Kevin began, then had to stop.

Ach, he couldn't back down now. There was only the one decent thing to do after all they'd been through together and all he'd learned about her hopes and dreams. And that was to call off the proposed marriage and give her back her freedom.

I can't! he cried in silent anguish. *I can't give her up, not now!*

But then Kevin told himself sharply, *Nonsense. Maybe you do love her, but—but she doesn't love you. It would never work out. You'd only make her miserable. Besides, she—she deserves so much better. A prince, maybe, a king, someone fine and noble and—and—oh gods, it does hurt!*

"Gwenlyn," Kevin began again, miserable, "when I first met you, we both knew things weren't going to work out between us. Now . . . well . . . I know it sounds trite, but I really do want you to be happy. And that means," he continued bravely, "that I—I—I don't want to force you into a marriage you don't want."

But to his amazement, Gwenlyn burst into a smile, her astonishing indigo eyes gone most wonderfully warm. "Who says I don't want it?"

"What—Gwenlyn, think! A Bard spends half his time with his head in the ether, listening to music no one else can hear, or throwing things around the room because the right words just won't get pinned to the parchment—"

"I've been known to throw a few things, too," Gwenlyn said. "And if you're going to keep your head in the ether, you need someone to keep you connected with the earth, don't you? We're probably going to have some spectacular fights, you and I, but let's face it: we'd both be miserable living apart. As Lydia would put it, we make too good a team to think of disbanding now."

Kevin stared at her in dawning, disbelieving hope. "Then you—I—we—"

"Exactly," Gwenlyn said. "I love you, too."

And before Kevin could say another word, she kissed him firmly.